Praise for The Leash and the Ball

"The chasm is there. But Samir does
ing about it—he does everything in
both to Leda and to the Netherland:
novel so digestible and so painful at ......, ...o..
of a comedy of manners about someone trying to integrate
than an indictment of the impossibility of ever succeeding at
that, which makes the criticism inherent in the novel hit all
the harder."
NRC Handelsblad

"Phenomenal."
RICK NIEMANN, *Jinek*

"Witty, sad, and beautiful."
MAARTEN 'T HART

"In *The Leash and the Ball*, Rodaan Al Galidi peels the layers
off his new compatriots. His style is visual, layered and
imaginative, full of humor but vulnerable too."
MO* Magazine

"Beautiful, intense, moving, funny—a valuable novel."
Allesoverboekenenschrijvers.nl

"A book that really touches you."
DWDD

"If Al Galidi shows anything about the many characters in this
riveting novel, it is that everyone lives in a mix of different
cultures in their own way, whether you happen to come from
the same country or city, or from the other side of the world."
Tzum

"*The Leash and the Ball* is at least as poignant as *Two Blankets, Three Sheets*. It, too, can be hilarious, though there's always that disturbing undertone."
De Leesclub van Alles blog

•

Praise for Two Blankets, Three Sheets

"A blunt and surprisingly humorous peek at an aspect of global displacement that remains largely hidden from public view."
Kirkus Reviews

"An absolute treat. Al Galidi has an eye for the absurd. It's all the more striking because of the lightness of the telling."
Irish Times

"No other book I have read makes the soul-destroying effects of European asylum procedures more vividly clear than this one."
Foreign Affairs

"Ably translated into English for an American readership by Jonathan Reeder, *Two Blankets, Three Sheets* is a deftly written and engaging novel that showcases author Rodaan Al Galidi's exceptionally effective narrative storytelling style."
Midwest Book Review

"At once funny and bleak, this novel by the Iraq-born Dutch novelist draws on his personal experiences to expose the cruel and often absurd procedural challenges that immigrants must endure. It's an engrossing and exasperating novel. *Two Blankets, Three Sheets* is a tale of belonging and what it means to be human in a world that deems people less important than government protocols."
Words Without Borders

"This frank and poetic account of a life in limbo yields a story with universal power that transcends borders and cultures, with more than a touch of *Catch-22*'s black humor."
Shelf Awareness

"*Two Blankets, Three Sheets* does for the beleaguered political asylum seeker stuck in legal limbo what Joseph Heller's *Catch-22* did for the hapless soldier trapped in a military at war. Translated from the Dutch into nimble and conversational English by Jonathan Reeder ... It is a tale for and of our time."
Los Angeles Review of Books

"*Two Blankets, Three Sheets* infuses tedious sufferings with drama, humor and life: the agony of waiting, the cruelty and pettiness of bureaucracy. It makes visceral the shameful ways we misuse our small powers over each other. I've never read a book that better illustrates the human cost of the European asylum systems. This vital, eye-opening work is essential to our collective education, as a history, as a call to action, bringing one person's suffering vividly to life in the imagination of strangers."
DINA NAYERI, author of *The Ungrateful Refugee*, for *The Guardian*

"*Two Blankets, Three Sheets* is an interesting, rich novel on fear, insecurity, arbitrariness and hopelessness."
GUUS BAUER, author of *Bird Boy*

"This is an unnerving, ironical book about how lives are grinded down by endlessly stretched procedures."
Leeuwarder Courant

"Al Galidi writes this novel based on his own experiences, but he manages to cover that up so well with his fluent writing style, a sense of humor and an absence of resentment. A real feat in his case. The lighthearted way in which he writes

about tragic experiences makes this a very impactful book."
KRISTIEN HEMMERECHTS, author of *The Woman Who Fed the Dogs*

"Book of the month? Book of the year! Rodaan Al Galidi has been writing beautiful books for years, but this is his absolute masterpiece. Loose, light, and humoristic, and precisely for these reasons the book hits home. Don't be mistaken: stylistically, too, this book is a testament to his mastery."
Bookseller Van Rossum

"Don't look any further, buy this book!"
Bookseller Hijman Ongerijmd

"The dilemma of the desire for survival set against one's moral compass brings to mind George Orwell's *Down and Out in Paris and London*; Samir's attempts to make the best of his protracted detention have much in common with the plight of the stateless Tom Hanks in Steven Spielberg's film *The Terminal*."
Dutch Foundation for Literature

"For all its heavy themes—the tragedy of miscommunication, loss of identity and meaning of life, humiliation, and the incapacity to truly connect—it is also a very light and humorous book."
Literair Nederland

"A challenging portrait of Dutch hospitality. Absolutely recommended."
The Correspondent

"You can write emails about refugees until you're blue in the face, but you can also, thanks to the unique power of literature, spend a few hours inside the mind and soul of one of them. By reading this tragicomic masterpiece. It will do you good."
De Limburger

"'The asylum center,' Al Galidi writes, 'is a grave where the time of a few hundred people is buried.' For this grave he has erected a memorable monument that functions as both a complaint and a mirror. And I, for one, was ashamed of what I saw in it."
TOMMY WIERINGA, author of *Joe Speedboat*

"Essential reading."
Trouw

"A stunning novel about the experiences of a refugee in a heartless regime: polder-bureaucracy thick as mud. Al Galidi holds up a mirror to us. A mirror that we should all look into."
ADRIAAN VAN DIS

"*Two Blankets, Three Sheets* is a valuable and rich novel about fear, uncertainty, arbitrariness, and hopelessness, written by someone who was, thankfully, able to use his new language as a lifebuoy."
Tzum

THE LEASH AND THE BALL

RODAAN AL GALIDI

THE LEASH AND THE BALL

Translated from the Dutch
by Jonathan Reeder

WORLD EDITIONS
New York, London, Amsterdam

Published in the USA in 2022 by World Editions LLC, New York
Published in the UK in 2022 by World Editions Ltd., London

World Editions
New York / London / Amsterdam

Printed by Lake Book, USA

World Editions is committed to a sustainable future. Papers used by
World Editions meet the FSC standards of certification.

This book is a work of fiction. Any resemblance to actual persons, living or
dead, or actual events is purely coincidental.

Library of Congress Cataloging in Publication Data is available

ISBN 978-1-64286-112-9

First published as *Holland* in the Netherlands in 2020 by De Vrije Uitgevers,
Amersfoort

This publication has been made possible with financial support from the
Dutch Foundation for Literature.

N ederlands
letterenfonds
dutch foundation
for literature

Twitter: @WorldEdBooks
Facebook: @WorldEditionsInternationalPublishing
Instagram: @WorldEdBooks
YouTube: World Editions
www.worldeditions.org

1

A glass door.

I walked into city hall holding the letter informing me of my residence status. Going to city hall might not seem a big deal for you, but for me it was the kind of everyday errand that terrified me the most. For a Dutch person, picking up a raw herring by its tail, lifting it above their head, and then lowering it into their mouth is a delicious snack, but for me it is torture. Torture akin to standing at the city hall reception desk.

Encounters that turn out to be crucial to my life always happen at the wrong place and the wrong time. The shed where I was living, for instance, smelled at that moment like Chinese takeout. I was wearing the striped pajama bottoms I had bought at the thrift store for a euro and a half, so with my chest hair I looked like a cross between an ape and a zebra. As I hadn't shaved yet, my chin sported an ambivalent beard of the Che Guevara variety and a resolute mustache like Saddam Hussein's when he was in power. About as unromantic as you can get.

My first encounter with Leda ... It was the most beautiful thing that had happened to me in all my life, and the most dramatic. What I couldn't have imagined then was that in that tiny, sleepy Dutch village, my head and my heart would take a terrible, simultaneous hit. A hit from which I still suffer, and will probably never recover.

A few weeks before that disastrous meeting in the shed behind her family's house, the nine years, nine months, one week, and three days I had been waiting in an asylum seekers' center for a residence permit came to an end. It looked like I would end up spending my entire life in that ASC, until one day, an ordinary day just like any other day, I received an official sheet of paper saying I could stay.

"Good afternoon," said the friendly-looking woman behind the desk after I sat down. She had gray hair, but her face was young and even friendlier than her voice. She exuded a kind of calm that didn't seem to fit with her job of handing out money, but would have rather suited a job where she handed out peace, light, or daily words of wisdom. She shook my hand and, smiling, introduced herself.

"Esther Jacobs. *Spreek je Nederlands?*"

"Yes, I speak Dutch. I lived in the ASC for nine years, nine months, one week, and three days."

"You can round it off to years," she said with that same friendly smile, as she scrolled in the computer to check whether what I said was correct. "So you didn't attend classes?"

"No, we weren't allowed to. Only minors could go to school."

"Okay, then you have the right to Dutch lessons," she said, perhaps more to herself or her computer than to me. She typed something. "And civics classes ..."

"Ma'am, I've only come to tell you I don't want to go on welfare."

"No welfare?"

"No. I can take care of myself."

"But Mr. ... Mr. Kareem, you've just come from the ASC. After more than nine years. That's a long time."

"I know, and that's why I don't want it. I want to go to the south of Spain. To Tarifa, a town I read about in the library. It's on the southernmost tip of Europe. They call it the Capital of the Wind, because it's always windy there and people fly over the water."

"What kind of residence permit do you have?"

"General amnesty."

"I don't think you can just go live somewhere else. For the time being you still fall under the Aliens Act. First you have to take Dutch lessons and civics classes, and then pass your citizenship exam, and once you've got Dutch nationality, in five years or so, then you can move around as you please. And you've got to have something to live off in the meantime, right? Since you spent so long in the ASC you'll get a two-year exemption from the job-search requirement ..." It was like going to the doctor for a sniffle and finding out I had some awful disease. I saw before me an endless bureaucratic tunnel where, if I entered it, I would never come out the other end. I wasn't about to let this happen to me again.

"And still, I don't want welfare," I said firmly.

"Well, if you insist ..." Esther Jacobs said. "I'll have to check how that works, because this is a new one for me. Just a moment." She got up and went through a door, behind which were undoubtedly yet more offices and desks. Soon she was back.

"It's not possible," she said. "You are required to have insurance."

"Insurance?"

"Yes, you have to have insurance, you know, health insurance."

"I was given a residence permit, not a disease," I said.

"I understand that, yes, but ... Say you get sick, or fall down the stairs and break your leg? Or develop some allergy? Then you really have to be insured, otherwise you'll have no end of trouble."

I listened to Esther Jacobs tick off a whole list of possible health issues, and tried to get my head around the fact that for all those years the Dutch system tried to protect civilian life from me, and now, suddenly, was intent on protecting me from civilian life! In the end, I left city hall uninsured. Esther Jacobs shook my hand.

"Watch out," she said as a friendly goodbye. "You don't want to get run over by a bus."

As I walked outside I thought of my ancestors, who survived two million years without insurance, and of my family in Iraq where more bombs fell, more injuries occurred, and more illnesses existed than there were written and unwritten rules in the Netherlands. After a few uninsured days I returned to Esther Jacobs with an insurance policy, so I was off the hook for welfare.

Now I had insurance, a sheet of paper that said I could officially stay in the Netherlands, and a garbage bag full of old photo albums I'd collected from thrift stores over the years. It felt like the spring breeze had liberated a frozen wave from the ice and released it into the great, wide ocean. I was on the way to my life.

2

But where to? My home was the ASC.

In my contact list were forty-seven telephone numbers for people whose place I could probably crash at for a night or two. I had acted as an interpreter for many of them in tight, distressing, embarrassing, or amusing situations. I started dialing.

"Hey Murat, how's things?"

"Hey Samir, long time no see."

"You bet. How are you doing? Where are you now?"

"In Turkey, man. Calling is expensive, for both of us. I'll be in touch once I'm back." In the background I heard the familiar jingle of a tram bell.

"Have they got Dutch trams in Turkey, too, Murat?" I asked. The line went dead. I deleted Murat's number and went to the next on the list.

"Hey Tahir, how you doing?"

"Samir! Long time no see!"

"Where do you live these days?"

"Me? In Turkey, man. Expensive to call. Samir, I'll be in touch once I'm back! Ciao!"

I deleted Tahir's number.

"Hi Rafid, it's Samir. What's up?"

"Samir! So long since we talked. How are things in the ASC?"

"I'm finally gonna leave it."

"Oh, too bad, man, I'm away for a while."

"Don't tell me: Turkey."

"How'd you know?"

"Say hi to Murat and Tahir."

One by one I deleted the phone numbers of my old buddies.

On my shrinking list was one name I couldn't place: Calvin. Who was Calvin? I couldn't remember if I'd met him in the ASC or somewhere else. How did his number get into my phone? Maybe it was left over from the previous owner, an Angolan guy who had sold me the phone when he left for Germany. I dialed the number.

"Hello?"

"Hello, this is Samir."

"Samir!" So he remembered me, at least.

"Who are you, and where do I know you from?"

"Och, man. We lived in the same camp for a month and a half. And when they chucked me out in the middle of the goddamn winter, you gave me your coat and seven euros. You waved at me from the window and shouted, 'Don't ever come back.' Remember?" I remembered my coat, and many others I waved off, but not Calvin or the seven euros.

"Listen, my minutes are running out and so is the battery, but I need a place to stay. Just one or two nights."

"Come out here, man!" he said, and gave me directions.

So I boarded a train with a delay of nine years, nine months, one week, three days, and fifteen minutes. Once I arrived I called him, and he gave me some more directions.

Two and a half hours and four phone calls later I got out at a bus stop in the middle of nowhere. From a distance I saw Calvin cycling towards me, his left hand on the handlebars and his right hand holding another bike. He stopped, dropped the two bikes onto the shoulder, ran over, and gave me a hug.

"Did you steal the other bike?" I asked.

"No, man. In this town there are four times as many bikes as people. If you say hi to a Hollander, the first thing he asks is whether you need a bike." He laughed a great big laugh and slapped me on the back. "Welcome to the real Holland," he said, and started laughing even harder. While we fastened my things to the baggage carriers, he told me that he and I were the only foreigners the village had ever seen.

"A Japanese tourist came here by mistake a few years ago, but he only lasted an hour. I think he's still in therapy. Whatcha got in that garbage bag? A body?"

"Old photo albums," I said.

"In a garbage bag?"

"Yeah, so it's clear to everyone I haven't stolen them, but found them in the trash."

My journey began long ago in that tiny village: a journey that I thought was about getting to know the Dutch people, but that I should now confess was really about getting to know myself.

3

The village looked nothing like the villages in the country where I was born. A stranger entering an Iraqi village is a real event for the residents. Something like the arrival of a Hollywood star in East Podunk. First you'll see and hear the dogs. Some of the dogs will bark, others will run up and bite you. As you approach the houses you'll hear the nonstop chatter. If you listen well, you'll hear the cries of a newborn, the cries of whiny, slightly older children, the cries of even older, whiny and fighting children, and the shouts of children who are almost no longer children. This potpourri of children's noises is then mixed with the bleating of goats, a squawking, quacking, meowing, lowing, and then some more bleating. Through all of this you'll hear the sound of water. Water means life. All the village noises make you think of water—the children, the animals, the squeak of the pumps, and the bellyaching of the villagers.

And this is what will probably surprise you the most. Villagers in Iraq gripe constantly, about themselves, about one another, and about life. They're all waiting for God to come up with a solution. If, for instance, there is a small canal where a few children drowned because two planks of the bridge were broken, then rather than repair it themselves, the villagers gripe that Iraq's government is useless and doesn't take care of them, and pray to God day and night to solve the problem. They expect Him to personally come down from heaven with a hammer and nails, a saw, and new planks to fix the bridge.

In an Iraqi village there are fruit trees and date palms, you see reeds everywhere, and it smells of clay. Most houses have loam walls and a roof thatched with palm leaves. A few of the houses—those families whose son is in the army—are made of stone. The roads are not paved, so drivers must take care to avoid all the potholes and ditches. Cars kick up dust clouds in the summertime and get mired in the mud after a rainstorm. As soon you see a paved road, you know it will lead from the home of a high-placed military man to the highway. A few old women sit along the route to the village with their grandchildren, selling whatever they have left over from their orchard and livestock. You never see young girls selling things, because the men make them either work in the fields, stay at home and make babies, or fetch water from the river. This is a village in Iraq.

You cannot compare a Dutch village to an Iraqi one. Whereas in Iraq the dogs lie in wait in order to bite you, in a Dutch village it's the solitude that lurks. To me, the word *village* means "factory for fruit, vegetables, meat, eggs, and soldiers" (since village children in Iraq do not go to school, the boys enlist in the army at eighteen). In a Dutch village you see tractors and barns, fields of potatoes, carrots, and onions, but not a single Dutch person sweating out in the fields, chasing his neighbor's cattle from his orchard, or struggling to coax more water out of the ground. It's as though the village runs itself. I was surprised to discover that even the smallest village in the Netherlands has a supermarket, where to my even greater surprise you can buy all sorts of fruit and vegetables without seeing the trees they grow on, or those trees having the climate they need.

That first day in the village, cycling alongside Calvin from the bus stop to his house, the only person I saw outside was the mailman. Elderly faces watched us pass from behind large, spotless plate-glass windows. I waved to an older man who was watching us from his window, and Calvin hissed, "Don't do that, man."

"Why not? Did you two have an argument?"

"Of course not, but the Hollanders don't like people seeing them sitting in their living rooms."

"But the curtains are open."

Calvin shook his head and chuckled. "Boy, have you got a lot to learn, Samir. I thought you'd caught on to the Dutch by now. Hollanders have windows so *they* can watch *you*, not so you can look at them. Those big windows are there to satisfy their curiosity, not yours."

"Spoken like a true native," I said.

"Man oh man, fortunately not," Calvin laughed. "This town's got enough psychological problems for the whole of Africa. Man, man."

We cycled past windows, behind which people stood watching us. As though we were the only thing that ever happened outside. I peeked at the windows out of the corner of my eye, without turning to look.

"How can you stand living here, with all this grayness?"

"Listen, Samir, you've got more of a chance with girls in a Dutch village than you do in the city."

"Get outta here," I said.

4

Calvin and I arrived at my first-ever Dutch lodgings: the home of the Van der Weerde family. We put our bikes in the shed, which was tidier than a museum. On one side was a large bike rack, with a separate spot for each bicycle. On another wall, tools hung like paintings, sorted by size and function. Pliers with pliers, hammers with hammers, screwdrivers with screwdrivers, saws with saws, hedge clippers with hedge clippers, and shovels with shovels.

"Do they know I'm coming to stay here?"

"Whether *they* know is not important," Calvin said. "What's important is whether Diesel knows." He called Diesel and at once a dog came running. It was one of those dogs you see pulling a sled. I have never seen a creature with eyes as extraordinary as Diesel's. They shone, reflecting the light to make the world brighter, and absorbing it in order to see everything. Were they azure, or light green? They were not the eyes of an animal, but of light itself.

"Hey Diesel, this is Samir," Calvin said excitedly.

He patted Diesel's head with both hands. When I spotted the sharp white teeth alongside the tongue dangling from the dog's open mouth, I became afraid of him because he looked like the wolves from my youth that farmers shot at if they got too close to the cattle.

"Pet him, man, he won't bite," Calvin said.

During my stay at the Van der Weerdes', Diesel was not only a dog to me, but a guru. That marvelous dog taught me much by how he reacted to the people living in the house, and the distance he kept from them. He was, in addition to being a dog and a guru, also a psychologist.

It was a big house. If you let two cocks fight and a couple of chickens peck around the yard, or had some frolicking lambs or goats, you could have called it a farmhouse. It probably was a farmhouse in the old days. The outside was stone, and the small windows had real working shutters. The back part of the shed, with a separate door at the back, had been converted into a living space. This was Calvin's room. It had a small shower, a toilet, a simple kitchenette, a single bed, and a gas heater. There was an old easy chair with fraying upholstery and two folding chairs that just about fit under a small square table. The prints of Dutch landscapes on the wall were certainly not Calvin's idea. A dried-out cactus stood on the windowsill. What definitely was Calvin's in there were the T-shirts, the socks, and the underwear scattered around the room.

Calvin and I left the shed, with Diesel at our heels and dancing around.

"Oh man, Samir, it's so great you're here," Calvin said. "For months I haven't spoken to anyone but Diesel. I speak English with him, and Portuguese, a bit of Spanish, and some French and Dutch, but all he does in return is bark. An asylum seeker only needs a few months to be able to gossip in Dutch, but this dumbo—" He stroked Diesel's head affectionately, and laughed loudly, which Diesel responded to with a short bark.

"Do the people who live there know I'm here?" I asked.

He shrugged.

"Shouldn't we go tell them? They'll get a fright when they see me."

I was the guest of a guest, and did not want to be underfoot. I didn't know then that my stay here would be more than just a brief visit.

"Okay, then, let's go," Calvin said, and we walked inside.

The house and the shed were no more than twenty-five meters apart, but they were two completely different worlds. Inside the house were diaries, photo albums full of births, growing children, weddings, photos of grandparents, children, and grandchildren. Before long, everything in the Van der Weerde house would be opened to me, a foreigner. As closed as the Dutch are outdoors, they are open in their homes.

5

The folks in this house had for generations been fighting a terrible enemy. And it was a battle they would never win. An enemy with a gray-clad army and able to break one's will: Winter. A row of winter parkas, raincoats, body warmers, and scarves hung on a coatrack, there were bins full of hats and gloves, and next to them a row of rain- and snow-boots, clogs, and shoes. The door to the Van der Weerdes' house was the frontier between them and their eternal foe, and that hallway was a battle trench. Winter's hostilities would never be entirely out of sight: even on the most beautiful summer's day you could still see a forgotten woolen scarf or a pair of gloves hanging on the rack. If the Dutch people can't defeat their enemy, then they turn him into an old friend whom they cannot ignore.

Calvin walked inside without knocking, and Diesel ran out ahead of us into a long hallway. One of the doors in the hallway led to an office. Calvin opened it. Diesel stayed in the doorway, panting, and I could tell he didn't dare go in until he got permission. So Diesel taught me my next lesson: while in Iraq, it's places of prayer that are sacred and off limits to dogs; in Holland, it's the office.

I went inside and saw a desk, with bulletin boards and a whiteboard on the wall behind it. The bulletin board was full of letters, bills, lists, receipts, and train or bus tickets. On the whiteboard, names and dates were written in different sizes and colors. Next to the desk was a tall filing cabinet. The walls were crowded with shelves full of books, binders, and dossiers, everything labeled in magic marker by year and category. The dossiers went back for years. There, it was immediately clear to me what the Dutch people's second eternal war was about: the war on clutter. But even a cluttered Dutchman is cluttered in a tidy way.

"Go away, Diesel," a woman, clearly the lady of the house, commanded as she turned from her desk toward the door. Diesel's inquisitive head was inside the office and his wagging tail was still in the hallway. Only the front half of his body being guilty, she was only half angry at him, but I was startled by Diesel's full fear of her half anger.

"Good boy ..." she said, looking at her watch. "It's afternoon already," she said to herself, and then, to us: "Good afternoon."

It's hard to imagine a colder introduction than that. Her hand felt cold, as if it did not belong to a body of 98.6°.

"Danielle van der Weerde," she said.

"Samir."

"He's staying one or two nights, otherwise he'll get sent back," Calvin said. She turned to me with an expression of deep sympathy and then to him with a silent, unreadable look.

Meeting Danielle in person did not clear up my impression of her. There seemed to be anger bottled up in her that she was able to vent on the dog, but aside from that her actions were kind, hospitable, and caring. She was a woman of fifty-six who for years had been living a prematurely autumnal life. She appeared to have decided that the point of her life was that there was no point to it. What confused me even more was that she never complained or had even an iota of self-pity. Her house didn't even seem like her own. When she was in the kitchen, the kitchen was a hasty, tasteless meal. When she was in the living room, the living room was like black coffee or white wine. When she was in the yard, the yard was her cigarette. She was the mother of three children and foster mother to one more, Mieke. On top of that, she was a mother to all the little children in the village, for she ran a day care in her house, *and* was also a mother to the mothers of those children. And yet, despite all those children she looked after, she radiated a sort of immutable rigidity.

6

Calvin's heart was only a few millimeters deep, which made it difficult for feelings to nestle in his bosom. On the other hand, his take on human nature was infallible, and he could pinpoint someone's character with just a few words.

"I'll make you more pathetic," he said as we stood outside in the cold between the house and the shed. "Danielle has got hundreds of things going on in her mind at the same time. How many nights you stay, where you go or don't go after that, she'll never be able to keep track of, but she *will* remember how pathetic you are. Then you can stay as long as you like."

What Calvin did was make jokes and put on little dramas to amuse himself. Or to amuse others, it didn't matter. In the end I discovered that these qualities gave Calvin an incredible advantage with women. He knew exactly how to make himself attractive. Not lovable or dependable, just attractive.

Back in the shed, he hurried to the shower, quickly dried himself off, and got dressed in a flurry of underwear, socks, and T-shirts. "Date," he said with a wink. "Sorry, pal, first date. Have to be right on time, otherwise she'll think I'm an illegal, and not the adopted son of doctors like I told her." Laughing, he pulled his cap down over his ears, and left.

I flopped down on Calvin's bed without taking off my coat or shoes. Through the wall I could hear the muffled whining of children in the day care, and from outside came the screech of crows. I fell into a deep sleep as if I'd been anesthetized. It was as though my body was given a sign that, finally, it could let go.

In my dream, I was an animal and was walking in the dark. The tip of my tail gave off light and I spun around, following that dot of brightness. I heard my eldest brother, who was killed in a bombing in 2014, say, "Samir, wake up, quit chasing your tail." But no matter how hard I tried to wake up, I just sank deeper and deeper into sleep.

I eventually woke to the sound of a gentle knocking at the door. Danielle. Her face was different. It was just like with the ASC staff. A Dutch person's face at their workplace is not necessarily their own face, but their uniform.

"Sorry to disturb you, Sa ..." She glanced at something written in ballpoint pen on her hand. "Samir. I'd just been interrupted by a telephone call earlier, it had to do with work, but now I can take a break." So even if a Dutch person works at home, even if they are their own boss, work is work and break time is break time!

"That's okay," I said. "Good that I can stay here tonight. Thank you."

"Of course! And if you need anything, just come around and help yourself. Shall I show you around the house?"

Also typically Dutch: The Tour of the House. Danielle showed me where the coffee was, and the five kinds of tea. The sugar (two kinds), the saccharine, and the honey in another cupboard. She opened the fridge and summed up everything in it; she showed me how the sparker on the gas stove worked. She spoke respectfully and kindly, as though I was a long-term houseguest.

At the end of the tour, she said Calvin had called to say he wouldn't be coming home that night. She gave me a duvet and bed linens, and when I answered that I didn't have my own towel, I got a towel, too.

She showed me where Diesel's leash hung, and the ball he liked to play fetch with. So even the dog was part of Danielle's hospitality. I immediately felt at home. She gave me a Chinese takeout meal just in case I got hungry later.

I went back to the shed, intending to sit down and eat, when I heard Diesel barking at the door. It was his way of knocking.

So I let him in. He sat down next to me with those clear eyes of his and looked from me to my takeout meal. What a polite creature! He took only what I gave him.

When I was finished, I flopped onto Calvin's bed without bothering to change the sheets. I flicked off a sandal, which Diesel then brought back to me. He could see I was tired, but kept nudging the sandal encouragingly into my hand. Whenever I was about to say something to him, I stopped myself, figuring he wouldn't understand. At which point he would bark, as though to say he understood me without words.

The heat was turned up high. I undressed, put on my striped pajama bottoms, and dozed off. Diesel lay down next to me.

Suddenly I woke up to a woman's voice. Someone calling Diesel. He pricked up his ears, got up at once, and barked just as the door was cautiously opened and he was able to wriggle through to whoever was on the other side. From the bed I could see Diesel jump against a young woman.

"Diesel!" she cried, petting his head. Now Diesel was nothing but tail, wagging and dancing around her.

"Sorry," she said. "He always gets so excited when he hasn't seen me in a while."

Her presence bowled me over. But for her part she didn't seem surprised by mine. "Easy, Diesel," she said, and then, to me: "You must be the new ..."

"The new Calvin," I said.

She reached over and offered me her hand. "Leda. How are you?"

"Pretty darn good," I said, still overwhelmed.

"Pretty darn good?"

Her look was chilly and her voice sounded irritated.

I thought it might be Calvin's socks, that she smelled them but I didn't. As my mind wandered to Calvin's dirty clothes I heard her call, "Diesel, come!"

That's how quickly it went. She left me befuddled. My

mind replayed my not-so-great first impression on her. I went to the window and looked outside.

Leda. Who was she?

7

From the moment I laid eyes on Leda, I did not want to leave, ever. She was the anchor that kept me fixed to the village seabed. It was definitely not love at first sight. I don't believe in that. But what was it?

It was tough not knowing how long I would have to wait to see her again, especially because I didn't want to let on that she was the reason I was sticking around. But Calvin reassured me that neither mice nor asylum seekers need permission to stay longer in the Van der Weerdes' shed. So those few nights I spent there turned into a whole lot more.

As with our first meeting, the second time I met Leda, I had been snoozing. There was a quiet tapping at the door.

"Come in," I said. Leda came in with the leash, but no dog. "I'm going for a walk," she said. "Care to come along?"

"On the leash?" I joked, but she appeared not to hear it.

"In ten minutes?"

I had the best reason in the world to go: Diesel and I would be taken out by beauty itself.

Precisely ten minutes later I was standing outside. Diesel came trotting up, wagging his tail. Right on time. I had to laugh to myself, because it reminded me of my introduction, long ago, to time. My father and I were at Baghdad's international airport to meet a Lebanese friend of his who had fled to Sweden during the Lebanese civil war and now visited us regularly. (The stories he told of that faraway land fascinated me. The most sensational of these, which he might have invented himself, was that in Sweden, people believe that if you go to hell, it's ice cold there rather than the more usual inferno.) When he arrived that day at the airport, he lifted me up.

"How you've grown these last two years!" he said. Then, without pointing, because there were more government secret agents walking around the airport than passengers, he told me to look at the wall clock.

"Samir, look at that clock. What time is it?" The clock stood at seven minutes past ten. He turned to face another clock on the far wall. There, it said quarter to ten. Yet another clock hanging in the arrival hall stood still at a few minutes past one. "Even at an international airport, time has no value. But in Sweden, it does." As it does in the Netherlands.

Had Leda also told the Dutch dog that he had to be ready in ten minutes? Could Diesel tell time? Questions only I could ask, and only Diesel could answer. I rocked from one leg to the other, like a stork, until Leda appeared. She had wrapped the leash around her left hand. Her expression showed no surprise that I was standing there—after all, she had invited me herself—but no enthusiasm, either. It was more the look of someone who thinks, well, I did ask him to join me, but was that such a good idea?

Leda had plenty of experience letting dogs out, but not asylum seekers. I had been sick in bed for the past three weeks and felt better now, but my joints were stiff. I walked for a bit and then stood still to rest. Leda zigzagged, oblivious to what was going on around her, as though she was walking in her imagination. Sometimes she would snap to because Diesel demanded attention, then she would throw the ball for him, which he brought back in return for a pat on the head. At a certain point she realized I wasn't keeping up with her.

"Come on, Samir!" she called with the same tone of voice as when she called Diesel. She came up to me and said with a laugh, "You walk like Michael Jackson." Then she caught herself and looked at me, her eyes wide. "But wait ... did you know who Michael Jackson was, in the ASC?"

Even my grandma knew who Michael Jackson was. "The first Black president of South Africa?"

"No, silly, that was Nelson Mandela. Don't you know him?"

"Of course I do. Before he was rejected for asylum, he lived with us in the ASC."

"Nelson Mandela rejected? That's not possible."

I burst out laughing. Leda tapped me on the head with the leash and laughed, too. Her laugh on a colorful autumn day was the best muscle massage imaginable.

"Leda, say you throw something and I retrieve it for you. Do I also get my head stroked?"

"Of course," she said, as she tossed a stick. I stood there. "So why are you so stiff?"

"Maybe because I'm not used to the calm here," I said, groaning.

"How long were you in the ASC, then?"

"Nine years, nine months, one week, and three days," I said.

"No, really. Seriously, how long?"

"Nine months."

"Whoa! That long? That's incredible. Once, we went to Milan on vacation. Danielle had reserved a hotel for three nights. But it was a terrible hotel, it was dirty and the beds were uncomfortable. I even saw a mouse. If I'd stayed there for nine days, I'd have been a basket case and my muscles would be ruined. And you spent nine whole *months* there? How many of you were there, in that place?"

"Five hundred and fifty."

"What?! Come on, be serious."

"Fifty."

"Fifty? Gosh. With just one other person you lose half your privacy, but how much is left when you have to share a building with fifty other people? Terrible! I went on a group trip to Peru with seven others. After a few days I just about went crazy from one guy in the group and my aunt, who had paid for it."

I looked at Leda's face, which stuck out above the pink scarf around her neck. I thought: how great is that, in Holland your worst troubles are with group vacations, crappy hotels, and Italian mice.

"Was there psychiatric help in the ASC?"

"Of course. And a sauna and a swimming pool with a huge slide. And a McDonald's. But unfortunately no coffee shop," I said, but she did not laugh, she just scrunched up her face, as though to reprimand herself for taking me seriously. I tried to change the subject, but that only made it worse. I asked her the name of the mouse in that hotel in Milan. She seemed annoyed that I would crack jokes in the middle of a serious talk. This is how my first discussion with Leda ended: with an anonymous Italian mouse and Nelson Mandela being denied asylum.

Leda made me realize I was like a guitar that still needed to be tuned before getting into conversations with Dutch people. I had met Spaniards, Portuguese people, Russians, South Americans, Greeks, Germans, and Belgians. And yes, with them, too, my strings might have had to be retuned. Sometimes one of my strings, sometimes one of theirs. But it appeared that to have a conversation with a Hollander, all the strings had to be tuned just so. Or, better yet: get yourself a whole new instrument.

8

Someone knocked at the door. Forgive me if I keep telling you about all this knocking on doors. In Holland you never enter a room without knocking, not even in your own house. It was Danielle. She invited me to join them for dinner. I was tired from the walk, but it would be impolite to refuse.

So that evening at six I was sitting at the dinner table with their son Maurice (15), daughter Tessa (17), and sixteen-year-old Mieke, who lived with them because there were problems with her own family. Leda, who lived in student digs in Utrecht, was Danielle's eldest daughter.

Danielle brought out a steaming pan of mashed potatoes and platters of meat and vegetables, none of which had any noticeable color or smell. Then Danielle asked me if I wanted to say grace. I would have taken it as a joke if her expression hadn't been so serious. Everyone looked at me. *What will he do?*

"Pray? I thought we were going to eat," I said, at which Danielle gave the sign that we could start.

The clank of cutlery on plates, the glug-glug of glasses being filled, forks and knives ticking against each other, and for the rest a heavy silence. It was like the cutlery's job was to cut up the silence and convey it to our mouths. The mouths chewed the silence and swallowed it. No belches, no laughs or shouts into the air above the table, accompanied by airborn grains of rice or droplets of soup— something I always enjoyed watching as a child. No one talked and chewed at the same time, no highlights of the day or tall tales were exchanged. Nothing was eaten with the hand, but only with a knife and fork, and I did my clumsy best to master the utensils. I noticed that Tessa winced at the sounds I made. She clearly saw my contribution as a chainsaw during a classical concert. The others all ate in the same rhythm, like members of an orchestra.

I couldn't imagine getting through this deadly meal of potatoes and vegetables. So I took three pieces of meat from the platter.

Looking around the table at how the others ate, I noticed that Mieke didn't have any meat. I asked if she was a vegetarian. She shook her head.

"I don't always feel like meat," she said with a polite smile. When I had finished my three pieces of meat, I wanted another, but the plate was empty. I looked at Danielle's plate—no meat there, either. Only then did I realize that there was exactly enough meat for one piece per person. And even though the meal had just begun, I had already eaten half of it.

Danielle asked Leda about someone named Tim. Leda said he was doing better after rehab. Since I figured I hadn't been invited to dinner to keep quiet, I tried to join in the conversation, and asked Leda:

"Who's Tim?" My voice came across as loud and belligerent, because my mouth was still accustomed to Arabic sounds, and also because I was still chewing.

Leda had just taken a mouthful of food. She was taken aback by my question, and because she could neither swallow or spit it back out, she looked up, startled. Clearly she was not familiar with the Arabic technique of talking and eating at the same time, whereby you divide the food in half, pushing one half into each cheek, like a hamster. Or just park the whole thing in one cheek, so you look like someone with an infected molar. Her mouth stayed immobile. She put one hand in front of her mouth and used the other to gesture for me to wait, as though to apologize for not answering immediately. I saw how much trouble that bite of food was causing her and her throat, where that poor chunk was being forced down. Her eyes bugged out and she took several deep breaths.

"Sorry, what was your question?" But by then, the last thing in the world I wanted to know was who Tim was.

"How long have you lived in Utrecht?"

"You asked something else just now," she said, laying her hands alongside her plate.

"He asked who Tim was," Danielle said.

"Oh, Tim. A good friend."

That was it. Her expression said that Tim was not worth nearly choking for. I thought she just didn't feel like talking, but when her plate was empty she took a few sips of wine and told the others about our walk with Diesel. It sounded like she thought it was great. She even repeated my joke about the name of the mouse in the hotel in Milan.

By the end of the meal, there wasn't a single morsel left. No crumb for an ant, a mouse, or a chicken that had snuck in to do the dishes. As though Danielle had gone through everyone's mouth to their stomach and measured their hunger to know exactly how much food to prepare. The meal was quiet, the table was quiet, and the five Dutch people at the table were quiet. Even Diesel's tail was quiet.

There was dessert and coffee and tea, but I excused myself and went back to the shed. I had exhausted enough energy for one day. I lay down on the bed and thought about how hard it was to take each member of the Van der Weerde family into account individually, rather than to think of them all as one whole entity. I was used to being exuberant and exaggerated with my emotions. Whenever I was happy to be somewhere, I would repeat over and over how happy I was. Not only to the people, but to the walls, to myself, to my cup of tea. If I liked someone, I would tell them this constantly. For just one gram of good feelings I needed ten kilos of words. But there, in the Van der Weerde house, this was not going to be possible. The words you uttered were *your* words, and you were responsible for them. How tiring.

In Iraq, what you feel is a balloon, and what you say is the air that fills it. Sometimes your feeling explodes, and it evaporates because of all those words you pumped into it. In Holland, what you say is your own ATM card, and your emotions are your PIN code. If the two do not match, nothing comes out.

9

I thanked fate and Calvin that I ended up with this family, but after a few weeks I found it impossible to stay any longer. Whenever I saw Danielle it felt like I was living not in the shed behind her house, but on her shoulders. I decided that I either had to find some way to pay for staying there, or leave.

I called my family in Iraq, but I knew they had nothing to exchange into euros. Old friends from the asylum seekers' center, the ASC, proved to be unreliable. Inside there, you got to know your *me* but forgot about your *us*. The friends I made when I was on the run—those were real friends. I had met them in the darkest times of hunger and fear, and in those terrible times, they remained loyal. But that was before the days of Facebook, cell phones, and internet, and therefore we had lost track of one another.

During one of Calvin's sporadic spells at home, I told him I was planning to leave soon.

"Stay, man. Why leave? Spend the winter here. It freezes outside, and here everything is free."

"That's just it. Poor Danielle works day and night, and I'm just a freeloader. I don't want that."

"Nonsense. You cost her less then Diesel, man," he said. He wrapped a towel around his neck like a scarf and left the shed. Half an hour later he returned to say he had discussed the matter with Danielle, and if I wanted to stay, I could clean the day care center in return. Fantastic! Then I didn't have to say goodbye to Calvin and Diesel. Or Leda.

I'd like to tell you about the difference between a job in the Netherlands and a job in other countries where I've worked. But in truth, it's easier to explain the difference between an Iraqi date palm and a Dutch potato. But one thing is for sure: working as a cleaner in a day care center in Holland is more dignified than working as a civil engineer in Iraq. In Holland you pay with your time in exchange for money. In other countries you give everything you have, even your dignity, and sometimes you don't even get paid. You can work for one day and spend a week begging for your wages. I never experienced this in the Netherlands. Also, in the Netherlands there are jobs that do not exist anywhere else. I remember an Armenian who had been refused asylum but worked as a gene factory by selling his sperm to a sperm bank.

I assumed cleaning a day care center would be a gross job. Diapers strewn everywhere, kids peeing all over the toilet seats and puking on the floor. But it wasn't bad at all. I started work at eight in the evening. Already on my first day on the job, I saw how tidy it all was. It hardly stank at all and the tables were clean. I opened the window for some fresh air and went around with the vacuum cleaner. Not because it needed vacuuming, but to get the cleanliness clean. I had no experience whatsoever with either cleanliness or cleaning. But I had to do something. Danielle came in while I was working that first evening. She shouted my name, so I could hear her above the vacuum cleaner.

"Nice and clean!" she exclaimed, as though the crèche had never been so spick and span, and I pretended I was getting rid of years' worth of dust. She went off again, and I wiped down the kitchenette counter. I cleaned the coffee machine, rinsed the kettle, washed glasses and plates. I did the windows, both inside and out, and the frames as well, just to be busy for longer. After an hour and a half I called it a day. The next day I swept the patio and tidied up the shed, and the third day I did the paths and watered the plants in the greenhouse. Then I asked Danielle to buy some cement so I could take care of some odd jobs, in the day care center but also in the house and the yard. This went on for a while.

In the evenings I cleaned the crèche and during the day did whatever yard work or indoor jobs needed doing. I unclogged pipes, hung shelves, weeded the path, changed the oil in the car, and patched flat bicycle tires. I never started without checking with Danielle, and she invariably said, "Fine." I painted doors and window frames, and I even made creaking beds quiet.

After a while Danielle started recommending me in the village for incidental work, usually for older people. I never set a fee. They just paid me cash, and it was always more than I expected. Gradually I started finding work on my own. Or the work found me. Not only in the village, but also further afield.

The best jobs were for Mrs. Dotinga. She was eighty-five years old, used to be a GP, and loved roses. She could still drive but preferred not to. The first time I went to her place, she asked me to walk with her to the garden center, where she bought bags of dirt and gloves and overalls in my size, as though I had signed an open-ended contract. I was to dig up the old earth around her rosebushes, put it in garbage bags, and replace it with fresh dirt.

Her dog was deaf, and whenever he saw me he would bark until Mrs. Dotinga hoisted herself out of her chair, went over to him, and explained with gestures that he didn't need to bark. I know for sure that if that dog could talk, he'd have said to Mrs. Dotinga, "I don't trust that asylum seeker." The dog even knew when to put on his watchdog act. When Mrs. Dotinga sat napping in her chair he was more menacing. He didn't bark, just growled whenever I moved, as though to say, "Watch it, bud, I see what you're up to." I won't tell you his name, so that rotten dog can stay a nameless mutt.

As meticulously as that dog followed my every move, Mrs. Dotinga counted the minutes I spent in her yard, so that she could pay me down to the last second. Every second from the moment I knocked until I closed the gate behind me was counted, plus bonus time, as she called it. Even the time we spent walking to the garden center or drinking tea together was converted into euros.

I often cycled back to the Van der Weerdes' house loaded with money, where I would wait until Leda returned.

10

Leda was the reason I stayed in that village for so long, and Diesel was the reason she showed up every Friday. Diesel came to symbolize Leda's presence. He was the leash that pulled her from Utrecht back to that drab village, turning it into a place more beautiful than Bali. By now I was starting to act like Diesel: when I saw Leda, I wanted to leap, bark, wag my tail, and run over to her so she would run her fingers through my hair and stroke my head.

I lost my faith in God during the war, my faith in the world after crossing the Iraqi border, and my faith in myself in the ASC. But Leda made me glad of it, because it meant I had ended up in that village and met her.

I will never forget that winter up in the far north. It was the winter of Leda.

I remember her once noticing me sitting there sadly, and asking me what was the matter.

"Diesel."

"Did he bite you?"

"No, but I asked him to take me to Utrecht for a weekend to be with you, and he looked in his datebook and said he really couldn't fit it in." She laughed, which cheered me up.

"Good idea! Come to Utrecht. I'll show you around, take you to the cathedral square in the city center, where everyone hangs out." Her positive response cheered me up even more, but at the same time I was worried that Danielle might object. In Arabic culture, it's a woman's responsibility to preserve the family's honor. Women aren't to be touched, except by the hand of marriage.

So I was relieved when Danielle said, "Leda comes back more often since you've been here." The smile that followed was a green light, encouraging me to fantasize about taking things further with Leda. But as soon as I started thinking about it in the Arabic way, the green light quickly jumped back to red. So confusing. What was possible, and what wasn't? What were the limits? Calvin assured me that Danielle was really glad I had such a good rapport with Leda.

"I think Danielle worries. Leda can have hard times, but she told me recently how good it is that she can have such a good laugh with you."

"What do you mean, hard times?"

He said he didn't know.

I started to pay attention, and it was true that Danielle worried about her daughter. I didn't know if I could ask about it, because if she had wanted me to know, she would have said something by now. What went through my head was: is it possible that someone like Leda, who looks so happy and strong and carefree and rich on the outside, could experience hard times on the inside? I couldn't get my head around it then, and still have trouble getting my head around it now.

She came every Friday evening, often while I was still cleaning the day care center. Diesel gave the signal that she had arrived, and a bit later she would pop her head around the corner.

"Look who we have here, Diesel. Our diaper cleaner."

"I smell like baby poop! Go away!" I would shout, and she laughed at my standard Friday evening joke.

"You do stink," she said, and laughed for real. "I'll come out back for a cup of tea, but you have to take a shower first."

Then she would come by to flop down on Calvin's bed, where I had just tucked his underwear out of sight. Diesel lay on the floor next to her. Leda had no clue that the only reason I stayed in that town was to see her every weekend.

It wasn't easy to talk to her. It even seemed that the more we talked, the less we understood each other. For me, Leda was an ocean full of whales and starfish, ebb and flow, desert islands, dolphins and sharks. It hadn't occurred to me that Leda was in fact a faucet waiting to be opened so that she could gush forth, or waiting until she trusted me enough, so she could turn herself open. I always had to take a deep breath before submerging myself in that seawater. From our very first encounter, I never managed to form a clear image of her. Only later did I learn that she didn't want me to really get to know her, which is why it was such a struggle to understand her. Somehow it felt like she wanted to convince me that she wasn't as good as I thought.

But then, if I did say something critical about her, she surprised me by retorting that I shouldn't talk her down like that, because she had a good side, too. If I only looked at her good side, she would remind me of her bad side, and only when I saw both her good and bad sides simultaneously did she accept what I said and not think I was sucking up to her or exaggerating.

Apparently I had learned to either look at someone's negative side, which made their positive side negative, too, or at the person's positive side, which made the negative side positive. So a person was either entirely bad or entirely good. Leda forced me to adjust my way of thinking.

My image of Leda was that she was a beauty on the inside as well as the outside, without the one getting in the way of the other. But the inside turned out to be darker than I had imagined. I didn't realize this at the time, and I regret it to this day.

11

As a diversion I repaired fountain pens or I opened up my trash bags full of old photo albums. I hadn't added any new albums since moving to the village, because I either bought them at thrift stores, of which there weren't any here, or found them in the garbage, and in this village people did not throw out such personal treasures.

I was ignorant about art, so I started reading art history books to learn something about it. I ended up understanding art history, but not art. An artist once told me you don't have to understand art, but *feel* it. So I stood looking at many paintings, but felt nothing except my sore legs. Once a volunteer from the Dutch Council for Refugees took me to Amsterdam. We went to the Rijksmuseum and he talked a lot about Vermeer's *The Milkmaid*. The only thing that struck me about the painting was that the milk the woman poured was not really white, so it must have been whole milk. The volunteer was rather disappointed in my limited capacity for observation.

"What a pity," he said. "You understand the cow, but not Johannes Vermeer."

That eternal stream of whole milk made me realize that the brain cells responsible for art are dormant, or maybe even totally absent, in me. What I do understand well are photographs, especially portraits. I can gaze at them for hours on end, until I feel the flesh and blood that filled the scene while the person was still alive.

In real life, people's faces change every second. So you can never really see someone: he or she is always moving, even when they're standing still. But a photograph steals a face and nails it to the cross of time. A photo doesn't let me get lost in someone's many faces, but just that one face. And that one face in turn lets me see all the other living faces, and know who it is.

I remember once seeing a photo of a friend of my sister. That girl later fell out of a date palm tree and died. I stared at that photo until I could see her death in it.

"Look," I said to my sister. "I see a date palm in her eyes."

"I don't see any date palm," she said. "That's just your fantasy. If she had drowned in the Euphrates, you'd have said, 'Look, I see a river in her eyes.'"

I stared at the photo for hours longer, until I saw the river, ready for a different death for that girl if she hadn't fallen out of the palm tree. My sister had also seen a river, without realizing it.

In Iraq, people sometimes only had one or two photos taken of themselves in their entire life, and of those people who don't have a passport or ID card, often not even one photo exists. But in the Netherlands, I was surprised to discover, nearly everyone had their own photo archive. And not only of themselves, but also of their ancestors, all the way back to the invention of the camera. Pure magic. Every Dutch house was a museum. Oceans of photos on which you could sail further and further into the past, where the waves were faces and the beaches were baby announcements or obituaries. From face to face to face. Until one face brings you back to the present. What got me collecting photo albums was the first one I found, in a box alongside a garbage container. It contained photos dating all the way from 1871 up to 1999. For me, those albums were a treasure trove of time.

One Wednesday, Diesel came to the shed and started barking and leaping and wagging his tail. He was trying to tell me something. Something important not only for him, but for me, too. Then Leda knocked at the door, and Diesel charged over to her. I looked up from my fountain pen repair work, surprised.

"It's only Wednesday," I said.

"So?" she replied. I couldn't believe she was suddenly standing there before me, and that I couldn't prepare myself for her visit. "What's that you're doing?"

"I'm trying to fix this Waterman," I said, holding up the pen. She did not look at the fountain pen, but at the open garbage bag where I kept my photo albums.

"What's in the bag?"

"Families," I said. I took out one of the albums. She thumbed through it.

"Personal photos," she said to herself. It sounded like a reproach, like I had no business having someone else's photos in my possession. When I didn't respond, she said: "Dutch cheeseheads."

Then she bent over, petted Diesel, and went off with him. I tried not to let her irritation get the better of me and overshadow the joy of seeing her again. Half an hour later she returned with four photo albums.

"Voilà," she said, dropping them with a thwack on the floor. "Now you can have your fill of the bad tempers in this nuthouse," she said, whereupon she sat down on Calvin's bed. I just stared at her. "Don't look at me like that," she said.

"Why have you come in the middle of the week? That poor dog is beside himself, he thinks it's Friday."

"Danielle is taking me to the airport at four o'clock tomorrow morning. I'm going to Lisbon for the weekend."

She lay back and put her head on the pillow, reached under it and pulled something out. Calvin's underwear. She flung it away with an elegant flick of her hand. Then she felt under her back. Another pair of Calvin's underwear. Again it flew through the air. When she pulled the blanket up to her chin, another one appeared.

"That Calvin has more underwear than ..."

"Than a chicken has feathers."

"Don't exaggerate," she said, closing her eyes. "It was just three."

Then she did something that made the blood rush to my head. Her hands wriggled around under the blanket, and before I knew it she had tossed her pants onto the bed.

"I sleep better this way," she said. "I have to get up really early, so I'll just have a little nap." She fell asleep, her face to the ceiling and a smile on her lips.

I took the photo albums from under Calvin's underwear and quietly opened them, one by one. Leda appeared for the first time in 1914. A far-off September day. A bouquet of flowers in her hands. Behind her, a stately home. Then she vanished from the album until 1936, and thereafter she disappeared again. There she was as an eight-year-old girl in 1944, and then gone again. It was as though she appeared in this family only to disappear. In all those photos she had the same eyes, the same gaze into a void without a horizon. I paged through the albums. Not looking for the Ledas who appeared and disappeared over the course of time, but for the Leda who was now dozing in Calvin's bed. Ah, there she was: 24 July 1996. One photo made me stop. In it, she had the exact same expression as all the other girls and women I had just seen appear and disappear in various years. That photo, I later thought, should have been her last.

I went over to the window and looked at the gray outdoors. A crow cawed. I dared not look at her sleeping figure, afraid that she had already disappeared.

12

My time in that village changed me. It wasn't just Leda who made my head spin. The questions banging around in my head were not what or if I would eat that day, or how I would find shelter for the night, or whether I'd get picked up by the secret police, but rather things like: Who am I? What does life mean to me? What is the meaning of life in general? Am I ready to be in a relationship, or should I get to know myself better first? These questions had never entered my mind before, but Dutch culture had built a whole network of paths for them: highways, train tracks, bike paths, canals. These questions traveled effortlessly into my head and kept riding around in circles there.

One big question living in that Dutch family raised in me was: instead of *when*, *why* does the war in Iraq never end?

Suicide bombings were everyday occurrences in Iraq. Saddam Hussein had been driven from Baghdad in 2003, but instead of peace, only misery ensued. Not by dictatorship, fear, and torture, but by terror and suicide bombings.

I followed the news as little as possible, but the fact that buses were exploding and car bombs going off, I couldn't block out.

Danielle and the people I did odd jobs for often asked me how things were in Iraq, and if my family was all right. Usually I didn't go into it much, but one day I had seen the news and told Danielle what I had heard.

"Today, six hundred and eleven people were killed in various bombings in Iraq."

"Six hundred and eleven? Are you serious?" Danielle asked.

I nodded.

"That's horrible. Were any of the casualties from your family?"

I shrugged my shoulders. I preferred not to think about it. But for the rest of the evening and the whole next day, Danielle would shake her head and repeat, "Six hundred and eleven in one day. That's half our village ..." I started to get the feeling that I had become synonymous with war in that peaceful village. In any case, I had bombarded the composure of Danielle's mind. So I decided to no longer use my tongue as the loudspeaker for the war in Iraq, so as not to mar the gentle tranquility of my adopted village. Danielle said I *should* talk about it, to get it out of my system, but she could not convince me to do so.

Leda never asked me about Iraq. Sometimes she said that it was strange to think I had family in a distant land, and a mother who surely worried about me, but she never asked about them. After hearing from Calvin that Danielle worried about her, I started watching her more closely. I didn't know back then that Leda, like so many other Dutch people, was more open than I presumed, and that rather than watching her so closely I could have just asked the simple question, "How are you?"

But before continuing about Leda, I want to gradually introduce the other family members, starting with Calvin, who as far as I'm concerned was also part of the Van der Weerde family.

That this was not just my idea became clear when Calvin got picked up in Breda by the foreigners' police and Danielle spent many days and a lot of effort getting him back. Her maternal feelings for Calvin were what got him released from that cell. I still remember them pulling into the driveway that evening, Calvin getting out with that big smile of his, and Diesel running over to him and wagging his tail, as though he knew Calvin had been locked up.

"Where have you been?" I asked him back in the shed.

"On vacation."

"Was the cell cramped?"

"No, man, I was only in it at night. I spent all day in a big room or in an office. With Danielle. I think her head was in the cell, not me," he laughed.

We embraced.

"Has Nina asked about me?" he asked. "Or Elisa?"

Calvin was the local ladies' man. He had had them all, without a single one having had him. He went to bed with older women for money. Not that he got paid for sex, but because the women felt sorry for him, a poor asylum seeker without a green card. He then spent that money on the younger women. Even if he bought new shoes or expensive cologne, he said it wasn't for himself, but for the girls.

Calvin once told me that, like Danielle, he had his own business: his dick. He liked to boast about its business plan and direct marketing.

After a while I knew when Calvin's penis had to go to work, or out for pleasure. If Calvin wore shabby clothes and worn-out shoes and looked like an asylum seeker, then he was on his way to an older lady. But if he went out wearing snazzy clothes and a fine watch, and smelling nice, then he was off to one of his younger ones. Whenever I asked him about this, he said: "Not only the Dutch have rules in their business. My dick does, too. What he earns from an older lady goes to a young woman who's less well-off. In this way, the older generation takes care of the younger one."

13

Now I have to tell you about a dramatic event that befell the family: the death of Edward.

I was up early that morning, because Danielle wanted to go with me to buy supplies to repair the fence out back. However, the minute I entered the house I sensed that something awful had happened. Danielle was pale and in a state.

"Sorry, Samir, we can't go now. We'll do the fence some other time."

"Is something wrong?"

"Yes, Edward has taken ill. It's bad. And so suddenly." Her voice was shaky and she seemed to be fighting back tears. Tessa came into Danielle's office and without even noticing I was there, she hugged Danielle and started to cry.

Grief built a dark tent above the Van der Weerde house. It even got hold of Diesel's tail, which no longer flapped, but hung from his backside like a dead branch. But ... who was Edward? An uncle, a family friend, Tessa's best friend? The grief got hold of me too, and I was embarrassed to ask who Edward was. I went back to the shed and Calvin told me Edward was Tessa's rabbit.

I know that the death of a family pet can be painful, but in my mind Edward had been a man with spiffy clothes and a necktie. Now I had to totally reimagine him as a rabbit. I burst out laughing. I hope I don't give you the wrong impression, but Calvin and I had to tiptoe around the family during those days Edward lay on his deathstraw.

In Iraq I had seen all kinds of grief. Grief from war, murder, death. Grief from poverty, illness, or injustice. From the loss of a loved one who had disappeared or fled. But never did I see grief completely paralyze a family the way it did the Van der Weerdes. Calvin and I were afraid we would laugh at that grief, and we knew it was unkind. The fear of laughing only made it harder not to. So Calvin put his toothbrush, toothpaste, and a few pairs of underwear in a bag.

"Samir, I'm out of here. Just until that damn rabbit is dead and buried. Text me when it's happened."

When they decided that the rabbit mustn't suffer unnecessarily and should be put down, Tessa came to the shed for the first time. With tears in her eyes she said that if I wanted to say goodbye to Edward, I could do so until a quarter past twelve. I prayed to all the gods, prophets, and heavens that I would not get the giggles during my farewell to the rabbit. At ten to twelve I closed my eyes and did a backward meditation. You usually meditate in order to calm yourself, so you think of waterfalls, sunsets, or butterflies. But now I did just the opposite: I thought of bullet-ridden corpses, missiles and bombardments, of Chaweng Prison in Thailand, of the Dutch Immigration Services, of asylum seekers and ice-cold jail cells, and when I was pretty sure I could make it through the miserable affair without so much as a chortle, I walked over to the house. Everyone had put on nice clothes and I immediately saw how stupid it looked that I was saying farewell to Edward in my zebra pajamas and plastic sandals. Tessa's visible disappointment sent me back to the shed, where I put on my best clothes and Calvin's fancy shoes, despite the fact that his feet were a full size smaller than mine, and returned to the house to say goodbye to the rabbit.

"Upstairs," said Tessa. Up I went, thankfully alone. I smelled incense and heard gentle classical music. The curtains had been drawn, there was soft lighting and a few lit tea candles. It was impossible not to laugh, but suddenly, there in Tessa's room, the fear of laughing flipped into the fear of crying. Tessa had turned her room into a funeral parlor.

She had hung up childhood drawings she had made of Edward, handwritten poems, and photos of the two of them together. She'd had him since she was seven: that rabbit was Tessa's lifetime, her childhood years, and her emotions from age seven until now. It wasn't Edward who would be put down, but Tessa's childhood. This is what she had to say goodbye to. And that moved me deeply.

14

An eternity ago, or so it felt, our family experienced mutual grief. It was the last winter of the Iran-Iraq war. Until that evening, we were a complete family: a father and a mother, brothers and sisters.

One of my older brothers had graduated from university. However, that was not a reason for celebration. On the contrary, the mood was somber. Because now he had to choose between conscription into the army and fleeing the country. He chose the latter. My mother cooked his favorite meal. We all knew that if he got caught at the border he would end up in a cell run by the secret police and would be executed for treason. We would never see him again, not even as a corpse. But if he did succeed in escaping Saddam Hussein's Iraq, we would never hear from him again either. Aside from migrating birds and missiles, there was no contact with the outside world. Not even letters arrived unopened.

That was our last evening as a complete family. My brother was the first to flee the country; later, a younger brother and I would follow suit. My father died before we were able to see him again. My eldest brother was killed by a mortar, my sister died of grief a few months later. My youngest brother married his college sweetheart. He, a Shiite from the south, met her, a Sunni from the northern city of Mosul, at the University of Baghdad. Against all conventions, they married and had four children. A marriage you could compare to that of a German boy and Jewish girl during World War II. Eventually they fled, like many others, to Turkey. Except in our dreams, being reunited as a family was out of the question. Throughout that last evening together, at some point each one of us would go off on their own to cry. Then they would dry the tears, come back inside, and pretend they they'd only gone off for a pee. One of my brothers cried outside, dried his tears, and came back:

"Did you have to pee, too?" I asked him.

"Yeah, from my eyes," he said. And we all laughed extra hard, so we could also shed tears of grief.

Tessa came out to the shed, pale as could be. Before I could offer her something to drink, she asked an unexpected question, as though she had come out here for that specific reason.

"Have you ever seen the corpse of someone you loved?"

"Often," I said breezily.

"What was it like, the first time?"

"There was no first or second time. It's always *one* time that keeps repeating." She gave me a look that said, *That's not an answer.* But I took it as a sign to give her a more thorough reply, which I did with the following story:

Through the village where I grew up flowed a tributary of the Euphrates. Rather than teaching the children to swim so that they would not drown, the adults taught the children to fear the water. A good friend of mine, Shafik, wasn't afraid of anything. Not of the schoolmaster, even though he carried a stick; not of the soldiers who often trekked through the village, frightening off all the children; not of snakes, scorpions, or the dark; not of the wolves who came to snatch chickens at night; not even of his father. One hot summer afternoon, Shafik and I were hanging around with Daoud, another friend who was more of a fraidy-cat. Daoud told Shafik that he was probably only faking not being afraid of anything, and that he was surely afraid of the deep water.

"I am not afraid of the water," Shafik said. "I just can't swim." He looked sharply at Daoud, who returned the provocative look.

"No, that's not it," Daoud said. "You can't swim because you're scared of the water."

I remember that at this point in the story it occurred to me that it wasn't right to tell all this to Tessa. The rest might be too much for her, and she might think that because of what happened, I have a fear of water. As soon as you relate an everyday Iraqi anecdote to a European, they do not listen to it in the context of life there, but rather try to pin a psychological illness or trauma to it that you must have suffered as a consequence.

Tessa sensed my hesitation. "Maybe it's too emotional for you talk about it, Samir," she said.

"In difficult situations, and there are a lot of them, I think back on that brave Shafik. Maybe his bravery at the beginning of his life spared him all those wars and disasters that he would have otherwise experienced."

"Why do you say it like that?"

"Because he only died once. Me, I've died at least a thousand times. That is the good thing about heroes: they only die once."

"Do you think there's life after death?" she asked. She was clearly wondering if I thought I would see Shafik again, but before I could answer, she said, her eyes teary, "I so want to see Eddy again."

"Eddy?"

"Little Edward," she said, choking back the tears.

I had to bite my tongue, but Tessa deserved an answer.

"I am convinced that there is something after death. Heaven or paradise. And Edward will be there."

15

One thing about Tessa was she couldn't sit still. She would often get up from the table at mealtime, and you might see her doing a headstand, or standing on one leg like a stork. Mieke told me that Tessa was the smartest and most talented one in the family, especially at sports, languages, and general creativity. That was why Danielle signed her up for all kinds of classes: violin, piano, drawing, gymnastics, four languages, athletics—the list goes on. In fact, all those lessons had stifled her talents, they were jammed into too-small pots without being allowed to grow. So Tessa's talents became Tessa's boredom.

Tessa never came out back to the shed without a specific question in mind, which she then posed the minute I opened the door. When she ran out of questions she would sometimes bring her younger brother Maurice along, as though without a question she was afraid to knock on my door by herself.

One day, when Tessa's cell phone started pinging, as it often did, she and her pings went outside and left Maurice behind with me. He sat at the table and looked like a tourist who only realized when he got to the beach that he'd forgotten his bathing suit. I assumed he was just shy and unsure of himself, but this turned out not to be the case.

I don't think Maurice was ever a child. I only saw him three times in all those family albums. Once in a military uniform, and each time with the same fiery look in his eyes and the same narrow face.

He was tall and skinny and had a pale complexion. He always wore black army boots and clothes with a camouflage motif. Maybe he wanted to look macho because on the inside he was weak and naive. But when I looked into his eyes I saw strength, which made me forget that pale, skinny body. I can't put my finger on it, but I could tell right away that he had a militaristic spirit. He had been born in the wrong place, a provincial Dutch village, where war was only fought in people's minds, not in the sky above their head and not on the ground under their feet. Maurice was a fan of war movies. Once he and his friends, who were also skinny and wore camouflage clothes, were supposed to get together to watch a war film, but at the last minute they didn't show up. So he asked me if I'd like to watch it with him, and out of politeness I said yes, because he'd never invited me over before. But the scene where someone was tied to a stake in the midde of a town square and executed was too much for me. I leapt up and ran, trembling, out to the shed. I scrambled to find the Ventolin inhaler and took two puffs. Maurice came out. He stood in the doorway.

"Sorry I spoiled your film," I said.

"No problem, man, I left it on pause." His voice sounded like a teenager's.

He watched me. While the Ventolin did its job, he smiled faintly.

"I thought that people from war zones, who had seen it all with their own eyes, wouldn't be shocked by a scene in a film," he said, genuinely interested.

"It reminded me of an execution on the football field next to our high school," I said. "The man there had a cigarette in his mouth, just like in the film. Coincidentally," I said, and shrugged.

"Interesting," Maurice said, to encourage me to continue. But I did not. So he said, "Want to tell me some more?"

"I would, but I'm not sure you can handle it," I said.

He looked straight at me and said, "You'd be surprised."

So to cover up my embarrassment at running away from that scene in the film, I told him about the time soldiers, armed with automatic weapons, charged into our high school and forced the students from the classrooms out onto the football field. Maurice was not so much interested in the circumstances of the man about to be executed—what he looked like, whether he was frightened, whether or not he begged for mercy—but rather in the soldiers that had tied him to the left goalpost. How many of them there were, where their captain stood, did he also have an automatic rifle, and what kind? I told him that they cut the net of the goal with knives and tossed it aside. I told him how close the soldiers were to the man. I answered his question as to whether the captain shot him in the head after they had executed him. He informed me that the bullet through the head was called the *coup de grâce* and proceeded to recite all sorts of historical facts about executions, as though he was a tour guide in the Colosseum. He told me how much blood a person has in his body and how long it takes for a person to bleed to death after being executed. And on he went. Maurice stopped to ask me the occasional question, not in order to find something out, but to confirm that his knowledge tallied with reality. I answered him, but hid my shock.

His interest in me was to hear about real-life war, not the kind in films, documentaries, or computer games. My interest in him was to learn about the war that is not real, but plays out in the mind of someone who has no reason to need to know about it. And despite everything, Maurice was a nice kid. He had a calm exterior, he was intelligent and polite. This fifteen-year-old boy had been born far from war, both in time and distance, but his fascination with it made me realize something that can make me despair to this day: that there is war because people are born to wage it.

When I was patching the back tire of his bicycle a few days later, Maurice struck up a conversation, as though that leak in his tire was the trigger we needed to get a conversation going. He asked me about the war in Iraq.

"Tell me, do you like war?" I asked him. My question hit him like tomato soup on a wedding dress.

"Not war," he said, irritated. "I'm interested in the army."

"That sounds like someone who says: I don't like alcohol, but I'd be interested in being an alcoholic," I said. "Watch out for your soul. War never brings anything good."

His eyes burned into me, and I could feel that in that moment I had lost his respect and trust. I then learned that a Dutch person can ignore you even if you live in the same house. From that day onward, I was invisible to Maurice, even when I sat across from him at the table.

16

My contact with Tessa and Maurice was like lightning: it hit quickly and was over in a flash. But with Mieke it was like an apple tree: it grew slowly. She was, until she became a mother, not only a good friend but also a kind of sister. I feel the kind of warmth for her that you only feel for family. Once we became good friends, I would often ask Mieke about the details in Leda's life. I thought she was reticent about it because it was painful for her. She said I should ask Leda, not her, but when she realized it wasn't just curiosity but that I was in love with her sister and found her hard to understand, she opened up to me somewhat. For instance, she told me that Leda was not grateful for what she had, but focused on what she did not have. And that she was quick-tempered. Whenever Mieke told me something like this and then saw that I was taken aback, she added something positive to balance it out, such as that Leda had the best sense of humor in the family.

Mieke was also the one Danielle talked to the most. Once, I was in the kitchen, doing some odd job under the counter, while Danielle and Mieke sat drinking coffee. Danielle chattered away, Mieke listened. She would interject with a question now and again, maybe so the conversation would sound less like a monologue from Danielle.

What a difference with Leda and Danielle. I remember seeing Leda walking home from the bus stop one Friday afternoon. Danielle was working in the yard. Leda shouted to Diesel, who trotted off excitedly to greet her. Danielle greeted her daughter with a word like a hailstone: "Hey." And Leda responded with the same word. Danielle called to me to come over for a cup a tea. When Diesel fell asleep at Leda's feet, the conversation between the two women also dozed off. I looked at the two of them with no idea how to revive the connection.

What I had not noticed earlier was that Leda and Danielle spent most of their time trying to avoid conflict. When they weren't together, Danielle spoke of her daughter with all the love in the world, and Leda likewise spoke of her mother with bashful pride. But as soon as they were in the same place, they would walk on eggshells. As though what connected them was the thinnest of threads, and they were more concerned with the thread than they were with each other.

Leda saw in her mother what she could become if she didn't watch out, and if she gave her weak points too much room to grow. Danielle saw in Leda what she could have become if she had nurtured her strong points. What existed between them was a mystery to me. Was it worry, or love? Hate, or pity? It was like Leda really wanted her mother to see how much she loved her, but all that came out was irritation. It was the classic mother-daughter love-hate relationship, and a new language would need to be invented if they were to communicate their feelings for each other.

One Thursday in February I asked Mieke if she thought Leda was ready for a relationship.

"I don't know," she said. "But she's doing well these days. She spends more time here, and has a better relationship with Diesel."

If Leda had a good relationship with a dog, did that mean she was ready for a relationship with an asylum seeker?

17

I spent hours perusing the Van der Weerdes' family photo albums, with Diesel at my side. Tessa was the only family member I could not spot among the Van der Weerde ancestors. I paged through generation after generation. I saw the man who must have been her father at two different points in time. Even Mieke, though technically not an official family member, appeared here and there, but not Tessa. Tessa was a kind of drifter, a migratory bird who strayed from her flock and settled on a branch for the night, only to continue her journey with the first rays of the morning sun.

One Saturday afternoon while I was paging through the photo albums, Leda came in.

"You're a curious one, aren't you?" she said. "Old ladies in an upstairs apartment sometimes have a little mirror angled down to the street so they can spy on passersby. That's you." She came and stood next to me. I had not seen her in a week and had turned to the photo albums to distract myself from missing her, but I didn't want to let on.

She pointed at a picture of Danielle's great-grandmother, Johanna. "Why are you looking at her? Do you think she's attractive?"

"Actually, I was looking for Tessa but can't find her anywhere. Maybe Tessa has the same expression as Johanna. I can't look into Tessa's eyes long enough to find out."

"Why not?"

"Because her cell phone always steals them from me."

Leda smiled. "Nonsense," she said.

I set the photo album aside, and she flopped down on Calvin's bed. I poured her a cup of tea. She held the warm mug between her hands as if to capture all the tea's warmth. Her eyes fell on an open book next to the bed.

"What's that book?"

"Poetry."

"Could you recite some for me?"

It was a poem by César Fernandez Moreno. The Spanish original was on the left page and the Dutch translation on the right page.

Leda corrected my pronunciation of some words as I read. Then she got up, took the book from me, and started reading it out loud in fluent Spanish.

"Stop!" I shouted.

"What?"

"Stop! What time is it exactly?"

"One thirty-six p.m. Why?"

"Because at exactly one thirty-six p.m. I fell in love. With you. I am surely the first person in history who can pinpoint the exact minute he fell in love." Leda laughed so hard that the tears rolled down her cheeks.

"And now," she said, "it is one thirty-seven p.m. The exact moment I discovered what a jokester you are!" It was clear that the moment she discovered I was a jokester was more important to her than the moment I fell in love with her, but for me, my discovery was more important than the apple that fell on Isaac Newton's head.

"That's a pretty dry response to my declaration of love," I said.

"Because it's not even true, I've heard you've been in love with me for ages and ask all sorts of things about me." She wiped her face dry.

As a diversion I went back to paging through the album in search of a past Leda. She got up from Calvin's bed and glanced over my shoulder.

"Look, here you are in 1951," I said. "Look how angry you are."

She stared silently at the photo.

I looked into her eyes. "How are you?"

"Me? What do you mean?"

"I mean, how are you, *really?*"

She took her last sip of tea. "To be honest ... really bad."

It was as though she had seen that question coming. She looked me deep in my questioning eyes, and I in turn in her sad ones. I saw her as I had never seen her before.

She's unbound by the world around her, but imprisoned within herself, I thought.

Outside, it drizzled. The tears that had just wetted her cheeks in laughter now did the same, but in sadness. She cried. But this time she didn't wipe the tears away. Maybe she did not want me to notice. The tears made it impossible to just sit there and say nothing.

"Have you ever seen the dead body of someone you love?" she asked. It was exactly the same question Tessa had asked just after Edward died.

"By 'someone' do you mean a rabbit or a person?" I asked seriously, taking into account the family's grief surrounding Edward's demise. Tessa and Danielle would not have seen my question as impertinent, but Leda did. She gave me an angry look.

"Forget it," she said. Her face had changed from sad to angry. Perhaps not angry at me, but at herself, because she had opened up to someone and it was met with a misunderstanding.

She got up and left without a word. I wondered how she would have reacted if I had told her I'd seen thousands of corpses in my life, at least a hundred of them of people I knew.

"She is terrible," I said to myself out loud. "What am I to do with her?"

"Wait a second, Samir," she called from the house.

"Five minutes," I shouted back, "and not one second longer."

"I'll be right there," she said, and returned wearing knee-length boots and a raincoat draped over her shoulders.

18

We walked without Diesel, but Leda talked about him anyway. Especially about when he was a puppy. How she had picked him out, and what she liked about him and how exhausting he was at first. Once we left the village behind us she started talking about herself, as though we were no longer in Diesel's territory. It struck me that she talked about herself in the exact same tone of voice as when she talked about Diesel.

She used a term I had never heard before: *biological father.* Something you would never hear in the Middle East. Rather than feeling sorry for Leda, I started to feel sorry for her mother.

Danielle had once gone to bed with someone when she was drunk. Nine months later, Leda was born. When she was fourteen, Leda wanted to meet her biological father, and Danielle did her best to fix up a meeting. It was traumatic for both mother and daughter. All Leda could think the whole time was: yuck, how could my mother go to bed with someone like that? Danielle wondered the same thing all those years ago, when she woke up the next morning in a smelly bed, and got dressed quietly so as to slip away unnoticed, not aware then that no amount of distance could separate her from that man, because something had started growing inside her.

That man became a barrier between Leda and Danielle. He also became Leda's shame.

"Think about it, Samir," she said, shivering in the drizzle. "That man is my biological father ... I have his genes. I would go out of my way not to sit next to him in the train, he's that kind of man. And Danielle went to bed with him and made a child with him. An unwanted child. Danielle always calls me a 'happy accident.'" She said this with a bottled-up anger that covered an ocean full of loathing.

"I think it's marvelous that Danielle could produce such a beautiful child with a filthy man," I said. "She's more talented than Picasso, because Picasso turned a beautiful woman into a monster. Not your mother. On the contrary. She slept with a filthy bastard and produced a gorgeous child."

She stared at me blankly.

"I really do think you're more beautiful than an abortion," I said, and she burst out laughing. "I mean it," I continued, happy to have cheered her up. "I couldn't go out for walks, laugh, or fall in love with an abortion, but I can with you." This made her laugh even harder.

"You're silly, but fun," she said. "I guess I think too much sometimes."

"All you people *do* is think." I said. I looked at my watch. "Two forty-six p.m., the exact time we stood close enough together that we could kiss, but unfortunately my breath stank of garlic."

I was proud of my silliness, because it made her clear blue eyes twinkle. I had never been so happy. It wasn't only my heart that pounded for Leda, but my socks, too.

"Don't think so much about your father," I said. "It's not good for you."

"Now you sound like a schoolteacher; or no, more like a preacher."

"Don't think so much! He's just one link in an endless chain. I have the same mother and father as all my brothers and sisters. There were twelve of us, if I remember correctly. My father was a good father and my mother a good mother, but one of my brothers is a jerk. You would never think we came from the same two parents, but we did."

"Enough about garlic and families," she said with a dismissive flick of her hand. "If you keep going on like this it'll take us six years to get around to kissing."

Whenever Leda talked about herself, she would always start full of self-confidence, but gradually become more insecure, as though the words were less about herself than about a stranger she was only getting to know. She saw herself as an appliance in search of a user's manual.

But even when her thoughts got closer to my ears, it was as if the physical distance stayed the same. There was something in the way, some grim barrier between her body and mine. But I had no idea what it was.

19

The days advanced, slowly but surely, towards spring. I looked forward to it, and at the same time I was grateful for the receding winter. It was the first winter in my life I had spent surrounded by nature, warmth, and the gentler aspects of life, like love and yearning.

Calvin, however, began to tire of winter, and I saw less and less of him in the shed. He told me he wanted to go to Canada, and encouraged me to leave, too. But leaving was not an option. I couldn't get Leda out of my head. My doubts were not about whether I should stay or go, but about whether I was good enough for that Dutch girl.

Calvin said he was finally starting to realize there was no future for him in Holland without a residence permit. That sounded strange, coming from him. I wanted to know the real reason he chose to leave, and found out that his brother had made his way to Canada and wanted Calvin to join him.

"I'll really miss you, Calvin," I said.

"Miss me? What, are we lovers or something?"

"No, man, I'll miss you as a friend."

He laughed. "We'll keep in touch. And if life is good there, I'll bring you over. I promise."

I strummed a sad little tune on the guitar Danielle had lent me. Leda hadn't shown up that weekend.

"Such a sad song, Samir."

I sighed. "I'm so in love."

"With Diesel?"

"With his owner."

"Oh, no, Samir, no! Never ever fall in love with a Dutch girl, man. Leda will become a wheel boot. She'll anchor you to this damn town, man. You, Samir, you don't need an wheel boot, but a zero-to-sixty turbocharger!"

"My heart is not a car," I sputtered. "Even if it was, I

wouldn't be able to find the stick shift."

"Ha! But you're playing with fire, Samir," he said. "Leda is the most dangerous woman in the village. Except for Helma."

"Helma?"

"Oh, just some *trut*," he said with a dismissive gesture. "Lives down the road. You've probably seen her, but didn't take any notice. Keep it that way."

So it surely wasn't for Helma that Calvin was primping for one of his last dates in the village. While he fussed with his clothes and cologne, he asked, "Tell me, Samir, what do you think is the link between love and sex?"

"I'm not as experienced as you. But let's say that love makes the man think he has the best of all women, and makes the woman think she's found Mr. Right."

"Say love didn't exist, man, just sex. That would be so much easier."

"Still, I think the two need each other. Look at it this way: love is the car and sex is the driver's license."

"No, man," Calvin countered. "Sex is the car and love is the license. Or no … wait … sex is the car and the license and the fuel and the highway, and love is the cruise control, the traffic jams, the fender benders, and the speeding tickets." He burst out laughing.

"You know, Calvin, from the moment I laid eyes on Leda I was convinced that Dutch women are the most beautiful in all the world."

"Bullshit, man, then you haven't met Helma. But Leda is a decent model, even though you'll pay more for the inspection sticker than for the car itself. She hasn't been driven so long that the chassis is rusted through."

20

Helma made it clear to me that my image of "the Dutch woman" was off the mark. I'll tell you about her here, but I'll keep it short, because I don't want her to take up as much room in the book as she did in my life. I hope her poison does not seep from these chapters through the rest of the book.

One weekend in March, Calvin and I were standing in the checkout line at the local supermarket when Calvin nudged me and said, "Look, that's the *trut* I was talking about." The word *trut*—something like *bitch* but not quite as bad—didn't mean much coming from Calvin, because he called any woman who did not go to bed with him a *trut*. But the ones who did go to bed with him were *truts* as well. Go figure. I was curious to get a glimpse of Calvin's *trut* and saw Helma in the next checkout line. A woman in her mid-thirties, I guessed. Quiet and polite. A ready smile, to give you the idea that she was friendly. After that first time, I noticed her a lot. Mostly walking through town in her coat with the fur collar, into which she partly buried her face. She never looked at me or said hello. She didn't give our eyes the chance to meet.

Not long thereafter, on the first nice day of spring, Leda and I were out walking Diesel. As we laughed and talked, I heard someone greet us. Helma. Her smallish voice did not tally with her height. She chatted with Leda and patted Diesel on the head. Me, she didn't give the time of day, but from then on she did say hello if she passed me on the street, and if I was out with Diesel she would stop and chat. That is to say, she talked to me while she petted Diesel. But it wasn't long before she stuck out her hand and said we hadn't been properly introduced yet. After that she would stop to chat with me and ignored Diesel. She even pushed his head away if he came over for a sniff.

The increasing terrorist attacks in Iraq made me antsy, so one evening around eleven I decided to go out for some fresh air. The village was deserted, with the exception of Helma standing in front of her house.

"It's about to rain," she said. "Come on in, we'll have some tea."

It was to be the most expensive cup of tea I ever drank. It would cost me the new path I wanted to take in my poor, aimless life.

An automatic light popped on at her front door. This seemed to annoy her. She fished through her pockets for her key. I was surprised at the speed with which her face transformed, from friendly to annoyed.

"Damn, where's that key?" she hissed to herself.

"Everything okay?" I asked, my mind still on those recent blood-drenched images I had seen on the internet.

Maybe she needed to use the toilet really badly. Or knew the storm clouds would burst open any second. But then, just as abruptly, she was friendly again. She quickly opened the door and invited me in. We were hardly inside when she gave me a sultry look and her lips attached themselves to mine. It all happened so fast—my body did not give my brain any time—and in an impulse I shoved her away from me, so hard that her back banged against the doorframe. Her passionate, yearning look from a moment ago flipped instantly into one of childlike innocence, with a shot of pain thrown in for good measure. I had been in a tight spot hundreds of times in wars and prisons, but I had never been as beside myself as at that moment with Helma.

"Sorry," she said with her childlike voice.

"I'll go now, if you don't mind," I said, feeling claustrophobic. "Maybe we'll drink tea together another time."

"But it's going to rain," she said. Or maybe I thought she said it.

In any case, I didn't reply. I turned and left.

I got home soaked to the skin with rain and sweat. This Helma situation was totally new to me. I had no idea how to deal with it. I could only think: Did I push her too hard? Did I hurt her? Was she angry?

And: Should I tell Leda? Would she believe me if I said that Helma made moves on me and I pushed her away?

In my culture you would never, ever find yourself in such a situation. First of all, a woman does not live on her own, and second, a woman would never invite a man inside. I was utterly flummoxed. It would soon become clear that Helma was not a woman, but a 5'10" bottle of poison.

21

I had to find out if what happened with Helma was going to be problematic, but the strange thing was that now I never bumped into her, Diesel or no Diesel. Just as I had never noticed her until Calvin pointed her out, now she was back to being invisible. I checked the lights in her house every evening, so I knew she was still in town. I racked my brains to figure out why we no longer crossed paths. Was she afraid of me? Or was she embarrassed? Had I put the wrong idea in her head, that I fancied her?

A few weeks after that evening, when I had given up all hope of bumping into her, I spotted her in the supermarket. I said hello. She asked how I was, and how Diesel was. We made small talk, and I concluded that I had got myself into a state over nothing, maybe because I was still a greenhorn in Dutch social life. I had spent many days in utter confusion, but after just a two-minute chat with this woman I was so scared of, everything seemed fine again. I had not seen Leda in two weeks, and now instead of dreading it because of Helma, I started to look forward to the weekend.

"Samir van der Weerde!" she exclaimed, smiling, as she got off the bus. "I've missed you!" She gave me a big hug.

"More than Diesel? Or less?"

"Less, of course." I was so happy to see her. "How are things here?" she asked as we walked home.

"Maybe I should leave this place," I said.

"Too quiet for you?"

"Not really, but I'm going to look for a room in Utrecht so I can see you more often."

"Sometimes I don't even have time for myself. You see me more here, I'm telling you. And besides, you'd miss Diesel."

"I have a practical question."

"Go on."

"Say we like each other. When can we kiss?"

"You had your chance," she said, smiling.

"And I blew it?"

"Now you'll have to wait until I'm drunk. A second chance needs alcohol."

That evening in the shed, I tried to keep a discreet eye on her wine glass. She had drunk not even an inch of wine. But I brought my face closer to hers anyway. The seconds that followed, I could not describe in a hundred eternities. It was life. Bliss. After so many years of being on the run.

My lips touched hers. Just. Gently.

She pulled back cautiously, looked at me, and said, "Now that we're at this stage, there's something you should know about me." During my trek through southeast Asia I had kissed girls from Florence, Tokyo, Montenegro, and Canberra, and I can tell you that there is not a woman on earth as capable of ruining such a blissful moment as a Dutch woman.

She started talking.

When she was twenty-one she had a relationship with a certain Gerard. Three months later she dumped him for someone else. Shortly thereafter, Gerard threw himself in front of a moving train.

Leda spent months shut up in her room, and finally Danielle bought Diesel for her, so that she would at least have a reason to go outside. From that time on, she had not had another boyfriend. Our "kiss" was her first since she was twenty-one.

She went into the house and came back with a photo of Gerard. I looked long and hard at this guy, who had entered my life already dead. He looked robust and honest. I could imagine him being someone who would sacrifice his life for something he believed in. During my years in the asylum seekers' center I knew people who took their own life, but that a strapping young Dutch guy would do it—this was new for me. As I sat there looking at the photo with all sorts of questions in my head, Leda said: "Penny for your thoughts."

"Why did he do it?"

She shook her head. "No one knows. But not a moment goes by that I don't think of him and his death. If I had known what he might do, I'd never have left him." Her voice trembled.

"He is ..." I said, "... he turned his life into a few hours' delay for the train and a few years' delay for you."

"More than a few years," she said, doing her best to swallow away the lump in her throat. "Do you think it's possible for me to ever have another relationship, knowing I was the cause of someone's death?"

"You are not the cause. Millions and millions of girls have dumped millions and millions of Gerards. But only one Gerard threw himself in front of a train. Should all those millions of girls stay single on the outside chance that one ex-boyfriend might kill himself?"

Leda looked at me and smiled through her tears.

"Do you have a driver's license?" I asked.

"Yes, why?"

I thought to myself: *We'll buy a secondhand VW bus. I'll build a bed and a kitchenette in it. And we'll drive to Tarifa. To the southernmost tip of Europe.* I thought this, but did not say it out loud.

"Why do you ask?"

"Just curious."

I wondered if we had actually kissed or not. Did she like me? Did she like me enough? Was she in love with me, too? I said nothing because I didn't want her—like she had just turned our first kiss into a drama—to turn that vw bus, which was already driving south on the highway of my dreams, into a roadside breakdown.

22

"Are you going to meet Leda at the bus stop?" Danielle asked.

Diesel barked and I said "yes." (I think Diesel's bark was also a "yes.") At ten to eight we were there; and Diesel barked again, and my heart did too, when we saw the bus approaching. Diesel ran over to Leda when she got off. She patted his head.

"Let me give the other dog some attention, otherwise he's come for nothing," she said as she hugged me and kissed my cheeks three times, left-right-left, and then a short peck on the lips. She was mine, I could feel it.

"I've got a present for you," she said.

"A leash and a ball?"

"No, but you can have those, too."

"And your picture?"

"Okay, but no more than that!" We walked hand in hand to her house. At the door she said, "Wait a sec."

Before she went to her room, and me to my shed, she gave me a small package, then she nipped into the house and came out with an old leash of Diesel's, a chewed-up toy ball, and a photo in an envelope. The present was a teach-yourself-Spanish book. In the envelope was a picture of her I hadn't seen in any of the family albums. Leda was smiling into the camera, and Diesel was looking up at her, his tongue hanging out of his mouth.

At ten that evening she came out to the shed.

Together we laid the mattresses, mine and Calvin's, side by side.

"There," she said. "Now we have ..."

"A relationship?"

"No, a double bed," she laughed.

Leda got undressed down to her panties, got into bed, and pulled the sheet up over her breasts. I stood there looking at her. She did not say, "Come lie down next to me."

Looking back on it, I can't say she was pretty. No, she was everything. And everything was beautiful: me, the shed, my life, the village. What I'll never forgive myself for is that at that heavenly moment I was so stupid not to think of myself, or of Leda, or of the universe, but of what Danielle would think if she knew Leda was lying with me in bed.

I did not sleep a wink all night. Leda woke up six hours later. I shut my eyes and pretended to sleep deeply, to let her know how fine it was that she was next to me. She climbed out of bed, got dressed, and left. I was relieved to hear the door close: all night I tried to lie still so as not to disturb or wake her, until my body was one huge cramp. I had just stood up to stretch my muscles when she came back in and saw me standing there. I got a fright.

"You awake, too?" she said.

I did not want to embarrass her, so I yawned theatrically. She picked up her bra and left again. I had hoped that she would put it on on her way outside so no one would see her bare-chested, but through the window I saw her swinging the bra in her hand as she walked through the dawn light.

After lunch we took Diesel for a walk. Leda inched closer to me, putting her hand on my shoulder and, later, an arm around my waist. Since hearing about her drama, I was glad to be near her and to have her near me.

Suddenly Helma appeared. She said hello, but did not stop for a chat, like she had always done in the past. This time—also unlike before—she did not ignore me, but rather looked at me with a long, strange gaze, so overt that Leda couldn't possibly miss it.

And sure enough, as soon as Helma walked on, Leda gave me a questioning glance. I didn't know what to say.

Where I grew up, it was not the done thing for a man to argue with a woman he doesn't know. Maybe Helma could sense my anxiety and knew I couldn't bring myself to confront her. And maybe the fact that I was walking arm in arm with Leda, and that I was obviously sticking around in the village for her, evoked jealousy or some other kind of feelings in her.

In hindsight, years later, I know I should have told Leda exactly what had happened that rainy evening, and not just Leda but Danielle and Mieke and Diesel and all the dogs and cats in the village. If I had told everyone, down to the last details, what had and hadn't happened, then Helma would not have had a leg to stand on. But I didn't. I was a dead duck.

A week later I was out walking again with Leda and Diesel. She walked about five yards ahead of me and threw the ball for Diesel. I spotted Helma walking straight at us. Not at an ambling pace, so I knew this was not a coincidence. She stopped and said hi to Leda in her quiet, childlike voice. Then she came over to me with a pained look. She said, louder, and with an urgency that suggested she had tried repeatedly to catch me, but in vain: "Can we talk? I'm still in pain from last time."

Was she talking to me, or to someone else?

"Diesel, come!" Leda called.

Diesel came running. Leda clicked on his leash and walked off. I just stood there, befuddled and paralyzed.

To my surprise, Helma also turned and marched off without a word.

"What pain are you talking about?" I called after her.

"Forget it," she replied as she walked off and waved her arm in the air without looking back. Now I realize she could be one of those women from the Old Testament, the kind who demands the head of a man who has spurned her. But at that moment I didn't know what had hit me. Do you know Manet's painting *The Dead Toreador?* A man, once so proud and full of life, lies immobile on the ground. In him, you see life and death united. This is how I walked back to the Van der Weerdes' that day.

I knocked at the door. Danielle opened it and I asked if I could see Leda.

"I'll ask her," she said. When she came back she said Leda was tired and needed to rest. Danielle looked disappointed. I knew my days in that house were numbered.

I waited restlessly in the shed. I could hear the cawing of crows and through the window saw that the tree had been turned into a black umbrella. When I saw Leda and Diesel come outside, I went out immediately and asked if I could join them. She nodded. For the duration of our walk she never once looked at me or said a single word.

I didn't see her anymore that weekend, and I wondered whether I was still welcome in the house. Leda did not come home for three weeks in a row. I tried phoning her, and when she didn't answer I blocked my number ID. Then she answered. Her voice was ice cold. I told her I could come to Utrecht if she didn't want to come here. I waited silently for her answer, but when that silence lasted longer than necessary, I didn't dare ask again. I wished her a good day and immediately deleted her number from my phone, so I wouldn't call her in a moment of weakness only to hear her cold voice on the end of the line.

I thought: if I stay in the village any longer, Diesel will have to wait that much longer to see her. I knocked on Danielle's office door to thank her for everything. I was holding my bag of belongings (which now included the leash, the ball, and the picture) and the garbage bag full of photo albums.

"You're leaving," she said, as though she already knew, or had expected it.

She took an envelope from the table and opened it so I could see the €50 bills. "Your wages for working in the day care center."

"That's not necessary," I said.

"You worked for it, Samir." She handed me the envelope. "All the best."

I left the envelope on a small table next to the front door where mail sometimes lay. Then I said goodbye to Diesel. He kept jumping around me, until Danielle called him.

I looked around the place that had been a fresh start in my life. A place that could have been a new life. If you had asked me at that moment to choose between being an emir in an Arabic country, a mayor on Bali, a Hollywood star, a happy Buddhist, or the dog Diesel, I would without hesitation have answered "Diesel." Then I'd have said farewell to humankind, not in a wooden box, but with a heart and a tail. And I would always be close to Leda, without having to do anything to win her over.

23

Maybe hell is when the hope that had momentarily lifted you up dies.

Our house in Iraq was an address for misfortune. A bus stop for shrapnel wounds. A station for tears and grief, where the train of one's life sometimes stood motionless for years on end. I did not believe that happiness existed on this planet, except in books and movies. But in the home of the Van der Weerde family, where there was no fear of a general, a president, or poverty, and the place where Leda was, I believed happiness really did exist.

I called Calvin to ask if I could crash at his place, wherever that was, for a few nights.

"Of course you can, Samir. But you'll need to find a good smuggler."

"Are you in ..."

"Yeah, man. Canada."

"Since when?"

"Now, just now. I have a really good passport. Its owner won't report it missing for a month. That was the deal. I could send it to you, but the picture will be no good, I'm afraid." He laughed. "Come over here, man."

Oh, how I needed Calvin at that moment. Even if it was just for a week.

Aside from the Van der Weerdes, there weren't many people in the village I would miss, but before I left I went to say goodbye to Mrs. Dotinga. I had visited her regularly lately, just for the fun of it. While I was there she usually thought up some odd job that needed doing, so that my visit would earn me some money. But once I started to get the feeling that my visits to Mrs. Dotinga were making her poorer and me richer, I stopped going and only phoned her once in a while instead.

When I arrived at her house, her little dog barked at me from behind the window, and when he saw I was taking the path up to the front door, he leapt off the windowsill and continued barking from behind the door. Mrs. Dotinga's rosebushes were full of buds, even though it was still chilly out.

"Calm down, calm down," I heard her say in her crackly voice. She opened the door and the dog kept barking at me. "How lovely to see you, Samir," she said. "You've got your things with you. Are you leaving town?"

"Alas, yes," I said, swallowing hard.

"Leda has been through a lot. Maybe the time wasn't ripe for you two. Perhaps later," she said, without me having to explain anything. News traveled fast in this village.

She looked at my holdall, and the dog sniffed at the garbage bag.

"Where will you go?"

"I want to go to the south of Spain, but I need other papers for that."

"So where will you go now?"

"I don't know yet, but as soon as I get to the station, I will," I said.

There was something about Mrs. Dotinga that made her rise above everyday life and everyday chitchat and everyday pain that repeats itself until it stops hurting. Mrs. Dotinga had been through the war. Maybe that made it possible for me to tell her about my own pain without having to minimize it, without giving her the impression I was fishing for sympathy. Maybe that is why she understood me, even without words. I could tell her something painful and then a little later we would laugh about it. She understood that the loudest laugh comes from the deepest hurt.

Mrs. Dotinga looked at me with her peaceful, old eyes. She saw the pain of my loss. Since I didn't want to talk about

Leda, I talked about Iraq. The strange thing was that I could use the same words for the drama in Iraq as my own drama with Leda. In retrospect I realize how deeply the war had nestled into me. Deeper than love or happiness. I had never experienced the anguish of love, only the pain of war. And in some way the feelings resembled one another.

"What does your soul want?" she asked. A question that no one had asked so far. And yet I did not need to think about the answer for very long.

"To get away from people, just for a while. Someplace where I don't have to think about anyone else. But no such place exists in this country."

"Oh, but it does. Would you like to go there?"

"Yes, please!"

"All right. Just give me some time to arrange it."

24

Mrs. Dotinga arranged a room for me in a monastery. It was the first time I had ever set foot in one. I had no contact with the outside world. I slept, and looked at the small window or the chair or the table. There were other rooms and the communal dining room, but at first I did not see any of the other residents. Only Lea, a woman with azure-colored eyes that lit up the way night animals' eyes glow when light shines in them. She was there to receive me when I arrived.

I spent the first few days at the small table in my room. I tried to repair fountain pens (that old hobby of mine), but I kept breaking the nibs or damaging the pens because my mind was more on Leda than on my work. I paged through the photo albums to distract my thoughts, but in vain. My mind was fixated on Leda, who might at that moment be sitting in a pub on the main square in Utrecht chatting about Danielle or Diesel. Lovesickness is a terrible thing.

One day, around lunchtime, I heard singing. Classical songs. I quietly opened my door so it didn't squeak, and tiptoed in the direction of the music. I walked to reception and saw through the office window that Lea was singing. Every day I sat on the stone bench in the corridor while Lea sang during her lunch break.

I had no sense of time in that monastery. So I didn't know what day it was when an old, gray-haired man came into the dining room. He nodded politely. I wondered what I should say if he asked what I was doing there. I thought it was strange for me, a Muslim, to go to a monastery to find peace. But the man only asked if I wanted something to drink. I said I did not. Then a young woman with a roundish face came in. She introduced herself, but I can't for the life of me remember her name. You might wonder why I'm telling you about my stay in the monastery so many years ago, but those days were vital to me.

I'll call the young woman Miriam, because it's the first thing that pops into my mind when I think of her. She greeted the man. So now there were three of us sitting at the table. The other two with a cup of coffee, me without. There was a pleasant silence in the dining room that was occasionally marred by a noise from the kitchen.

"Are you a nun?" I asked Miriam. She smiled a bit at first, and when that wasn't enough for what she felt, she laughed out loud. The old man also smiled.

"In body, yes," she said. "But not in spirit, unfortunately."

"So, are you a monk?" I asked the man.

"Priest."

"What's that? A male nun?" I asked. Miriam laughed again.

"A … priest … is the …" the man said with a measured voice. I couldn't let him finish his sentence. In the monastery, the sentences were long and you needed to be patient for them all to come out. And patience was not my forte.

"Is he a preacher for the Catholics?" I asked like a schoolchild trying to show off his worldliness to the teacher.

"Something like that," said the old man.

He started coughing. His coughing fit lasted a while and his face went all red. Then he stopped, and the red slowly faded. A woman shouted something from the kitchen, at which he got up, nodded to us, and left.

"And you?" asked Miriam. "Who are you?"

"Leda's last ex, if you can say that. Her first one threw himself under a train and this last one has ended up in a monastery."

"So you're here to put Leda out of your mind?"

"No, I thought I'd be the world's first and last Muslim monk."

"Interesting," she said.

"And you? Why are you here?"

"To finish my thesis."

Miriam turned out to be pleasant company. Later, I heard about her background. She had been an "accident." The father did not want her, and even her mother wasn't sure if she wanted to keep the baby. But after spending a weekend in this very monastery thinking things over, her mother had decided to keep her, Miriam, after all. So Miriam had this place to thank for her very existence. Without the peace her mother found here, Miriam would probably have never been born. From the time she was nineteen, Miriam regularly visited the monastery for a few days or more. She took me to see the room where her pregnant mother had stayed.

"She slept here on this bed. It's here that she decided to keep me. And now I'm sleeping in the same room. Funny, huh?"

Miriam's presence was stronger than the monastery's silence. She laughed a lot or had a big smile on her lips. She was gentle and kind. She was clever, and she radiated the kind of peace that our surroundings also radiated. I took walks with her among the oak trees or in the orchard. The place was thus never totally quiet, but after she left—she hadn't finished her thesis, but said it would turn out fine—the silence returned. I had never been silent for so long. Day and night. Without saying a word, mostly because it wasn't necessary to say anything. Even though my room was small, it never made me think of a hostel or a police cell. It was the only room I ever stayed in that you could measure in spirit and not in square meters.

I had experienced the loss of loved ones through war or flight. I always felt terrible pain, but afterwards that pain turned into a kind of relief. But not with Leda. She had been the water that quenched my thirst—and not just a dryish mouth, but the thirst of the desert. Leda dominated my thoughts, and even when I did not think about her I realized I was not thinking about her. To my surprise, I missed her when I got distracted from thinking about her. As though the pain of losing her was the last link with Leda herself. I wanted to spend my time in the monastery focusing on her completely, precisely so it would hurt the most. I thought after that, she might vanish from my thoughts. Like a Band-Aid that you yank off in one go.

After a week or two I thought I would sink into a kind of grief that could last indefinitely. I realized that with Leda I didn't feel just one big pain that would one day dissolve, but many pains that would keep returning. So I decided it was better to ignore my loss of Leda, and felt that to do this it was necessary to leave the monastery. Because in the outside world, where I had to work to survive, I wouldn't have the time to think about her.

I had spent twenty-one days in that monastery. Exactly the same amount of time a chick spends in an egg creating itself. I found out that the problems I had were just the right problems for me, that they suited me perfectly. The only thing I had to do was get moving and stop entertaining my self-pity. I left the monastery no better and no worse, but just as I was, and this was the best I could do.

Lea gave me an envelope from Mrs. Dotinga. In it was a card and some money, intended, in her words (which I couldn't read because of her old-fashioned handwriting, but Lea could, with difficulty): *to learn to stand on your own two feet again.* But at that moment, I could already stand, and even walk.

25

I have written for you, and will continue to write for you, in the past tense about what happened and is over and done with. This does not go for Leda. She is the only person in the book whom I have written about, and will continue to write about, without her being over and done with.

For a long time I was convinced that love would be the solution to my problems, but after my experience with Leda I realized that love was not the solution, but the problem itself. The idea that after every failed relationship with a Dutch woman I would have to hole myself up in a monastery to find myself again frightened me. Fall for a few Dutch women, and I would end up as a full-time monk.

Lea explained how to get to the bus stop. The bus came once an hour. Walking through the cornfields, seeing how they colored the landscape green until they blocked the horizon, I thought to myself: I have to get out of this country.

I hoisted my sails, but did not catch any wind.

Now I have to explain why I stayed in the Netherlands and did not make a beeline for the border. Because 26,000 people had been given residency in one fell swoop in the "general pardon," things had not gone entirely smoothly. For instance, I had not yet received an IND card. That's an ID card from the Immigration and Naturalization Service that allows you to arrange your affairs. So I had a letter from the Ministry of Justice telling me that I had official permission to remain in the Netherlands, but no ID card. I did not go to the IND to ask for one because I was afraid it would jeopardize my residency status, nor to the Ministry of Justice to ask for one, out of fear of the same, or worse. I decided to let sleeping dogs lie.

This is how I ended up dangling between the open sky of

the Ministry of Justice and the solid ground of the IND.

So this is how things stood. My residence status was printed on a sheet of paper, but I had no card. Residency in the IND's computer, but not in my pocket. The fish was neither still swimming in the ocean nor lying in a pan in my oven.

I took the bus and the train to Amsterdam, thinking that after three weeks in the monastery I could do with a stroll around the city. But to stroll in Amsterdam you need money. I walked from street to street, and all around me Amsterdam was ravenous for euros. It's a huge city where every street corner asks you what you want. You can have anything, if you can pay for it. And if you can't pay, you can neither ask nor have. Muscular guys in tracksuits asked if I wanted hash, or pills, or a woman. If I said I wanted a cheap place to sleep, they all pointed in the same direction: Central Station.

So there I stood in Central Station, my bag on my back and the garbage bag of photo albums in my hand, and I looked up at the large blue departures board without any idea which train to take. A train that had a twelve-minute delay caught my eye.

"That is my train," I said to myself. "It has waited twelve minutes for me."

Like many asylum seekers do, I bought a ticket with 40% discount, even though I did not have a discount card. Pretty much every Dutch person has one, and they can take three fellow travelers with them for the same discount, so usually it wasn't difficult to find someone in the train who would share his discount card with you. I got on the train and saw a girl reading a book called *How God Vanished from Jorwerd*. She was about halfway through it. I sat down next to her. The title intrigued me, which made me fail to notice the hardness of her face. She glanced at the garbage bag next to me and then made a face like she had just smelled a kilo of peeled onions.

"I see you're halfway through the book. So now do you know half the reason God vanished from Jorwerd?" I joked, hoping to strike up a conversation so I could ask if I could mooch off her discount card.

She looked up, irritated. At once I knew my plan to get onto her discount card was going nowhere. Just as I got up to move on, the conductor appeared.

"Ticket, please," he said. I handed him my ticket. "And your discount card, please."

"I'm traveling with her," I said, pointing to the girl next to me.

"No." She was curt and on edge.

"Sorry, sir," the conductor said, "you'll have to buy a new ticket without the discount, plus a €35 fine."

The girl opened her book and continued reading. I paid €22.50 for a new ticket plus a €35 fine. The conductor stamped the ticket and went on his way.

"Sorry about that," I said.

"Never mind," she snapped back.

"I always travel with my own ticket and on someone else's discount card," I said, by way of an explanation that what I did was not so strange. I smiled, to let her know I didn't hold it against her. "I can't buy a discount card myself because the IND hasn't issued me an ID card yet. And traveling full fare is so expensive."

"Sorry, what?"

I repeated it, but she did not understand. Then I tried in my poor English, and she seemed to get my drift. I used the Dutch word for things I didn't know in English, then continued in Dutch, which she suddenly did understand. English was the door that opened a conversation with her. I told her I was in this train because it was delayed by twelve minutes. Even though I could tell she wanted to get back to her book, I kept chatting, and said I didn't know anyone in the city where we were headed, and didn't even know the city itself. That I was looking for a cheap, small room to rent, preferably as a sublet, because you needed an IND pass to get a proper rental. She listened to me the way a dentist listens to the radio while they're pulling a tooth. I had no idea if she was interested or irritated.

Then she put her book away and chatted with me for the last twenty minutes of the journey. Her name was Christel. She was on her way to Nick, whom she was hopelessly in love with. Just saying his name made her eyes glow. In the end, even though I couldn't make use of her discount card, I got to make use of something far more valuable: her heart.

"Come with me," she said on the platform after we arrived. Nick was waiting for her. He was so in love that he didn't even get a fright when he saw Christel get off the train with an asylum seeker carrying a garbage bag. Nick kissed Christel and Christel kissed Nick, and I stood there awkwardly, looking the other way. Then I heard Christel tell Nick that I was looking to rent a cheap room.

"I happen to know of a tiny room in the student house where a friend of mine lives," he said. "Would that be okay?"

I nodded. Nick called his friend.

"Hey, I've got ..."

"Samir."

"... Samir with me. He needs a room. Can you let the owner know he's interested? Yeah. Yeah, I'll tell him." He turned to me. "It's two by three meters. You sure that's not too small?"

"No, it's perfect," I said.

"Yeah, no problem. Yeah, two by three. Okay, I'll text you. And you'll call him? Dope. Yeah, we'll do that. Later." He turned to me again. "Give me your number. Our friend will call you. And if he doesn't, you call me back, okay?"

He shook my hand and they left. I had never seen such magical love as Nick and Christel's. It gave you not just butterflies in the stomach, but cheap lodgings as well.

26

Ten minutes later I got a call with instructions to report to Molenweg 26 at 4:30 p.m. It wasn't far from the station, and standing on the sidewalk I could see through the large front window. It was a room with a washbasin and the filthiest dark-blue carpeting I had ever seen. As I was much too early, I walked around the block so as not to alarm the neighbors who were already peering out their window. At precisely four thirty a car pulled up in front of the house. In the back was a cage with a huge dog in it.

"You the new renter?" the man asked, eyeing my garbage bag.

"Yes."

"Student?"

"Sort of."

"What do you study?"

"Dutch."

"Aha," he laughed, "that's why you're so hard to understand."

But I was the one who had to listen hard to understand him. He was in his seventies. Strong and practical, like a Dutch farmer.

"Where did you live before this?"

"In a monastery," I said.

"Huh?" He looked at me, then pulled out a bunch of keys. There were at least forty of them and he had to search for the right one. But before I could explain about the monastery, he had opened the door and we were inside. "You can paint the walls and put in new carpeting if you want. But listen good: the curtains mustn't hang lower than the windowsill because of the gas heater."

He repeated this a few times, that the curtains must not be allowed to touch the gas heater, otherwise eight students and I would be burned alive.

"No, not just the nine of you, but half the street as well, if it happens at night. Those students do nothing but drink. They're always forgetting to turn off the gas in the kitchen. And if the house catches fire, don't expect them to wake up. They drink themselves blind and are comatose until noon. What number Monastery Street did you say you lived at?"

"Not a street, I lived in a monastery," I said.

"Yeah, yeah, sure, but what number?"

"139."

He turned and walked into the hallway, without another word about the room. The hallway was nearly blocked by five parked bicycles.

"It's strictly forbidden to bring bikes inside," he said. "Bicycles have to be parked outside on the street. And not up against the window."

Further down the hall was the kitchen, and next to that a lavatory. He said there was a shower upstairs. I heard a cat meowing.

"House pets are forbidden," the man said. "No house pets." The meowing cat appeared on the stairs, and behind it, another one. He bent over, petted them, and looked straight at me. "House pets are strictly forbidden."

He led me back to the front room, pointed to the gas heater, and repeated his warning about the curtains not getting too close to the heater.

"All I need is your ID card."

"I don't have one."

"Passport?"

"Nope."

"Bank account number?"

"I don't have a bank account."

"What was your last address again?"

"Monastery Street 139."

"Okay, next time, next time," he said. "The rent is two hundred and eighty five euros a month. I'll give you the account number so you can pay. Rent is due on the twenty-fourth of the month."

"Can I pay by cash?" I asked.

"Why?"

"I'm waiting for an ID card from the IND, and once I have that I can open a bank account."

"How long will that take?"

"I wish I knew. Soon, I hope." He gave me a skeptical look.

"I'm a civil engineer," I said. "If anything breaks, I can fix it."

"Then the rent is two hundred and fifty euros. If any of the students complain about you, you'll have a month to find someplace else. Oh, and I ask a month's deposit, too. Do you have five hundred euros?"

I took out Mrs. Dotinga's envelope. He could see there wasn't much money left, so he gave me back the deposit.

"No deposit, so no problems, okay? And don't forget about the curtains."

"Mr. Hofkamp," came the singsong voice of a girl from the far end of the hall. "The kitchen drain is clogged."

"Hello, Marga," he called back. He looked at me, winked, and shouted back to the girl, "Call me tonight if it still hasn't been repaired."

As soon as Mr. Hofkamp was gone, I unclogged the kitchen sink. Eventually I fixed so many things in the house that he lowered my rent to €200. I saw Mr. Hofkamp once a month. He came to collect the rent, but I also got the feeling he dropped by to chat. He asked about my family and Baghdad, how much money I sent them, and how much I earned here in Holland. Sometimes he gave me back part of the rent money, to send home. Even after I stopped telling him about the situation in Iraq, so that he wouldn't think I was unable to pay the rent, he lowered it again, this time to €150. I'll never forget how he looked me deep in the eyes and said quietly, "I know what war is ..."

I had the best landlord a person could want, a room of six square meters with its own washbasin, and eight housemates I didn't know. I had never been so rich.

27

I hadn't the foggiest idea about student life in the Netherlands, even though I had once been a university student myself. I studied civil engineering in Erbil, as the Arabs call it, or Hawler, in Kurdish.

Next to my university were two buildings, one surrounded by a high wall topped with barbed wire. This was where the female students lived. The building without a wall was for the male students. It was forbidden for the women to go out after eight in the evening, unless there was an acute medical reason. So a female student needed an ambulance to go out on a date. The young women therefore often had food poisoning or a ruptured appendix, and the ambulance would race to the dormitory to pick them up. On the way to the hospital, the pain would miraculously disappear and the woman would get out of the ambulance. One of the ambulance drivers in particular was known to be a sympathetic guy, and he would ask the girl where her date was and take her straight there instead of to the hospital. No man ever set foot in the women's dormitory, except during the summer break or to repair something.

The men's dormitory was home to students from all over Iraq, plus a few international students, maybe fifteen at most. Their parents were members of the Ba'ath Party in other Arabic countries, and they got a stipend from Saddam Hussein to study in Iraq. We were four to a room. At the beginning of the academic year they would assign two Arabic and two Kurdish students per room, but a month later we would secretly change rooms, Arabs with Arabs, and Kurds with Kurds. Later yet, there would be another room switch: the Kurds would regroup by dialect, and the Arabs by religion: Sunni, Shiite, or Christian.

There were frequent brawls in the men's dormitory. If two Arabs fought, or two Kurds, then it would be resolved within the group. But if there was a fight between a Kurd and an Arab, the melee would spread throughout the building, which made it not only a student dormitory but a martial arts academy. Boxing, karate, jujitsu, kung fu, you name it.

In that building I learned what brings people together. Not religion nor ethnic background, but food, music, and literature. Encounters via food last for a meal. Encounters via music last for a concert. Encounters via literature last a lifetime. I already enjoyed food and played the guitar, and at university I became even more fond of reading. This way, I made friends from all cultures and religions. We were a group of six or seven, and we belonged everywhere and nowhere. We read books. Whenever a brawl broke out in the dormitory, nobody bothered us, because we were friends with all sides. I would often stand shaving at my leisure in the shower room while behind me the Kurds and Arabs picked fights with one another. That same evening I would see the warring parties sitting together in the cheap neighborhood kebab joint.

I was carrying out the repairs in the kitchen when I heard someone come in. I turned and saw that it was the girl named Marga. She wore her hair in a medium cut on the left side and down over shoulder on the right. The first thing I noticed were her bunny-rabbit slippers. The softness of her slippers and her velour pajamas were not enough to soften her face. She asked me peevishly how much longer I would be.

"A half hour at most," I said.

"Okaaaayyyyy," she drawled, and left.

Half an hour later she came back. By now the kitchen stank to high heaven because I had unscrewed the siphon trap under the sink and it was clogged with rotten food. She scrunched up her face while she looked at me, as though I was the cause of the smell. I hurried up, and another half hour later I had the sink back in order. She came back, switched on the exhaust fan, and opened the window, glowering at me all the while, as though I still hadn't got rid of the smell.

She took me for a repairman, not a housemate, because (as I later heard) my room was so tiny that no student lasted there longer than three months.

"Oh, do you *live* here?" she asked when she saw me open the door next to the kitchen. From then on, contact with Marga was uncomfortable, and I often got the feeling that she thought I stank, even when I had come straight from the shower.

The first order of business was to fit out my room. My room looked out onto the sidewalk, so it was impossible to sleep without curtains. It was important to find some that were not too long. The first day, I went to the thrift store and bought a pillow, two badly stained white bedsheets, and a blanket, all of it for less than five euros. If I'd had a cart, I'd have bought a single mattress for ten euros, but this was enough for the time being. I hung up one of the sheets as a curtain, and sure enough, within half an hour I smelled something burning. The sheet was singed along the bottom. I quickly snipped off the bottom, so that it hung well above the gas heater.

Even before the sun set on my first day in the student house, I discovered how hospitable Dutch streets are. In the *Thousand and One Nights* stories there is a magic lamp which, if you rubbed it, would produce a genie, and the genie would grant you wishes. But Dutch streets are even more magical. On every street corner you find something you're looking for. Looking for a microwave? Just keep your eyes peeled. How about a set of chairs? Within a week you've got them. A dining table? No problem. I went from street corner to street corner, and from dumpster to dumpster, and found all kinds of surprises: a color TV, a granny bike missing its saddle. Within no time I had furnished my whole room.

28

At first I mainly stayed in my room, because I didn't want to invite complaints. But because my room was on the ground floor between the kitchen and the front door, I inevitably got to know my housemates—or their faces, at least.

The kitchen was the heart of the house. But the students had a peculiar way of cleaning it up. They would cook and leave the dirty pots and pans and plates behind. So when someone else wanted to cook, they would first have to wash the plates and cookware (usually accompanied by loud cursing), which they in turn left unwashed for the next person.

In the middle of the kitchen was a large round table, which had been scribbled on and carved into. Hearts pierced by arrows, stick-figure drawings in positions you wouldn't even find in the *Kama Sutra*, sayings like *God is there if you need him*, and mostly names and dates. One wall was papered with snapshots of students current and past. Passport photos, group pictures taken at the table or in the backyard. Portraits with beer, without beer, with cigarettes, without cigarettes.

The most bizarre photo was a close-up of a penis, including hair and balls. Underneath, on a slip of paper, was written: *This is my dick. For rent if I run into problems with my student loans. Ciao, Ard.*

Whenever I was in the kitchen, I would examine the wall of photos. How many faces had been in that room? How many stories were behind them? They all looked set to go partying or do something crazy. The wall itself was a snapshot covering many years.

Out back in the unkempt garden was a shed full of stuff that former housemates left behind. And way at the back of the shed was a secret place the students called Schiphol.

There, they grew marijuana under strong lamps. After I discovered it, it dawned on me why the landlord always complained about the electricity bills. Whenever he came round he would turn off all the lights, but he had no idea it was "Schiphol" that was running up his electricity bill. They had hidden the secret cannabis grove well behind a thick, opaque curtain, so Mr. Hofkamp never discovered it.

If Marga was an outdoor café, then I was a cold front. Whenever she saw me, her face clouded over. If I cooked something and switched off the exhaust fan afterwards, she would turn it right back on again, even if she wasn't in the kitchen. *Maybe the spices I'm using are too strong*, I thought, so I started using less, but this did not change anything. The sound of the exhaust fan was the sound of her grouchiness. So now I was stuck with two Margas, one in the room next to me and an electrical one in my ears.

There was one large communal refrigerator. One day I noticed a bowl of food I had put in it had been covered with plastic wrap. Marga. I decided to avoid using the fridge after that. If this went on much longer I would quit using the shower or washing machine because of her.

I soon discovered that Thursday was an important party night for the students. The kitchen would be crammed with crates of beer, and these would be emptied between 9 and 11 p.m. "Pre-drinking," this was called. Then they would head out for the bars and only return home at around four in the morning. My room being right next to the front door, I would often wake up to their yelling and swearing as they tried to get the key into the lock. Once they managed this, they would slam the door behind them and make a ruckus in the hallway. Sometimes they would even sing. Occasionally they brought someone with them who proceeded to vomit all over themselves. It was often the girls who led the guys home because they had had too much to drink.

Sometimes they would stand on the sidewalk in front of my window and chat, argue, laugh, or kiss. I would also occasionally hear them groan with delight, but the alcohol was more likely to lead to vomiting than to orgasms.

It was unbelievable. Were they alcoholics? Did they not dare scream without being loaded? Did they have some buried aggression that could only be released with drink? At their age, in a free country, I would only think of kissing, necking, and falling in love. Why did they bring the prettiest girls home with them only to puke together? If they weren't occupied with beauty, love, and intimacy at this age, when would they be?

But then I discovered that not all of them were drunk, that some of them played along just to act tough. Alcohol was a sort of disguise to mask their insecurities and prove to the others they were finally freed from their families: strict mothers, uptight fathers, cranky siblings, Bible-bashing grandmas. Later, when I saw how cows would leap about wildly when their farmers let them out of the barn for the first time in spring, I understood the students.

After getting to know them a little, I realized how rigid their home life must have been. What's worse, I thought, is that pretty soon they'll graduate and have children of their own and will repeat the cycle of strictness, and their children will end up in a student house, too, and will vomit all over themselves. In the Netherlands you only have from age eighteen through twenty-five to let loose.

By 6 a.m. the house would be quiet, so I could go back to sleep. A house that for hours had felt like a disco had been transformed into a cemetery. It was dead quiet until halfway through the afternoon. They would wake up at about three and hang around in the kitchen, pale and bleary-eyed from their hangovers. Later in the afternoon most of them would leave for their parents' and would return, revitalized, on Sunday.

I would always listen carefully before leaving my room, in order to avoid Marga. Since the door to my room was so close to the front door, I could slip in and out unnoticed. I spent most of my time in my room repairing fountain pens and trying not to think of Leda. Or else I would think of Leda so as not to have to think of the Dutch Immigration Department. Or I'd think of the Immigration Department so as not to have to think of Iraq. It didn't really seem to matter to the students, or to their cats, that I lived there.

29

Now I have to tell you how fascinating the Netherlands is for me. After hundreds of years of working and thinking, the Dutch people have devised a system where no one needs to be a burden to another individual. Except in the name of love and psychiatric problems. But not financially. How amazing this is, is not evident when you are born in a place such as this, where every person is taken care of, no matter how physically disabled, how old, how solitary. Where no one is chucked out onto the street, or left to starve or freeze. No, everyone is cared for, not only until they breathe their last breath, but right up until they are well and truly buried.

In Iraq, the government robs its citizens. There is no state pension, no social services. It is every man for himself. And if he cannot manage, because of an accident or physical circumstances or whatever, then the family comes to his rescue. If his family cannot help, then perhaps his friends. And after that there is Islam, especially in the time of Ramadan, when fasting makes people realize how hard hunger is. When all other possibilities are exhausted, there is begging or stealing. This is the Iraqi social welfare system.

When I lived in Iraq, I did not realize how much my family did for me. I was a dreamer. I read books, lazed in bed, played the guitar, and occasionally worked in my father's business.

During my first year of university, the government paid for my studies and a bed in a dormitory. But this came to an end when the war broke out, and my family became my financial support. Except for the studies, which were still free, my family paid for everything: my room, the doctor if I got sick, my clothes, the bus to and from the university, even my weekly telephone call to them to ask for money. I never really gave much thought to how they managed this.

If you did not flee the country after finishing your studies, you went into the army and the government paid for everything. And after that—if you didn't get killed in the war—you would find a job and support your family. But because of the many wars, followed by terrorist attacks that killed or maimed family members, many young people fled, leaving behind households of children, the handicapped, and the elderly. In my family, too, there were fewer and fewer adult breadwinners around.

So when I got a phone call from my brother in Iraq to say he needed a thousand euros as quickly as possible, I knew they had already tried everything in their power to get it. They did not need that thousand euros for cocktails or restaurants or a vacation or a new phone. By now, the money Mrs. Dotinga had given me was dwindling. Every bill I broke just melted away in my wallet. "Everything will be okay," I said. If you're in a tiny boat in the middle of the ocean and someone sticks his hand up out of the water, you don't tell him the boat is too small.

To transfer money to Iraq, you don't go to a bank but to Western Union. You bring money to any Western Union office, show your ID card or passport, give them the details of whoever is to receive the money, pay the amount you want to transfer plus a huge commission to Western Union, and at that moment your family member can pick up the money, after presenting their identification at a Western Union office near them. But since I did not have an ID card or passport, I was forced to use "Mohammed Super Western Union" in The Hague.

Mohammed Super Western Union had nothing to do with the real Western Union. He was called this because he was faster and easier. You gave him the money, you waited while he called someone in Iraq, and that person would give the money directly to your family. Mohammed Super Western Union was cheaper than the real thing, and it was not necessary to show your passport. All you needed to do was trust him. Via Mohammed I sent everything I had to Iraq. Even though it was less than they needed, I was relieved to be able to at least send something. And I went on with my life. Sending those thousand euros to Iraq liberated me from my thoughts of Leda. Terror is the best distraction from love.

Hunger began to gnaw at me. In other countries where I had drifted, the poor people shared their daily bread with you. In the asylum seekers' center there were 549 other asylum seekers you could eat with. In the Netherlands, if you're hungry people think you're on a diet, or that you've wasted your money on hash or alcohol or gambling.

While drifting through Thailand and Laos, the offerings at Buddhist shrines provided for me if I was hungry and broke. But there was no such thing in the Netherlands.

I opened the fridge to see if there was anything I could help myself to, but I didn't know what was whose, and I imagined Marga's face if she discovered that something of hers was missing. So I shut the refrigerator door and went outside.

I cycled, as I often did when I felt like getting out of the house, to the petting zoo. My preferred time to go there was between six and seven in the evening, Dutch dinnertime. Then it was quiet. Lots of people went to the petting zoo with their children and bags of stale bread. There was so much of it that pretty soon the animals had had their fill. Next to the gate was a large container where you could put your stale bread. That evening the container was so full that there were even bags hanging off it. Enough for a week! White bread, wheat bread, raisin bread, baguettes. Stale, but not moldy.

I opened a bag and started eating. A goat came over to me. I tossed him a piece, but he wasn't hungry. He was just very curious: he was used to hands that offered bread, not mouths that chewed it. I smiled at him.

"Nice to meet you, I'm the new guest," I said. "We'll be seeing a lot of each other."

In Thailand it was Buddha who kept me from starving, in Malaysia it was the mosques, and in the Netherlands, the goats.

30

Just as goats provided a solution for my stomach, the solution for my wallet came from chickens. I still hadn't got an ID card from the immigration department, which made it complicated to find work. But one Tuesday afternoon I happened to see a van stop on the outskirts of town. Four dark-skinned men got out. They were covered in feathers and bird droppings, and you could smell them from across the street. I wondered where they had come from.

"Are you guys asylum seekers?" I asked.

"No, city councilmen," one of them answered, while the others laughed.

Right away, I said, "I'm looking for work."

"Be here, at this very spot, tomorrow morning at five. Not asylum-seeker time, either. Dutch time."

"And I can just go with you? Don't you have to ask first?"

"The boss asks us every day if we can't rustle up some more guys who want to work."

So at a quarter to five the next morning I walked down the tidy, clean sidewalks, my eyes still half glued shut with sleep, to the place where I'd seen the van. Aside from my footsteps there was nothing to break the silence. The other four were already waiting. They wore different clothes than yesterday, and while it was clear they had bathed, I still got a whiff of a strange smell. I did not want to let on, but the first thing one of them said to me was, "There isn't a soap or shampoo on Earth that can get the stench out. Get used to it." The others laughed, but it wasn't a joke, it was a warning.

"No problem," I said.

"Really? Can you stink wherever it is you live?" another one asked. They laughed again.

Of course, it would be a problem in the student house.

And not only for Marga, who already thought I stank, and for whom a real stench would only confirm it. But I needed money.

At twenty past five we got out of the van on the grounds of a poultry farm. A sturdy redheaded man wearing overalls and knee-length boots came over to us.

"We've got a new one," said Basil.

"Good," said the farmer.

"Now you're a chicken catcher," said Aziz to me.

Bert van Lier offered me the biggest hand I'd ever shaken. "You speak some Dutch?" he asked.

"Yes."

"Good."

He led me to a small office where he gave me a face mask and a small lamp that I was to strap to my forehead. I looked like a spelunker.

"Have they told you what you have to do?" he asked.

"Sort of," I replied, without saying that the only thing I knew was that I would stink to high heaven.

"I've never been checked, but if they do come around, always say it's your first day on the job and that I've asked for your tax number and that you'll bring it tomorrow."

"Okay," I said.

"You'll get ten euros an hour the first few days, because you'll cost me too many dead chickens."

"Too many dead chickens?"

"You'll tread on more of them than you can catch and put into crates. But you'll still get ten euros an hour." He tightened the strap around my forehead and showed me how to switch the light on and off. "And remember to turn it off when you leave the shed." I put on my face mask and followed him to the shed, to begin my career as a chicken catcher.

31

On the property was a huge, windowless shed. You could hear the chickens before you even went in. Inside I did not breathe air, but feathers. That shed was hell, the feathers were fire, and the chickens were the sinners and the pain.

The chickens were crowded together like Dutch people on King's Day in Amsterdam. It was impossible to walk without stepping on them. The smell was unbearable. Not unlike the smell of Yarmouk Hospital in Baghdad, where my brother and I once went to pick up the body of our old neighbor, who had accidentally got shot at a wedding. The hospital's electricity had been out for a few hours, so it stank in the mortuary, where bodies were lined up on the ground. The chicken stench permeated your body. I ran outside, threw up, and sank down against the wall.

"You okay?" Bert asked, bending over and switching off my forehead lamp.

"Yeah," I said, gasping.

"You want me to bring you home? Or do you just need a break, give it another go?"

"Another go."

"Good. Take your time. Plenty of chickens and plenty of time."

I washed my hands and neck with cold water and walked back and forth to get extra fresh air. All I thought about was those ten euros an hour. I put on the face mask, switched on the light, and went back inside. I would work until I had earned enough to send my family what they needed. A thousand euros equals a hundred hours of chicken catching. This was the only way I could manage to survive that chicken hell.

It was pitch dark in the shed, except for our five headlamps. More light would make it impossible to catch the chickens, because then they ran every which way. Behind us were crates, empty and full. Amid all the regular cackling, you could make out the "fright chorus" of the chickens being grabbed and the "pain chorus" of those being stepped on in the dark.

We, the morning crew, worked from five in the morning until one in the afternoon. Then came an afternoon crew, and after them, an evening crew, so that there was an almost round-the-clock capturing of chickens.

You were supposed to grab the chickens by their legs, five per hand. So ten chickens in all. You stuffed them into a crate, went and got ten more, and stuffed them in, and so on, until no more would fit. I was a beginner. The first hours I only managed to catch one at a time. More chickens ended up under my feet than in the crate. I would feel around in the crate to make sure the chickens already in it would have room to breathe and move around. I thought of the money I was earning and kept at it.

Suddenly I felt a heavy hand grasp me by the shoulder and pull me outside.

I yanked off the face mask, wiped the feathers from my face, and breathed deeply. Air. Bert van Lier switched off the lamp strapped to my forehead.

"Turn off the lamp when you're outside. Otherwise the battery will go dead before you know it," he said. He gave me a moment to catch my breath.

"I thought it was a policeman dragging me outside," I said, "because we're working illegally."

"No, man, there are jobs they don't check on, because no one except illegals will do them. What was your name, again?"

"Samir."

"Listen, Samir, you're doing it all wrong. Don't think of the chickens, think of the crates."

I went back into the shed and this time I thought of the chickens as little as possible, and not really of the crates, but mostly of Bert van Lier and his euros. Instead of one chicken, I managed two per hand, and soon, three. I shoved them into the crate and ran back to grab as many as I could. When no more chickens fit in the crate, I got a new one. Being bad for the chickens meant being good for Bert van Lier and his crates, and in turn for my own wallet.

Bert might not have been so nice to the chickens, but he was good to the asylum seekers. He had a frighteningly hard face and a belly like a piece of carry-on luggage, but he had a good heart. He was always moving and could only do two things at once otherwise he would get confused, and if he got confused you had to stay out of his way, because then he could snap at you for no reason.

After every hour of work, Bert gave us a fifteen-minute break. Sometimes we would forget, but Bert did not. He would stick his head in the shed and yell "Break!" and we would go outside for some fresh air.

Break time, whether in Bert's office or outside if it was good weather, was never quiet. We were a team of five or six men. Just as all chickens look alike, our conversations as foreign chicken catchers all sounded the same.

"How stupid the Hollanders are!" said Mamoun, the best chicken crate filler. "They live in the middle of Europe. No war, no Saddam Hussein, no Osama bin Laden, no America, no jihad, and what do they do? They set up house right here next to millions of stinking chickens! They eat cheese and bread and stay here, even in the winter when it's dark and freezing cold, even though they can visit three-quarters of the world without a visa and the euro is worth more than the dollar."

Everyone laughed, except Najif. He was in his mid-forties, skinny, and seemed smart and easily piqued.

"Why aren't you laughing?" said Mamoun. "Laugh!"

"Say something funny, and I will," Najif replied.

"Wasn't what I said funny?"

"Not at all. Bert van Lier is not stupid. Nor is his wife Arianne, their daughter Lisanne, or their son Joost. It's not true that they don't have war because they live in the middle of Europe—and by the way, this is the north, not the middle—but because they're so busy working. And you say they live here amid the chickens. Just look around, you fool. Are you blind? The sheds are here, far from where Bert van Lier's nose and ears live. And why shouldn't they stay here in the winter? It's their winter. They've got fireplaces and furnaces, and firewood and gas to run them. But look at us. We live here in the winter, even though it's not our winter. Can my mother ice-skate? Or your grandpa?"

"Ach, Najif, don't make such a big deal about it," Mamoud said. "I just said something to liven up the break."

But Najif didn't let up. "You, what did you study?"

"Civil engineering," I said.

"And you?"

Mamoun: "Master's in mathematics."

"And you?"

"Law."

"And you?"

"I was a soldier."

"And I had a master's in chemistry. Mr. Bert van Lier has managed to get five university graduates and a soldier to chase chickens for him. Is he not a genius? Our countries have turned five university graduates and a soldier into chicken catchers. Here in the Netherlands, Bert and his family live in peace. They have a good life. They've got a fridge full of fresh vegetables, a camper for vacations, four canoes, and a motorboat. And a van and a car. In their house is a piano, a guitar, and a flute. And you could search for three weeks and still you won't find a pistol or an automatic rifle or a dagger. Not even an old sword that belonged to some grandfather. In Iraq you can't live from chickens, not even if they lay silver or gold eggs or poop diamonds. And did you know that Bert told me his father was a Nazi sympathizer? And now just look. His father was not killed, and look how the son lives. In our country they'd have burned him alive, because the son of a traitor is himself a traitor."

"I'm glad my father sent me to the army and not to university," said the soldier.

This time, only Najif laughed. "That's the best the joke I've heard in three months."

I started working night shifts at the chicken shed. Eventually I got paid thirteen euros an hour. When I got back I would sometimes hear the students sitting at the kitchen table chatting and drinking. Then I would creep into my room, stinking and covered with feathers, and sleep like a log. If the house was quiet I would take a shower and wash my clothes before going to bed.

My plan was to quit that job once I had earned the thousand euros I wanted to send my family and kept some for myself. But day-to-day life cost more than I wanted it to, and the Iraqi jihadists kept sending me back to the chickens.

One night, during my shift, my telephone vibrated in my pants pocket. I always had it with me in case anything happened to my family. It was an anonymous number. I answered.

"Hello, Samir? I hear chickens and chickens. And more chickens. Is Samir there, or is it just chickens?"

I pressed the phone tighter against one ear and stuck my finger in the other. It sounded like Yelena, the Russian woman I knew from the ASC.

"Yelena?"

"Yes, who did you expect, Vladimir Putin? Hey Samir, I hear nothing but chickens."

Yelena! Her voice bowled me over and filled my heart—

just like during those long years in the ASC—with a warm and homey feeling.

"Wait a minute, I'll go outside. I'm in a shed full of chickens."

"What did you say? Has the Immigration Department sent you to a chicken center?"

"Just a sec, Yelena, I can't hear you. It's too noisy in here. I'm catching chickens."

"What, they've caught you with chickens? It's three in the morning and you're in with a bunch of chickens? What a place Holland is. Used to be asylum seekers and asylum seekers, now chickens and chickens."

"Wait a minute, Yelena. I'm stepping outside."

"Samir, I'll call you back in five minutes, when the chickens have gone to sleep. I've got good news," she said, and hung up. I didn't even think of her good news, because her voice alone was good enough news for me. Those five minutes lasted a long time. She did not call me back, and it would be quite some time before I heard from her again.

32

Before you become a vegetarian or develop an allergy to feathers, I'll bring you back to the student house. Sometimes I felt as claustrophobic there as in the chicken shed. It wasn't the foreigners police or the IND, nor the Dutch streets or the horrible weather, not even the spring hay fever that made it clear how unwelcome I was in the Netherlands. It was Marga. Everything about me annoyed her. Sometimes, from my room, I overheard her say things like: "That Iraqi guy next door to me smells funny." Or: "Kind of a strange one, that asylum seeker." She said it with the sweetest possible voice, but with an undertone that gave me the feeling that she was suffering from my presence in that house. Or she'd say: "That Iraqi spends all his time in his room. Twenty-four hours a day." Desperate censure packaged in muted resentment. Whenever I heard her talking about me, I'd try not to let on I was in my room. I did not want to embarrass her. But after a while I realized she was saying these things purposely so I would hear them, maybe because she knew I would then stay put in my room for longer.

All that time, I was a mouse in his nest, biding his time until it was safe to come out. I had no inkling that eventually I would land right in the middle of student house life.

One day someone rapped on my door. I was in my room, as usual, and I could hear there were lots of people in the kitchen. And now … was someone angry? I cautiously opened the door and saw a guy standing there.

"Ard," he said, offering me a hand. "Ow," he said, pulling it back. "Goddamn, man, you've broken at least two bones."

Ard sounded stupid when he talked, even when he said something clever. Later, I understood that his voice came straight from the heart. He turned out to be the sensitive type who tried to mask this behind a facade of rough talk.

"Sorry," I said, thrown off balance. My chicken-catching hands must have gotten stronger than I realized.

"No problemo," he said. And after a brief silence he said, "You want to come to the kitchen? We're having a house meeting."

All sorts of thoughts spun through my mind. Do the students meet in this house? About what? Why did I have to be there? Was there a problem?

But I couldn't refuse, so I followed Ard into the full kitchen. It wasn't just the housemates, but their friends and fellow students as well.

In front of the whole crowd Ard started in again about his hand. "Ow, my hand. This fucking asylum seeker just broke two bones in my hand. No, three." The group broke out laughing. When he felt that it was enough, he said, "I introduce you to … What's your name?"

"Samir."

"I introduce you to: Samir the asylum seeker." Then he flapped his sore hand and shouted, "And now how am I supposed to jerk off?"

"Do you do that left-handed, or right?" one girl asked.

"Left, actually," Ard replied. "But I finger with my right hand, so that's out for now." His voice changed from one moment to the next, from loud to soft, from normal to high-pitched. "Boys, girls, this is Samir the asylum seeker, who lives with us in this house. Ladies and gents and homos and bis, know that you are no longer safe in this house! I understand that this fucking asylum seeker is from Af-ghan-i-stan." This last word he enunciated with the tone of a schoolteacher, with one hand on my shoulder and the other in the air.

"I'm from Iraq," I said.

"Even worse, ladies. He is from I-raq. Girls: be on your guard. I repeat: warning, he comes from Iraq. So no more walking to the shower with bare boobs. And you, Ms. Right-Winger, did you hear? Your daddy's political party wants no more asylum seekers in this country, and now one is living with you under the same roof!" He said this, with a big laugh, to Marga.

Everyone laughed along, except Marga and a guy sitting next to her.

The table was full of beer bottles, glasses of wine, and full ashtrays. Cigarettes and joints went around the room.

"Bu-u-u-t-t-t ..." Ard continued, "I also have good news. Hofkamp called me and said to tell you that if the Afghan-Iraqi doesn't behave: report him! So once again: ladies, if you feel a finger between your butt cheeks, you know who it was. The asylum seeker! If you feel a tongue licking something with two lips that in this establishment is referred to as a cunt, do not turn on the light to see who it is. Have an orgasm and go back to sleep. And report it to Hofkamp the next morning. Because it was ... *the asylum seeker!* Anything gone missing, like your panties, a sanitary pad, or a bra, who do you think is the culprit?" Ard held his hands in the air like a conductor, and on his cue came the chorus: "The asylum seeker!"

Then he cracked open a can of beer and pressed it into my hand. "Cheers, man. To the Dutch asylum system!"

His own can in the air was the signal for a general chorus of "Cheers!" At which everyone started to drink and smoke and shout all at once.

What a difference between life in the ASC and in that student house. The Dutch people in the ASC called me "Sir" but treated me like an asylum seeker. In the student house they called me "the asylum seeker" but treated me like a Sir.

33

Later, I learned the phrase "baptism by fire," and that was exactly what I went through in the kitchen that day.

To show them that I wasn't weird or scary, I took a sip from the can of beer. It was the first time in my life I had drunk alcohol, and the cheap beer did not exactly go down smoothly. But I was surrounded by twelve students, all experienced drinkers, so I really had to do my best.

I shook everyone's hand. The kitchen was full of cigarette smoke and the smell of beer, wind, burnt oil, and rancid food. I sat down at the table with them and accepted every beer or wine or cigarette I was offered, to let the students know I was one of them. And sure enough, after that uncomfortable introduction it was as though I had lived there for years, like it had never been otherwise. They all talked at the same time, about their studies, about money and parents, but mostly about sex and politics.

I landed in a discussion about the ideal number of orgasms per day, or per week or per month, and the difference between orgasms in a relationship and outside of one, or while still in love or thereafter. In that conversation I heard Dutch words I did not know, because I wasn't used to talking about sex in the first place, let alone with a bunch of Dutch students half my age. One word sounded to me like a Greek philosopher or emperor: *Clitoris*.

"Sorry, quick question. Who is this Clitoris?" I said to the girl sitting next to me, whose name was Nellie.

"What? Don't you know? What kind of immigrant are you, anyway? You come to Europe without knowing what a clitoris is?"

The others laughed.

"Ard," said Nellie. "You claim that this asylum seeker is a danger for our nation's womenfolk, but he doesn't even know what a clitoris is. Can you please explain it to him?"

Ard got up and took two mini carrots and a grape out of the fridge. He shoved the bottles, wine glasses, and ashtrays to one side. Here and there, someone jumped up if Ard spilled beer or ashes on them.

"Let's say this is the cunt. These two carrots are the labia, okay? *La-bi-a*," he said, articulating clearly. "The only difference is that these two carrots here are good for your eyes, and the cunt is not. But anyhow, this here,"—he said, placing the grape in between the carrots—"this little piece of meat on top here. This is the Clitoris. With a captial C."

Then he took the grape and demonstratively popped it in his mouth. If I should ever forget what a clitoris is, Ard's demonstration will be forever etched in my memory. The most vitamin-rich sex education lesson ever.

One of the other girls was named Marit. She was the only one not drinking alcohol or smoking. She drank tea. Her serene expression would suit a profession like psychologist. Marit was religious. Not in the belligerent, macho way, like in Iraq, but in a feminine, loving way. She was not afraid of God, she loved Him.

"First time drinking?" she asked me.

"Yes, how can you tell?"

"You're chugging it. Slow down. Would you like some tea?"

"Please," I said, gratefully.

A small girl sat across the table from me. She looked about fourteen, but was twenty-one. Her name was Nina. She had short hair and surprisingly small lips that spread into a broad smile. I had no idea about fashion, but I could still tell she had an eye for it, because her clothes went well together and suited her. She sat at the table as though she was at an expensive restaurant. Nina lived in another student house, but, as I would later find out, she spent a lot of time at ours. What I found out, from Marit, was that Nina could not say No.

That evening, Nina was like a gazelle that had been separated from her herd by the tigers, and runs every which way but knows it's only a matter of time before she's a tiger's next meal. The difference between Nina and a gazelle was that the gazelle tried to run away. Nina just sat there smiling. What I later learned was that if Philip was around, Nina was his. If Philip wasn't there, then she was Ard's. If Ard had another girlfriend at that moment, then Nina had Levi, who would bring her to his room in the brief spells between his other girlfriends. If Levi was taken, then she was José's.

If Nina belonged to four people in this kitchen alone, how many would she belong to on the planet? Nina didn't seem to mind whose she was. Her gentle heart could accept anybody. But this mentality is lethal for someone like Nina. She becomes prey for the vultures.

Philip, who was twenty-three and had a restless face, lived in a student house around the corner. Since he was friends with Ard, he was a regular at the kitchen meetings. I wasn't sure whether he was still a student, but what I did soon learn is that whatever mind-altering substances you were after, Philip was your go-to guy. He sat next to Nina.

I watched them roll joint after joint and fill glass after glass. My own head was heavy, too, from the first alcohol I'd ever drunk and the first joint I'd ever smoked. By now, the kitchen had turned into an enormous joint.

When midnight had long since passed, Ard tapped me on the head with his can of beer.

"Come with me," he whispered.

He led me into the backyard and out to the shed. The light was on, and through the small window we could see Philip sitting on a chair and Nina, now wearing only a bra, on his lap.

"That dork doesn't know how to undo a bra," Ard chuckled. Nina smoked a huge joint as she heaved up and down. I was shocked. A short time ago, there was this mild-mannered person sitting across from me, and a bit of drink and drugs had turned her into a naked hunk of meat in a garden shed.

The joint dangled in Nina's lips. She took a deep drag and put the joint into Philip's mouth, then took it back, moving up and down all the while. Occasionally she stopped moving, but never stopped smoking.

"Hot, isn't it?" Ard said, his eyes still glued to Nina and Philip and taking swigs of beer. "If you want to jerk off here on your own, I'll go."

"No, thanks."

"I do, sometimes."

"But then everyone can see you."

"So? The last time I jerked off while Philip and Nina fucked, Marit watched me from her window. And she started to finger herself. And when Sep saw that, he jerked off too, and ..." He wanted to keep going, but burst out laughing and pulled me away from the shed.

The next morning, I experienced something new. A milestone, you could call it. When I woke up, my head had lost its virginity to the worst headache of my life. My first hangover.

34

My head and my body no longer felt whole. My head weighed
a ton, and my body could not hold it up. I turned over and
felt something next to me. Nina. Asleep. Naked. The blanket
went up as far as her navel.

My emotions and thoughts began to boil in the same pot.
I heard my heart pounding, not only in my chest and my
head, but under the covers. Sounds started to come out of
my hairy belly like the gurgling of water on the boil, the
result of a combination of hash and all kinds of alcohol and
mint tea and the presence of a naked girl in my bed, whom
I had not brought here.

Nina's easy nakedness was torture. What if she wakes up,
I thought, and sees a hairy asylum seeker next to her. She'll
take fright and bolt. I'll end up in jail. I slipped out of bed
and got up, still in my underwear. The most hideous underwear you could imagine wearing next to a naked girl. I had
bought it for two euros, on sale at Zeeman. Nina's clothes
were lying on the floor in the middle of the room. The bra,
the jacket, the pants, and her bag. And, what really scared
me, her panties. Still inside her jeans, like the panties were
wearing the jeans. Had she done that, taken off her underpants? Impossible. Me? No way. Did the panties take themselves off?

The only solution I could think of was to get dressed as
fast as possible and leave. Not just the room, but the house.

I wandered around town for a bit and went back home at
about one in the afternoon. The student house now felt like
a field of landmines. But when I opened the door, I heard
nothing, not a peep, just the usual silence the day after one
of the kitchen meetings.

I tiptoed back into my room, in the hope that Nina would

have woken up and assumed she had spent the whole night alone. But seeing her passed out in my bed sent me hurrying back outside, where I wandered for another two hours. If she was still sleeping when I got back, I decided, I would just wake her up. But when I opened the front door I heard the vacuum cleaner. Nina was vacuuming my room. She didn't switch it off, probably because noise was the ideal conversation between us after that crazy night. My room still stank of chickens, but I only smelled it when I saw Nina.

"I'm going to make tea," I shouted, above the din of the vacuum cleaner.

"Rooibos, please," she shouted back.

I went to the supermarket to buy rooibos tea, because I only had black. When I got back she said I shouldn't have gone to the supermarket specially for rooibos, any kind would do. She did not go to the kitchen to drink her tea, but sat on the only chair in my room.

"I slept really late," she said. "You, too?"

"Yes, me too."

How in heaven's name did she end up in my bed, I wondered. Why wasn't she wearing her underpants? Nina herself didn't seem to find any of it all that strange. I wondered if she even knew.

"Hey, asylum seeker. Get laid?" Ard asked me later in the kitchen.

"Not last night," I replied, "but I've been screwed all day long."

"Whatever. Doesn't matter who screwed who. As long as it was good."

35

I saw all sorts of love in that student house: love at first sight, at first orgasm, at first joint or first beer. I saw all sorts of freedom, all sorts of alcoholic drinks, and all sorts of drugs, but—and this surprised me—I never saw the students fight. At university in Iraq, not a month passed without a brawl. Sometimes not even a week. The Dutch did not fight with their fists, but argued with words. Even when the discussions got heated, they remained calm, as though they had built-in cooling mechanisms. We do not have these in the Middle East.

What was also new for me was that love and sex were trading commodities.

I always thought that if a girl communicated well with a guy, then her heart was likewise open to him. But that's not how things worked here. The girls talked comfortably with Stef and at length with Kenneth, who was quick to fall for someone. The girls gave their trust to Kenneth, but their body to Levi. When I asked Nellie how this all worked, she laughed out loud. Her answer could just as easily have come from Calvin, my old shedmate.

"Well spotted, Samir. Stef is an ear. Kenneth is a heart. And Levi is a dick."

One Thursday, Lisbeth appeared in the kitchen. At first she was quiet. Stef talked to her about the environment. She talked to him about herself and he listened attentively. I sat at the table across from them, and noticed that Kenneth was eyeing her. She also seemed to return the interest. If she mentioned a film, Kenneth knew a funny scene from it. If it was a book, then Kenneth had a quote handy. From a quarter past eight till twenty past nine, Kenneth proved that he was the cleverest one in the kitchen, and had the most knowledge about things that interested Lisbeth. Until Levi came in. He sat down across from Lisbeth. He looked her straight in the eye, while Kenneth, whether out of shyness or respect, avoided her glance when he talked to her. To avoid feeling uncomfortable with Levi's gaze, Lisbeth sought out Kenneth's, who in turn looked at the walls and the photos so as not to become embarrassed by her glances. Kenneth talked and talked to conceal his lack of confidence, and Levi looked deeper and deeper into her eyes to show how confident he was. Each time someone got up, Levi moved one chair closer to her. And with every chair closer that Levi became, Kenneth was one bed further away.

Levi started spreading himself over Lisbeth like an oil spill in the ocean, isolating her not only from Kenneth but from the rest of the table and the kitchen and the entire world. Nellie whispered in my ear, "Poor Kenneth. He's bombed out again. And he was so close." When Lisbeth got up to go to the bathroom, Levi got up as well. He took her hand, and instead of going to the toilet, we heard her footsteps on the stairs.

Kenneth continued to chat with Stef and the others and with the kitchen walls. Just as he had talked and talked to hide his insecurity, now he talked to disguise his defeat. Kenneth had latent insecurity and Levi had latent aggression. Apparently Levi's aggression won the girls' bodies while Kenneth's insecurity won their trust.

This is how it always went with Kenneth. The nicest guy in the house, and the one who would treat the girl the kindest, always went back to his room alone. I hope with all my heart that he has found someone who he'll be together with happily ever after. The chance of this is good, because I now know that once they're ready to have children, Dutch women in their thirties are more likely to choose the man with the good heart.

36

If there was one person that the guys in the kitchen admired or argued about, it was Noëlle. The name Noëlle occupied the kitchen long before the person did. Noëlle kept all the boys at bay, which only made them desire her even more. Levi called her a sweetheart, Ard called her a whore, others said she had a screw loose, yet others said she was spiritual. In any case, she was talked about so much that I became curious. When I finally met her, she surpassed my wildest expectations.

Noëlle was indeed something special. Sexy, exciting, well dressed, rich, and ethereal. She wore mod clothes, like in recent Italian films (or vintage French ones), and often had flowers in her hair. She caught everyone's eye, indoors or out. She smiled when people looked at her, and even when they did not. She always looked like she was on her way to or from a wedding. She had an open face, which invited people of all sorts to greet her on the street.

Whenever she saw something beautiful, she would become emotional and the tears would run down her cheeks. And when she thought something was funny, she laughed so hard the tears would roll. Her eyes were like a leaky roof. You didn't need to wait long for them to start dripping.

Noëlle's parents were wealthy, and had planned to buy an apartment for her when she went to university. Noëlle believed that everything had energy, either positive or negative. But all the apartments Noëlle saw either had negative energy, or not enough of the positive sort. Her parents became exasperated: every time they drove in from the rich suburbs to view an apartment they liked, Noëlle felt negative energy. So in the end, they let her go house-hunting on her own. She found a houseboat. Noëlle said that she felt positive energy the moment she walked into it. Everywhere on the boat. She was so overcome by the positive energy that the estate agent had to go fetch some toilet paper so Noëlle could dry her eyes.

The houseboat was moored on the canal. On the sidewalk and bank of the canal were so many plants that the boat was secluded. On one side was a small deck with a table and two chairs. Inside, it was not a boat, but heaven. Noëlle's houseboat had electricity, running water, and a wood stove.

I was struck that in the bathroom was a Paulo Coelho calendar, in the kitchen a photo of the Dalai Lama, and in the bedroom a statue of Buddha, with closed eyes (not, I thought right away, because of any inner spirituality, but so that he did not have to see what went on there). The boat was full of bookshelves. I saw books there I had never seen anywhere else, with black-and-white photos of the author on the back cover. Indians so scrawny they made Gandhi look fat. I haven't the foggiest idea where Noëlle got all these books from. They were by masters with names like Annamalai Swami, Ramana Maharshi, Swami Vivekananda, and Nisargadatta Maharaj. Noëlle would read the words of that master and then totally believe what he said. She absorbed the master's words and retold them as though they were her own.

But back to our student kitchen, where I first saw her. Noëlle had just made tea for herself when I came in.

Her spirituality meant Noëlle saw me not as an asylum seeker, but as energy. She had lit a stick of incense in the kitchen (she always had one with her) so that her energy would not clash with the energy of the universe, but so they would melt together as one.

She introduced herself, smiling. Before I could even say my name and shake her hand, she continued, in English, "Wait. Close your eyes." It was not a request, it was an order. I closed my eyes and felt her fingers on my eyelids, which were quivering because I had closed them without them wanting to be closed. "Your eyes are quivering from negative energy." She began caressing my face. "Open your chakras, calm, calm." I had no idea what she was talking about.

"I am calm," I said.

"Shh, I'm not talking to you, I'm talking to your chakras. Calm, calm," she repeated. The words came from deep in her throat, which gave her voice such a sexual quality—forgive me—that between this, the warmth of her hands, and the smell of the incense I was completely overwhelmed. She went on lightly touching my face. When she took her hands away, I opened my eyes and saw that she was still moving her hands just over the surface of my skin.

"What are you doing?" I asked, softly.

"I am caressing your universe, your aura is becoming clearer. But stay calm and keep your eyes closed, otherwise your chakras will close up again."

I was nonplussed. And at that moment I got the most unwelcome erection ever. I was afraid she would notice, or that someone would come in and see the bulge in my pants.

I felt her hand on my face again, which made me open my eyes. She whispered, "Your chakras are open, the energy has been released. It's flowing from you to the universe and from the universe to you. You are now the universe itself. Do you feel it?"

If I had wanted to tell her the truth, I'd have said that the energy was streaming through my body and straight into my penis. But at that moment, looking at her beautiful face, the truth was the last thing I believed in.

"Yes," I said. "For the first time in my life, I feel the energy of the universe flowing. It is a miracle."

One tear sprung from her left eye, and three from her right. She looked like she wanted to laugh and cry at the same time. She hugged me as though she'd just saved my life. This unnerved me, because it was now impossible to conceal my erection, but she wasn't fazed by it, she just kept hugging me. *What do I do now?* I thought. Stay put, or take her to my room? Just then, she pushed me away. I was startled: maybe she had read my thoughts. But she put her hand on my chest, on the left, on my heart.

"All your chakras are open, except those in your heart," she said.

She closed my eyelids with her fingers and began to whisper.

"Hare Krishna, Hare, Hare, Hare Krishna." She whispered with the most sensual voice I had ever heard in a kitchen. Then she stopped and asked, "What happened to your heart? Were you in love recently?" Just as she had hit the right spot sexually a few minutes ago, now she touched an emotional nerve.

"Yes, how could you tell?"

"I can feel it. And I see it in your aura. Your heart is not satisfied with just you, it wants to be shared with someone else. But you can wipe away the pain in your heart. That's easier than carrying it around with you."

"Wipe it away where? Into which garbage can?"

"Into the universe. Come around to my place to do tantra sometime. That can help."

"Tantra? It sounds like a kind of cake."

Noëlle laughed and explained what *tantra* meant. She proudly told me there were many ways of tantra, but that she had her own method. Two students came into the kitchen. My head was spinning so much that I didn't even notice who. Noëlle left after hugging everyone. I waited patiently for her to visit again, which did not take long.

37

Noëlle knocked on my door and gave me a handwritten invitation to join her that Saturday—not, unfortunately, for a private tantra on her boat, which was what I was hoping for, but at a farm owned by Stefanie and Kees. They were on a weeklong vacation and Noëlle was looking after the animals. I thanked her and said I would go. She handed out the invitations, one by one, to the others in the house, and on Saturday she pulled up in a van. There were five or six of us, and when we got to the farm, a few others had already arrived. What caught my eye was not the farm or the other guests, but the contact between Noëlle and one particular sheep named Herman. Herman the sheep was very much into Noëlle. He allowed her to cuddle him, but did not listen to what she wanted him to do. Herman and the other sheep were in the stall, where Kees and Stefanie said they should stay, but Noëlle felt they needed to soak up new energy from the universe, and outside the stall there was better reception. As though the sheep were cell phones. So they grazed outside, invigorated with fresh energy from the universe, and at five o'clock Noëlle led them back to the shed after giving each one a cuddle. Herman let Noëlle cuddle him, but refused to go back into the stall. Noëlle tried to lure him with lettuce leaves, carrots, broccoli, and several kinds of bread, whatever she found in the kitchen that a sheep might like. Herman ate gratefully from her hand, but go into the stall—no. She came into the house and informed the others of the predicament. Then fourteen Dutch people went outside to get one sheep back into his stall. But instead of convincing Herman to go to the stall, Herman convinced them to run around the farmyard for an hour. Sweating and panting, they went back inside, had something to drink, and held a meeting. They made a plan to nab Herman without, Noëlle insisted, damaging his aura or his heart or his wool. The sheep and I looked at the Hollanders. I am guessing that at that moment Herman and I were thinking exactly the same thing: the Netherlands will never win the World Cup if fourteen Hollanders can't even get a ball of wool—without either a goalie or defenders—into a stall. After lengthy deliberations, the group came back outside. This time they did not use the animal's stomach to get him to go into the stall, but his heart. Stef whispered, "Herman, sweetie, come now." Marit whispered, even more softly, "Please, Herman, come on, we need to cook dinner." Ard did his best sheep imitation. Herman bleated back to him, and I guarantee you he wasn't really bleating, but laughing at them. From inside the stall, Nellie made little *baa-baa* sounds the whole time, like a pathetic lamb.

After that, there was another brief meeting, where it was decided to let Herman be for now, because now he was stressed and this could lead to a burnout.

There was general consternation when they came out after dessert and did not see the sheep anywhere. They thought Herman had escaped. But when I told them he was in the stall, rather than looking at me like a hero because I had done single-handedly what fourteen Dutch people together could not accomplish, they cast doubt on my methods. How had I done it? Had I injured Herman, or frightened him?

"The sheep did not have any pain. Only his ear did," I said. "What?!" cried Noëlle. She ran into the stall and hugged Herman and kissed both his ears. "Which ear?" she called out to me.

"The left one," I shouted back. Not one of the fourteen Hollanders was curious as to how I got Herman into the stall, but every last one of them felt bad for his ear. How I did it is Herman's and my secret. Maybe he now has a mental condition and thinks he is Herman, and not a sheep.

I was afraid that the Herman incident would cost me

Noëlle, but it blew over. After dinner I decided to return home. Noëlle gave me a lift to the bus station. She gave me a spontaneous hug and said, "Your chakra is more trapped than Herman is in that stall. Come around to my place next week."

And that is how I got to see her on her boat.

It was as though I had been transported to a tropical paradise. There was gentle music with waterfall sound effects and the chirping of songbirds. The music came from all sides; there must have been hidden speakers everywhere.

"Nothing in the boat must stand in the way of the energy," Noëlle said. She explained that she had left everything as it was when she came to live on this houseboat, so that it could remain itself. "Sit wherever your energy leads you." I wanted to say that my energy led me to her bed, but instead I chose to sit in a rocking chair. She made tea for me and said she had a bad connection with the Wi-Fi of the universe, or something like that.

"I'm not getting any connection with the universe," she said. "I have to cleanse my own chakras first." So unfortunately I went home without having experienced the tantra.

"When will I see you again?" I asked her as I left her houseboat for the first and the last time.

"Follow your chakras. I'll follow mine, and maybe they will bring us together."

I did in fact follow my chakras, but instead of bringing me back to Noëlle's houseboat, they sent me with a second-class train ticket to the city of Utrecht.

38

If I thought of Noëlle for one minute, then my thoughts would drift to Leda and I would spend an hour thinking about her instead. Was Leda so much a part of me? I followed my chakras, and while I had never dared go to Utrecht earlier, now I went once or twice a week in the hope of bumping into her.

I ambled through the city center, always ending up at Domplein, the square in front of the cathedral, because Leda had told me she often went there. I drank tea in one of the many cafés on that square, but never caught sight of her. I decided to give Mieke a call.

I had kept in touch with Mieke. I'd call her now and again, and she would tell me what she was up to. She had a boyfriend, studied obstetrics. She lived in a dorm but returned to the village on a regular basis. Mieke said it was high time she went to visit, she wanted to see Leda, too, and would keep me posted.

One Wednesday she called and said that Leda had taken Diesel to Utrecht and would be bringing him back that Friday. Mieke figured that since Leda always liked to get to the village in time for dinner, she would have to take the 4:48 train from Utrecht. Platform 7.

The station was busy that Friday. I was standing on platform 7 an hour early, just in case she took an earlier train. And sure enough, I spotted Leda and Diesel coming down the escalator. Diesel recognized me and barked, but Leda didn't seem to know why, and tugged on his leash. He stopped barking.

I was torn between fleeing and running up to her. But I didn't dare do either. She stood on the busy platform for perhaps two minutes. I approached them from behind, cautiously skulking among the passengers. I got closer and closer, until there were maybe five people separating us. She looked straight ahead. I took another step and could see Diesel, his tongue hanging out of this mouth. He saw me, wagged his tail, and barked again. I quickly turned and left, afraid she would look back and see me. I nipped into one of those glass waiting rooms, and hoped the train would be delayed, the longest delay ever, but it arrived right on time. Maybe that Aruban man in Nieuwegein was right when he said that Dutch trains are always late when they are bringing people together, but always on time when there's a goodbye involved.

Leda and Diesel boarded the train. I heard the conductor's whistle. The doors slid closed, and a few seconds later I was alone on the platform. The train pulled out, leaving only emptiness behind.

When I called Mieke the following week to thank her for the tip, she said that during dinner, Leda had told Danielle she had seen me on the platform in Utrecht station. Danielle asked if we had spoken.

"No, he pretended not to see me. Even after Diesel barked hello at him, twice. He probably had a date and didn't want the other girl to see us together."

A while later, Mieke told me Leda had a boyfriend. And after that, that she was single again. Then I heard that she got back together with the first boyfriend, and then was single, and was now just good friends with the second boyfriend and had an on-again, off-again relationship with the first one. After that I couldn't keep track of which one was just a good friend and which a sometimes-boyfriend. Mieke also had a hard time telling the boyfriends apart, and I'll bet Leda did, too. The love of her life, and her best friend, was still Diesel.

Before Mieke became a mother and stopped calling me, I started to understand that Leda always left a bit of her heart behind with a lover. She never left someone with her heart entirely intact. Maybe this left open the possibility of going back. Over time, I thought, Leda's heart would be divided up among so many men that there wouldn't be any left for herself. I would have so liked to keep a bit of her heart, so that she might come back to me, but all I had was a leash and a rubber ball.

39

My time in the student house—the first time in my life I had an address of my own—also came to an end. It could have gone on for longer, if I hadn't received a phone call one day that would cost me the room. Abdulsalaam, an old friend, had been made to leave the ASC and came to stay with me.

Abdulsalaam was already living in the ASC when I arrived, and he was still there when I left nine years later. All those years of waiting had made him crazy, but he was an old friend, and in my culture when someone needs your help, you don't ignore them. I clearly remembered the day I left the ASC, and that was no picnic, so when Abdulsalaam called to tell me he was being thrown out and had nowhere to go, I went to pick him up.

You should know that Abdulsalaam was in fact, in his mind, still in Yemen. In the ASC he had neither been given nor had he taken the chance to acclimatize himself to Dutch society. So you can imagine that after all those years in imaginary Yemen, life in a student house was an enormous culture shock for him. Not only for him, but for Marga, who no longer dared to go into the kitchen in her short pajama top and rabbit slippers, and for Levi's cats, whom Abdulsalaam kicked every chance he got.

So it didn't surprise me at all when, a while later, the students said that Abdulsalaam had to go. But he had no one and I couldn't bring myself to leave him in the lurch. He was my responsibility. If that hadn't been the case, I could have asked him to leave, but there was no way he would survive on his own, so sending him packing was not an option. I grew up in an extreme society where your best friend could easily become your victim, or where you'd rather drown together than run away and regret it for the rest of your life.

So I packed my things, put my key in an envelope with Mr. Hofkamp's name on it, and set it with the rest of the post. I called him up and said I was leaving.

"Okay then," he said, cool and businesslike. "Make sure the room's emptied out, yeah? Good luck now."

I brought everything out to the street and set it next to the dumpster. Half an hour later all that was left in the room was the carpeting.

Then I knocked on every door in the house and said good-bye to my housemates. Nellie and Ard called whenever there was mail for me. I think mail for me is likely still being delivered to that student house at Molenweg 26.

40

Just as Don Quixote and Sancho Panza trudged through the mountains of Spain, Abdulsalaam and I made our way through the Dutch streets lugging our belongings in carry-alls and garbage bags. Only I didn't feel like Don Quixote, but like his emaciated horse.

I had no plan. I walked ahead and Abdulsalaam followed. Walking alongside Abdulsalaam irritated me, so I kept my pace up to stay a few steps ahead of him.

His pots and pans and plates clanked in the garbage bag like a drum set. We were a spectacle to behold, and everyone—Hollanders, cats, dogs—watched as we passed. Old women opened doors and stared. One woman even went out to the middle of the street behind us—was it to check that we didn't leave a trail of blood from the two garbage bags? One of Abdulsalaam's pans clattered onto the asphalt and made a cat leap into the bushes in fright.

"Look at all these huge houses, Samir," Abdulsalaam said. "Even the smallest one has at least two bedrooms, some of them are three stories high. I'll bet every one of them has an empty room. Or two or three, or a whole floor. But do you think a Dutchman will shout to us that he has a room in his house for us? Not a chance."

We walked further in silence.

"Aren't you glad you're finally out of that little room?" he asked a while later.

I didn't answer.

"You really should be relieved to be out of that filthy house full of cat shit and rancid food."

I picked up my pace again, to be as far from him as possible.

After wandering for a couple of hours, we ended up at the train station. We drank a cup of tea and Abdulsalaam started calling people on his phone's contact list. After each brief telephone call he told me which asylum seeker it was, and where he was living now—Turkey, Jordan, Libya, or Greece—and that they would call us as soon as they were back.

I knew things were seriously wrong with him when he said, "Now for the last number," tapped the button, and held his phone to his ear. My cell phone rang and he shouted, "Hello! It's Abdulsalaam! Samir, man, where are you? Have you got a tenner on you? Come with me!"

He led me to the taxi rank outside the station.

"We're going somewhere warmer than that lousy train-station joint," he said. "We're going to God."

Fifteen minutes later we arrived at the mosque. Abdulsalaam walked up to the entrance and came back, disappointed.

"The door's closed. Locked. How strange. God is different in the Netherlands than in Yemen. There, he works 24/7. The mosques are always open, but here the door is locked and there's a sign with opening hours."

"Maybe God works 24/7 in Yemen because the people don't. That might explain why things are such a mess there."

The mosque finally opened its doors at three in the afternoon. Abdulsalaam asked the imam if we could sleep there. He replied that that wasn't possible, but that after prayers he would, *inshallah*, help us find a solution.

"See, Samir? God works quicker than the IND. Our problem will be solved after prayers, not after a thousand gray hairs."

That is how I met Jafar Kalaf. He was an Iraqi who brought a disabled Libyan man to the mosque once a week. He offered to take us home with him after he had dropped off the Libyan.

Jafar Kalaf was the only asylum seeker I had ever met who had become a complete Dutchman. I noticed it after about ten minutes in the car with him. It wasn't just that he peppered his Arabic with a lot of Dutch words, it was his whole manner of speaking.

"It sounds like they've turned you into a Hollander," I said to him. "Or were you born here?"

"No, I came here when I was about twenty. You know, some people come here as an Iraqi and want to be treated like an Iraqi. Like having an Iraqi flag flying above city hall and a war raging on the border, just so he'll feel at home. Oh yeah, and a secret police post a hundred meters from his house. Not me. Holland gave me everything I needed to remain a person."

"The Hollanders are arrogant," said the Libyan. "They want foreigners to adapt to their country, but they refuse to do the same somewhere else. I know a Dutch guy who has lived in Libya for years and only speaks English. Not a word of Arabic, except *salam alaikum*."

"Mustn't dredge old asylum seekers out of the canal," said Jafar in Dutch, laughing as he paraphrased the local saying "don't dredge old cows out of the canal," meaning in turn "let bygones be bygones." He was the only one who laughed, because none of us knew that saying. "You guys fled your country, hungry and scared," he said. "And what did you bring with you?" He waited. "You've got to change! Change, now! Become a person. Period. End of story."

He talked like he was in a hurry. He had the kind of routine haste that Dutch people often have. As though he was always running late.

"Give it a rest, Jafar," said the Libyan. "You act as though we know nothing and you know everything just because you've become a Hollander. Believe me, that's the easy way: become one of them. But not everyone wants to. Birds also fly from one forest to the other without changing their ways."

Jafar Kalaf switched on the radio and turned up the volume.

"You don't want to listen, do you?" the Libyan continued. "Because you know I'm right." He chuckled and turned to us in the back seat. "When I get out he'll tell you I'm ungrateful. He thinks he's one of them, but even if he bleaches his hair with a hundred kinds of blond dye he'll still be an asylum seeker."

We stopped in front of his house. Jafar Kalaf helped the man out of the car and said, "See you the same time next week."

"What an ingrate," he said as we drove off, just like the Libyan had predicted. "They gave him everything here: a house, people who come to take care of him, a welfare check. And not once have I ever heard him say anything positive about the Netherlands."

He stopped at a Chinese restaurant, bought a takeout meal for us, and drove us to his house.

Just like Johan Cruyff or Yogi Berra, Jafar Kalaf invented his own sayings. Whenever he laughed, he held his belly like it was a soccer ball. When he was angry, he would slap the steering wheel. He had come to the Netherlands as an asylum seeker in 1979, when Saddam Hussein had just become president. He married a Dutch woman, had a son and a daughter, and was now divorced.

I was curious about asylum seekers from those days. When Jafar told me about the warm welcome he got at Schiphol Airport, I realized the Golden Age of Asylum Seekers was long past.

His house was just as Dutch as he was: the framed photos of his son and daughter neatly arranged on the wall, an equal number per child, in identically sized frames, at exactly the same age and with the same expression; the books and knickknacks; the paper-recycling bin; the variety of glasses in the kitchen, one for each specific drink. We were even given a tour, just like Danielle van der Weerde had done.

"You guys can sleep here," he said. "I live at my girl-friend's. She lives in the next town. If you want to go, just leave the key on the table, but you're welcome to stay. There's nothing of any value in the house except Doortje, my cat. She goes in and out through the cat flap, and you only have to feed her twice a day. Good thing Muslims don't eat cats," he laughed as he left.

Only later did it become clear that Jafar Kalaf should have given Abdulsalaam instructions on how to treat the neighbor's dog.

41

The very first time the cat tried to rub up against Abdulsalaam's leg, he kicked her like Cristiano Ronaldo taking a
penalty shot. Screeching, the cat flew through the air, hit
the wall with a splat, and ran off with the most terrified,
drawn-out meow I had ever heard. Not even the wholest
whole milk could lure her back inside, and from then on
she would come no closer to the house than the back fence.

Next door to us lived Inge van Duinhoven and her little dog
Mario. A skinny, hairless, trembling Chihuahua. Inge was
in her late sixties and had recently gotten a new hip, and
since she wasn't able to take the dog out for walks, she let
him do his business on the sidewalk outside the front door.

"Say, Samir, why is the neighbor's dog so tiny?" Abdulsalaam asked.

"That's just how he is, he won't get any bigger than that,"
I replied.

"That dog is far away and up close at the same time. It
makes me dizzy. So when he came up to me, I gave him a
little kick. Not as hard as the cat. Nice and soft. Just to see
how close he was."

That same day Abdulsalaam resumed his show of ignorance by asking if such a small dog could bark.

Jafar Kalaf said Inge was a nice woman. However, I had
the impression she was afraid of us, or maybe just afraid of
the unknown. She would loosen up once she got to know
us, I figured. But now Abdulsalaam had botched it up.

So, after Mario's encounter with Abdulsalaam, I set out to
restore neighborly contact with Inge van Duinhoven. When
I saw Mario outside, I called him and he trotted over. I opened
a can of dog food and he gobbled it up. I patted him on the
head. Inge watched all this through her front window, but

before I could greet her, she turned away. Still, she didn't call the dog back inside.

Fortunately, it won't take Mario years to get used to asylum seekers, I thought. Making friends with him is simply a matter of a few cans of food.

In Jafar Kalaf's roomy house, Abdulsalaam began to feel something he had never experienced since coming to Netherlands: solitude. He went out into the yard, came back inside, went upstairs, came back downstairs. Sometimes he stopped halfway and I lost track of whether he was going up or down. So did he. Sometimes he said it was strange that there was no Reception here, or I would hear him talking in his sleep to an ASC staff member. This reinforced my theory that in his head he was still in the ASC, and that those seventeen years were still not over for him.

If Mario occasionally barked, even just one little yap, Abdulsalaam complained that he couldn't sleep with all that racket. He then told the neighbor that the dog kept him up at night, and that in Yemen, dogs that barked too much were shot. So in a single sentence, he once again thwarted my attempts to befriend Inge van Duinhoven and her dog.

He related this to me in Arabic, and that being his mother tongue, there was some nuance to it, but I knew for sure that in Dutch it must have sounded like a terrorist threat.

"And what did she say?" I asked.

"She apologized."

That same afternoon, Jafar Kalaf came around. He took me aside and said that maybe Abdulsalaam needed psychiatric help. Jafar had heard that Abdulsalaam told the neighbor that if a dog barks, its owner gets shot.

"That's a serious threat. Now we have to go calm poor Inge down, before she has a heart attack."

"Abdulsalaam meant to say that in Yemen they shoot barking dogs, not their owners."

"That's just as bad! This is Holland! People here skip a vacation because they don't want to leave the dog behind. Listen, I don't want to have to kick you guys out, but this is unacceptable."

At four o'clock that afternoon, Jafar returned with his wife, Hilly ten Hoor. Hilly had been a child psychologist, and after retiring she volunteered with Vluchtelingenwerk, a support organization for refugees. Hilly was a sturdy woman, with enough energy to run an entire circus. She told us she had devised her own therapy, which involved talking and doing something physical at the same time. This, she said, could solve any psychological issue. So Hilly started chatting with Abdulsalaam. She listened to him, asked questions, and hugged him, keeping him moving all the while. She said "sit" and he sat, she said "stand" and he stood. She got him to turn in circles while he talked. First clockwise, then counter clockwise. And he talked as he turned. She put on some music and led Abdulsalaam around by the hand, to teach him to dance and talk at the same time.

Jafar Kalaf and I watched in amazement. Not only at Hilly's approach, but mainly at how Abdulsalaam responded. After a few minutes, he got sweaty and dizzy from all that spinning around.

Hilly kept saying, "Come on, Abdulsalaam! Keep going!"

She took both his hands and twisted him left and right, while salsa and disco and all kinds of music blared from the speakers. She pressed up against him, let him loose, pulled him back by a finger, pushed him down with one flat hand, pulled him back up, threw him in the air and caught him. He was like a half-dead mouse in the claws of a cat.

"Come on, Abdulsalaam, faster! Swing!"

I was afraid that I'd be next, and that this tigress from Vluchtelingenwerk would devour me, too. I tried to sneak off to the kitchen, but Hilly intercepted me. She got all kinds of utensils from the kitchen, gave Jafar and me each a pan and a spoon, and asked us to bang to the rhythm of the music. Between us with our pans and spoons and Hilly with her sturdy, agile body, Abdulsalaam flailed around like a drowning victim. She flung him around the room; when he was about to fall, she would support him, and if he stood, she let him collapse. But from that salsa concert, a new Abdulsalaam was born. I witnessed the miracle with my own eyes.

"Music cures everything!" Hilly exclaimed. Now I had broken into a sweat, too.

Once Abdulsalaam was really worn out, she took him to the backyard. They talked for an hour and then went over to Inge's house to drink tea. Another hour later, I saw Hilly and Abdulsalaam and Mario walking down the street together, Abdulsalaam holding the leash and the dog pulling him along.

In the weeks that followed, Hilly came around every day, for an hour or so. She talk-danced with Abdulsalaam and after that had him talk to Mario. Abdulsalaam would say "sit" and Mario sat. Then he said "come" and Mario went over to him. Abdulsalaam found it hard to believe the dog understood him, but then he danced with Hilly for fifteen minutes, and soon enough was convinced that Mario wasn't a dog at all, but an extraordinary kind of Hollander that could listen, but not talk.

Not only did Mario start communicating with Abdulsalaam, but Inge opened up. She even started talking to Abdulsalaam in "asylumseekerese," that pidgin language all asylum seekers spoke among themselves and that Inge had picked up from Hilly. Abdulsalaam regularly took Mario out for walks, and the more Mario became Abdulsalaam's dog, the more Abdulsalaam became Inge's dog. The asylum seeker, the older Dutch woman, and the dog all listened to one another. This was the key to their happiness.

Eventually, Abdulsalaam no longer needed Hilly's intervention. He would take daily walks with Mario, sit in the park, and share with him all his woes and complaints.

42

Jafar Kalaf would not accept any money from us for staying in his house, not even for utilities. But since he knew I was keen to do something in return, he started taking me with him to his ex-wife, Toos Simons, to do odd jobs.

Just as Jafar's house looked like a Dutch house, Toos's house looked like an Iraqi one. The walls were hung with Middle Eastern calligraphy and paintings of women in colorful wraps, with similarly vibrant curtains on the windows. Cushions and rugs everywhere. There were bowls of nuts and sweets on little tables, and she served tea from an Iraqi teapot and in typical Iraqi tea glasses. The most striking differences from a Dutch house was that there wasn't a light bulb less than a hundred watts, and in the bathroom you could choose between toilet paper and water.

I was amused that I did not get a tour of Toos's house, like at Jafar's and the rest of the Dutch houses I had visited. The only thing Toos showed me was where the bathroom light switch was.

Jafar had been transformed into a Hollander and seemed happy with it; Toos likewise had become an Iraqi, only she was not happy with it. She was like a foreigner in her own country. Toos spoke Arabic well, and the Iraqi dialect passably. The downside of her transformation was that she had acquired the Iraqi penchant for talking. By this I mean allowing not even a moment's silence, repeating things ad infinitum, jumbling everything up, and padding her stories. She talked just as gladly about what she had bought that day as about her deepest spiritual feelings or what she was planning to eat the coming week and a half.

I liked going around to Toos's, not only because I felt at home there and enjoyed the Iraqi hospitality, but also to fantasize what life with Leda could have been like, even though I knew Leda would never become someone like Toos Simons, more likely someone like Jafar Kalaf.

Toos was also happy to have me there, because it meant she could talk my ear off. Besides, I wasn't much older than her two children, and she seemed to enjoy having contact with a "full-blood Iraqi," as she called me.

I once asked her how she and Jafar had met.

"Oh, I remember it well. It was April 4, 1981. I had taken the 14:15 train from Alkmaar to Amsterdam for a party. When my mother saw me getting all dolled up, she joked to me, 'Don't come back pregnant.' She wasn't far off the mark, because I met Jafar that day and less than three months later I *was* pregnant. Jafar got on, drenched from a downpour, and sat down across from me. 'The rain in Baghdad doesn't make people this wet,' he said. I wanted to ask if they use umbrellas there, but the word *Baghdad* sparked something in me. And so did the young man who said it. I already had butterflies in my stomach by the time the train pulled out."

"How come? Was he more handsome back then than he is now?" I joked. Toos smiled. Not only at my little joke, but also in a sort of loving way, as if recalling her feelings from that moment.

"A long time ago, before there were any real Iraqis here, the most famous Iraqi was a donkey in the Antwerp Zoo. The sign said: *Donkey from Baghdad.* I walked up to it, and it approached me. I patted its head. I felt like we had a connection. But soon enough I knew what that click was: the white rose in my hair. The donkey was eating it." She laughed out loud. "I'll bet you want to know if I was in love with the donkey."

I nodded.

"Absolutely! I wanted to take him home with me. I had read *One Thousand and One Nights* and lost myself in that magical world. I dreamed of a land where people flew around on magic carpets, where you found a buried treasure wherever you dug. A ship in every harbor that would take you away, and only bring you back after you had seen the whole world." Toos's eyes glistened.

"Good thing that Antwerp donkey didn't tell you that in Baghdad only the wealthy neighborhoods have sewers, and half the city smells like a clogged toilet."

"I didn't know that then," she said.

"So what happened next? Did Jafar remind you of that donkey?"

"Seeing Jafar brought me back to the first time I read *One Thousand and One Nights*. I thought: *I want to kiss him.* Maybe Jafar sensed that, because at the next station he took my hand—without even asking my name—and in a corner of the station he pressed his lips to mine. I was totally bowled over. No Dutch boy would do that. It was one of those moments that changes your life forever." She sighed and paused. "Our time together was the best time of my life. I introduced Jafar to my Dutch friends, he took me to meet his Iraqi ones. I started to tire of my own friends and become more attached to his. In the end, we basically swapped friends. By that time I was pregnant, and when Tameem was born we already realized we didn't belong together anymore. Fortunately Tameem was an easy child. He was a good reason to stay together. But things were different with Sumaya. She was more difficult. Jafar complained about the child, and I complained about him. If we had stayed together we would have become enemies. We both knew this. So we split up. And stayed friends."

One day I asked her if I might page through the photo albums I saw on the bottom shelf of the bookcase.

"Of course," she said, and went on with her needlepoint, after she had put a pot of Iraqi tea, with cookies, raisins, and dates on the table for me.

In the photo albums I saw, in addition to many faces, a

variety of houses. It was like Toos's family had always been searching for a home but never found one.

"Eat something. And drink your tea before it gets cold," she said as I looked at a card with a date, a time, and a long name on it. It was her birth announcement. *Cornelia Eleonora Antonia Maria Simons. We call her Toos ("priceless").*

"Thanks," I said. I took a sip of tea and went back to the album.

"Eat."

Every time my thoughts got lost in the photos, Toos's voice would bring me back.

"And?" she said.

"What a nomadic family you have. Always moving."

"No, I meant: do you like the cookies? Homemade." She went back to her needlepoint, and finally responded to my comment. "There was always a new job, and we had to move," she said.

"This man is restless," I said, holding up the album and pointing to an Anton Simons in 1908. "And the cookies are delicious."

"They were all restless," she said. "As far back as I can remember." I closed the photo albums and put them back in the bookcase. She insisted I take the cookies with me when I left.

43

Occasionally, I saw Tameem and Sumaya at their mother's when I was invited over to eat. Tameem spoke passable Iraqi, Sumaya did not. She refused to even say the words she did know out loud.

Sumaya, who went by "Sum," regretted not having her mother's last name, Toos being the last of the Simonses.

That brother and sister did something that you would never see Iraqi siblings do together: they shared a joint, like friends. An Iraqi brother and sister would never go camping with friends in the Ardennes or take a day trip to the beach. They would live together under one roof, but lead completely different lives. Tameem and Sumaya did not live in the same house, but the stories they told and the questions they asked one another showed how much they coexisted. She was definitely not the family honor that needed protecting.

And yet there was a kind of distance in that family. Their communication was neutral in a way that sidestepped any kind of disturbance or disagreement. They were exaggeratedly diplomatic and overly respectful, saying things like, "What do you think?" and "Do you like this?" and "Did you ever find your bike?" An Iraqi diplomat in an embassy anywhere in the world would not have been as diplomatic as these people were with each other.

Jafar Kalaf called me up once to say that Toos would cook for us. Iraqi food. Tameem and Sumaya would be there too. I asked him if I wasn't barging in on a family affair, but he said it was better if I came along. That way Sumaya would be nice to him, rather than snarky. I was surprised by his openness—it wasn't usually something you would hear an Iraqi man say about his daughter.

We arrived at five thirty. Toos was busy in the kitchen. I had just sat down with Jafar to drink tea when Tameem and Sumaya came in.

"Smells delicious!" Tameem called out to his mother.

"Iraqi food *again* ..." Sumaya grumbled, so that Jafar could hear but not Toos, as though it was Jafar's idea. Jafar had told me that Sumaya blamed him for all her and her mother's problems, and was sore that he had turned Toos into an Iraqi wife. And that once she had become one, he'd abandoned her and the two children. I noticed she did not like the fact that her father had had relationships since the divorce, but her mother had not.

After chatting about this and that, Tameem and Sumaya talked about internships they did not get because their last name was Kalaf. Tameem's tone of voice was gentle and jokey, but Sumaya's was bitter.

I did my best to cheer Sumaya up, making jokes and speaking Dutch as much as possible, despite the fact that Tameem liked hearing me and his mother speak in Iraqi. And yet, all Sumaya seemed to radiate was: *What's he doing here, anyway?*

Meanwhile I thought about the house where Sumaya was raised, and where I was staying. I had seen her vast collection of cuddly toys, how many beautiful photos had been taken of her, how often she had been read to as a child. All those frog princes, the rhymes, the rabbits that married moles. All those years of childhood bliss, and what was left? A spoiled brat. With parents like Jafar and Toos, two cultures full of love, warmth, and understanding. Where did this cold anger come from? She had more luck than ten Iraqi villages combined, but not an ounce of happiness.

Tameem sat next to her. How exuberant he was, how optimistic! In him I saw the best of both Iraq and the Netherlands rolled into one. Not only did he polish up things that were already positive, but he even found something positive to say about negative things. After every bite he said, in

Iraqi, "May your hands live long, Mama." When Sumaya went off to the bathroom, he asked after his father's girl-friend, and if she had recovered from her appendix operation.

Tameem shone a light on things. We could have become friends if I had stayed longer in Jafar Kalaf's house.

44

Mario was Abdulsalaam's barking residence permit. He was doing so well that I felt I could leave him behind in Jafar Kalaf's house with a clear conscience. I told Jafar I wanted to leave because my lengthy stay in the ASC made it hard for me to settle down anywhere for very long, not because of Abdulsalaam. It was a cheap excuse, but it turned out to be true. When I said goodbye to Abdulsalaam, he said that if I ever needed a dog, I could call him.

"Jafar told me you waited to leave until you were sure your friend, that Yemeni man, would be okay on his own. That's why I trust you," said Jafar's friend Asker Shaheen when he came to pick me up to visit a possible new place to live.

But first he took me to an Iraqi restaurant. The aroma of the grill came out to greet us as soon as we got out of the car. In an Iraqi restaurant you need a gas mask and two towels for your perspiration, but the food is delicious. The bread is freshly baked, you choose the meat, and they grill it right in front of you. You don't go to an Iraqi restaurant for long talks. You order, eat, and leave. A Dutch restaurant, where you talk and eat at the same time, makes an Iraqi enjoy neither his food nor the conversation. If you want to talk, go to a teahouse.

Asker chewed, made phone calls, and talked to me all at the same time.

"If you're smart, you'll be a lord in Holland. If you're stupid, you'll be a slave," he said.

"But whichever you are, you're always free," I replied.

"Yes, yes, you're always free in the Netherlands. But only if you can use the rules to your advantage, not the other way around. And that only happens if you know how. I've got a house for you, you'll share it with two other Iraqis.

Three hundred a month. I'll tell you exactly what you have to do."

The curtains were closed when we got there. Inside, it smelled of spices that were nice in the food, but not in the air. The house was rented to Nadhem and Ghazwaan, two cousins who had both been denied asylum. It had taken them four and a half years to get from Iraq to a Dutch ASC. After another six years without an answer, they went to Norway, got caught, and were sent back to the Netherlands. Having left the country illegally disqualified them for asylum and the general pardon.

After being introduced, I was told what I "had to do" to be able to live there. Asker Shaheen and his wife Zakiya were officially divorced, which entitled her to this council house and welfare payments. But in actual fact they were still together. This way Asker could pocket the welfare *and* sublet Zakiya's house. Should the council come to check, it had to look like she lived there. So every day, we had to pack up our things and stow them in the basement, so the house would look like an older Iraqi woman lived there.

There was a wardrobe with Zakiya's clothes, there was shampoo and a toothbrush in the bathroom. There was even a pair of knitting needles on the armrest of the sofa, a reading lamp and reading glasses and a cup that we had to keep half filled with tea, to make it look realistic. There was a small rug for her feet, a retro granny-telephone, and on a side table was a toilet kit full of medicine that Asker Shaheen replaced whenever the sell-by date approached. It went without saying that we had to keep the curtains closed at all times, and have no contact with the neighbors.

45

"That snake Asker is using his wife to rip off the government," Ghazwaan grumbled as I brought in my things. "If she still had milk, he would milk her, too. *And* he's taking advantage of us asylum seekers."

When I went to put my things in my room, I was surprised to see a few men lying on mattresses. They spoke among themselves in muffled voices, and greeted me with the same hushed tone, as though they were listening to a classical music concert. Ghazwaan brought me to the kitchen and asked another man who was cooking if he could leave us alone. He turned the gas to low, and left.

"How much are you paying Asker Shaheen?" Ghazwaan asked.

"Three hundred euros," I said.

"If you rent out the mattresses in your room, you only pay a hundred. Is that okay?"

"More than okay."

"Since you rent directly from Asker, you get the bed. And if he drops by, you don't have to sneak out through the back door. That's only if the council people come around."

This place was a kind of mini-ASC, even with the occasional wait for the shower or the toilet. We had to be cautious and speak softly, so the neighbors or Asker Shaheen would not catch on that so many men were living here. There were sitting men, reclining men, cooking men, whispering men. I never knew who was renting a mattress or who was just visiting. But I was free, and the rent was cheap.

Our life in that house depended on that of Zakiya. The men were obsessed with the ruse that Zakiya was living in the house. They turned on her reading lamp at the right time of the evening, so it would be visible through the closed curtain. They turned her bedroom light on and off at just the right moment to make it look like she was going to bed. They moistened her towel, as though she had just showered, and sometimes someone lay on the sofa as though Zakiya was catching forty winks. They were constantly occupied with the presence of that absent person. They had heard that the authorities could come checking unannounced, so they made it look like she let illegals in to bathe. It was as though I lived in that house on my own, because everyone was busy camouflaging his own existence.

Sometimes I really wanted to open the curtains, but this wasn't possible. What would the neighbors think if they saw all those men in Zakiya's house? We crept into the house like mice, once inside we were transformed into stealthy cats, and we crept back out like mice again. If there was anyone out front, we would use the back door. And if there was someone out back, we would use the front door. I'm pretty sure the neighbors knew what was going on, and if that was true, then in the end our Dutch neighbors offered the best cover ever, because they turned a blind eye.

46

Fearing inspectors, we never answered the door. Usually the person would give up and go away, but one time someone rang and didn't leave. We heard the metal letter flap clatter, and a knocking at the window. One of the Sudanese guys went upstairs to have a look, and came back down in a state of shock.

"It's not the police or a council inspector, it's a young blonde woman in green flip-flops," he said.

"Hello? Is anyone home?" she called through the letter flap. I decided to open up, and indeed, there stood a young blonde woman.

"Sorry," she said. "I'm Femke Slagter. I live at number 22." She pointed to a house a few doors down.

"I'm Samir Karim and I do not live here," I said. "What can I do for you?"

"I think Snoutie is in your backyard," she said.

"Snottie?"

"*Snoutie.*"

"Your child?"

"My rabbit."

"I'll go have a look."

I hurried to the kitchen, my heart aflame with fear. I looked for Snoutie in the pans, in the fridge, and in the freezer. I opened the garbage can in search of organs. I was sorry that I couldn't look into my housemates' stomachs, but was relieved not to find Snoutie anywhere inside, where instead of being considered cute and fuzzy he would mostly be seen as tasty.

I finally found him, a spotted brown rabbit with droopy ears, at the back of the yard. I tried to catch him, but he hopped off quicker than I could grab him. I called for Nadhem and Ghazwaan, and they called for the others. Five illegals, three undocumented aliens, and one asylum seeker with a general pardon but without an ID card, all running around after a single rabbit. Snoutie got the fright of his life when he realized the embarrassment of the European Union was chasing after him.

The neighbors watched this unlikely chase scene from behind their upstairs windows and from over the fences.

"Hey!" one neighbor lady shouted, annoyed.

The five illegals, three undocumented aliens, one asylum seeker with a general pardon, and Snoutie the rabbit all stopped running. The woman reached over the fence and opened the gate.

"Snoutie, come," she coaxed. The rabbit hopped over to her. She picked him up, held him against her chest, and demonstratively shut the gate behind her.

Thanks to Snoutie, the whole neighborhood now knew how many asylum seekers were living in Asker Shaheen's wife's house. Fortunately, no one reported it.

Once I had gained Asker Shaheen's trust, I asked him if he knew a way I could get my hands on an IND card. Rather than asking why I didn't just call the IND, he simply said he needed a copy of the document with my general pardon and my second asylum interrogation.

A few weeks later, Asker told me that in my case, because I had the right residency papers, an IND card would cost €3,500.

"I can front you the money," he said, "and you can pay me back in monthly installments." I agreed.

About five weeks later, Asker Shaheen handed me an IND identity card.

"Forged?" I asked.

"Are you kidding?" he said. "It cost three thousand five hundred euros. Of course it's real. A hundred percent. Would have been much more if you didn't have residency status." He looked at me as I stared at the ID card. "Now you can go and do anything you want, but wait a year before you go to the IND with it."

"How come?"

"Just because." He smiled and patted my shoulder. "In Holland it's not a matter of beating the system, but of speeding up the procedure."

How simple my life could have been if I had met Asker Shaheen my first year in the Netherlands. Or better yet, my first day. Asker Shaheen taught me that no matter how watertight the system is, there are always men and women who know where it's leaking. Those leaks are worth thousands of euros. Oh, how wonderful corruption is when it liberates a person. For the first time, and for just €3,500, I no longer felt as though I was living in an IND dossier, but in the European Union. And please don't tell me I shouldn't have gone about it this way because it's fraudulent. You don't ask a person who has lost a foot why he uses a cane.

47

Asker Shaheen had five grown children. His eldest son and daughter had both left for Dubai as soon as they got their Dutch passports. The son on his own, the daughter with a cousin from Iraq she had married in order to bring him to the Netherlands. Asker Shaheen married off his second daughter to an Iraqi man he had met in the asylum seekers' center.

The third daughter, Ferdous, had a council house, like her mother. Asker sublet her place to two Egyptians who had to pretend that Ferdous lived there, and they in turn rented out mattresses to others. Ferdous lived with her parents, although she was desperate for a place of her own, either in Amsterdam or Haarlem. She had two complete lives: one as a traditional Iraqi daughter with headscarf, and one as a bare-headed Dutch girl. You could make two separate Ferdouses from her.

The fact that she had been born in Holland and was in fact a Dutch woman made it more difficult for Asker Shaheen to marry her off to someone of his own choosing. She was twenty-four and single (thus already six years too old for marriage, according to Asker). He often told me how happy he would be if she married a nice Iraqi man—by which he meant someone of Iraqi heritage who hadn't become a Dutchman.

"In Iraq, society is dangerous for a girl; in Holland, a girl is dangerous for herself," he once said.

He also told me he had a building company and that his second son, Ehaab, worked for him. This turned out to be an "Iraqi misunderstanding," because the business actually belonged to Ehaab, and his father worked for him. But in Iraq, the son is the father's property, so this includes the son's business.

Asker worked the Iraqi way, in which the system and the government are enemies. Ehaab worked in the Dutch way, meaning the individual is the system and the government. This also meant being as honest as possible. These two methods often clashed. As Abdel Nasser, the ex-president of Egypt, once said, "Arabs agree to never agree." So it was between father and son.

"You must be honest with the smart customer," said Asker, "and devour the stupid one."

Ehaab felt that you should simply be honest with clients, without first sussing out how smart or stupid they were. Just draw up an estimate and let the client decide what was right for them. Asker earned thousands of euros the Iraqi way, and Ehaab earned hundreds of euros the Dutch way. But those thousands of euros seemed to make Asker poorer, while the hundreds of euros made Ehaab richer. The father earned money but lost the customers' trust, the son earned both money *and* trust.

Just as the dog listens to whoever feeds it, I listened to Asker, because he was the one paying me when I went to work for their company. I did exactly what he asked me to, and did not feel guilty if it was different from what Ehaab wanted. Though I would have preferred to work for Ehaab, because he was more straightforward. Let's put it this way: my wallet wanted to work for the father, and my heart for the son.

We were paid eight euros an hour to work for their construction company. But then, sometimes Asker lent us money, even as much as a thousand euros, and would send it to Iraq at his own cost.

He would also organize railway discount cards and bank accounts for undocumented or illegal aliens who worked for him, and send them to an Iraqi dentist if they had toothache or to an Iraqi doctor if they had a sore throat. Asker himself was a system.

After a while Asker offered to give me a raise, to ten euros an hour, if I didn't tell the others. When he found out I was a civil engineer and knew a lot about buildings and houses, he upped my wages to thirteen euros an hour, and left me to work alone with Nadhem and Ghazwaan. The more he trusted me, the more he let me do. I wished I could make him trust me less, because I really didn't want all that responsibility. But it was good to be able to send money to Iraq through him, even when I didn't have any. So I worked in order to pay him back.

Ehaab was married to a Dutch woman, Rebecca Noordhoek. They had three children: sons Ayid and Seef, seven and ten, and daughter Senna, three. Her father was a real-estate agent and had helped Ehaab start his construction company, which mostly bought up old dilapidated houses and refurbished them. Then, with the help of Rebecca's father, they could resell them for a profit.

They lived in a big place on the edge of town. It used to be a farmhouse, with two large sheds and a garage. Everything in their house was in perfect order, very Dutch.

Ehaab also bought secondhand building items online, and had his employees (including me) clean and paint them to look like new. He kept these things in the sheds to be installed in the old houses he fixed up. Asker drove us around in the company van to pick things up, but mostly I worked in the sheds. In this way I got a peek into the goings-on in Ehaab and Rebecca's house.

48

Ehaab was Dutch and Rebecca wanted to stay Dutch, but Asker Shaheen and his wife were anxious that their grandchildren be raised as Iraqis. And because they lived close by, and because Asker worked in Ehaab's business (or vice versa, if you asked Asker), they were often at Ehaab and Rebecca's home.

It was one of Asker's pet subjects when we were on our way to pick up secondhand items somewhere.

"The Hollanders have no respect for women. Just look into the history of any Dutch family and you won't find one single Dutchman who murdered his daughter's or sister's rapist. Their society is like their cheese spread: squishy and insipid."

"I think Dutch women are far better off than the women in Iraq."

"Really?" He looked at me in amazement.

"So many women in Iraq are forced to marry a man they don't want to. Isn't that lifelong rape?"

"What are you talking about? Are we the children of rape? You must be crazy! Of every hundred Iraqi women, there might be one who is made to marry against her will. But at least she had children. Here, plenty of Dutch women have a husband they don't want, but stay with for the mortgage. And how many of them are childless, because the husband has abandoned her?"

"The Dutch woman makes her own choices. Right? Not in Iraq."

"Women here don't make their own choices, either. Their psychological problems make the choices. Hang-ups they learn from their parents. So it's her parents who choose. Just like with us. But we make better choices. We at least make the woman a mother and a grandmother. For us, the woman has value. If a man insults her, we kill him." Asker was getting worked up over my opinion, and gave me a hard look. "Listen here, Samir. You have to watch out! Leave everything behind, but not your culture or your values."

A while later he said, "Just look at Ehaab. Even after years of living with a Dutch woman, he still hasn't convinced her to wear a headscarf."

"But Ehaab isn't religious. Why should his wife have to wear a headscarf?"

"Because it's tradition. His sister wears a headscarf, his mother wears a headscarf, all the women in his family wear a headscarf. For fifteen hundred years, every woman in his family has worn a headscarf. And now Sir Ehaab comes along and says, no headscarf. If his wife doesn't wear one, his daughter certainly won't."

"But you don't wear traditional Iraqi clothes, do you? Come on. Dutch women are mostly honest and pleasant. And as far as I can see, Rebecca is a good mother and Ehaab is happy with her."

"Fair enough," he said. After a long silence he concluded with, "Never marry a Dutch woman."

Sometimes Rebecca unwittingly brought thunder and lightning down on Asker Shaheen's head.

Ghazwaan, Nadhem, and I once had to sand and paint a set of secondhand window frames. The sun was out in full force that day, after weeks of overcast skies. We had unloaded the window frames from the van and were busy sanding them outside the shed when Rebecca appeared from the house wearing sunglasses. She brought out a reclining plastic lawn chair and lay down on it. Then she rolled up her pant legs to above her knees and hitched up her shirt to just under her breasts, so her skin could finally, after all those cloudy weeks, soak up some sun. We witnessed this disaster in the making and kept pretending to sand the wood, knowing full well that Rebecca's bare skin would rescue us from this hard work on such a hot day.

Asker came out of the shed and got the fright of his life. This Dutch woman was his daughter-in-law, the mother of his grandchildren, so according to Iraqi tradition she was his honor. And there it was, that honor, peeled half naked just to catch some sun, without the slightest concern whether anyone could see her.

"Boys," Asker said to us, "into the van. Hurry up."

We feigned ignorance. Within one minute we were all in the van. He leapt into the driver's seat, tore out of the driveway, and drove the whole way back to our house without saying a word.

From that day onward, we did not work at Ehaab and Rebecca's house when the sun was out.

49

Asker would often launch into his usual tirade about Dutch women to try to convince me I was better off marrying an Iraqi one, in particular his daughter Ferdous. He must have mentioned this to his son, because Ehaab started asking me about my life in the asylum seekers' center. My stories seemed to jog his memory, for he had come to the Netherlands with his parents when he was a child. They had lived in an ASC, too, and he had been allowed to go to school. At school, the teachers treated him a lot differently than the ASC staff treated his family.

For instance, at school he was asked, for the first time in his life, things like "But what do *you* think? Do you like this? Or that? How do you feel about it yourself? What do you want?" Ehaab made friends with a boy named Daniel. His mother was a stewardess. Daniel talked about his mother being in the sky, Ehaab about his mother in the ASC.

"Right now my mother is in the sky between Amsterdam and Rio de Janeiro."

"Right now my mother is in room 31–3."

Ehaab started to become ashamed of his mother, who was always either in that one room or in the kitchen on the third floor, while Daniel's mother was forever traveling from one sky to another. The shame became acute when he went to Daniel's house to play and realized that his schoolmate lived in a real house and not in a building like his. A building where people were stacked up in rooms and fought all the time or paced the hallways yelling or crying. Then Daniel invited Ehaab to sleep over. Daniel's parents and older brothers treated Ehaab like one of them. He saw how much space a child had in that house and in life. He saw that this family did not scream at each other, but explained things calmly. In Daniel's house, Ehaad became a Dutch child.

"That boy is ashamed of us," Zakiya had said to Asker. "We mustn't let him spend nights with the Hollanders."

"Let him go," Asker had replied. "Better there than in the Dutch sewers." By this he meant the ASC.

If we worked at Ehaab's place when he wasn't around, Rebecca seemed relieved, and came out to chat with us. This is how I found out that at first she was attracted to Ehaab precisely because he was so Dutch, but that since they'd had children it had become a problem.

"Why not before you had children?" I asked.

"He had his work, I had mine. We never saw his family. Well, Ferdous came around now and then. She was nice. Spontaneous. And once we visited his mother in the hospital after an operation. But they never did birthdays, and I avoided the religious holidays because I had heard that the women all wore headscarves and sat separately from the men. But after we had Ayid, his parents were suddenly there. I didn't mind so much—they're sweet and always make time for the children. More than my own parents do. But Ehaab has a problem with it. Or, should I say: *problems*."

"How strange," I said. "You'd think it would be the Dutch partner who had problems with the Iraqi family."

"Not me. I like them. My parents and my sister don't deal with them so well, though. It's not really a problem, more an incompatibility."

"As in ...?"

"My parents don't get involved with how we raise the children, as long as I have a good relationship with Ehaab and the kids. But Ehaab's parents meddle in everything. They want the children to be Iraqis. Ehaab doesn't even want them to learn Arabic, to make sure they don't get brainwashed by the jihadists. Even though it's such a beautiful language. And ..." She sighed. "I appreciate that they're keen to babysit, but they spoil the children rotten. All day they do whatever they want, eat candy and cookies, watch whatever they like on TV, no matter how unsuitable it is. Once they're back home, they're hyperactive and completely unmanageable."

Ehaab's parents had more trouble with Dutch culture than Rebecca's parents did with Iraqi. Dutch culture is an ocean: on a summer's day you can lie on its beach in a bikini, swim in its water, sail on its waves, you can go places on it, lose yourself, disappear into it; whereas Iraqi culture is a cage that keeps closing in on your soul until there is no room to move. And where there is certainly no place for a bikini.

Ferdous maneuvered effortlessly between the ocean and the cage. All she had to do was be occasionally dishonest, but Rebecca, who had learned to always be herself, felt powerless in that cramped Iraqi cage, where it was hard to stay and hard to leave. I think that if she and Ehaab had not had children, she would have long ago opted for freedom.

Oh, the bikini needs an ocean to be a bikini, and cannot work full-time as underwear.

50

I did not feel at home in Asker Shaheen's house, even though I had been living there for some time. It was starting to feel like I was living with his wife Zakiya. I got a fright when she wasn't on the sofa knitting, even though her lamp was on. Or if I heard oil crackling in a pan, I thought she was the one cooking. On top of it, you never were quite sure what you rented there. A room? Not really. A bed? No—I often came home to find someone else lying on my mattress. Renters, subletters, and mysterious itinerants who came and went.

So I spent as little time there as possible. When I wasn't working, I was in the public library. They had magazines and newspapers, and tea and coffee. It's too bad there wasn't a place there to cook or sleep, otherwise I'd have done just that. How wonderful it would be to live among all those written words. Sleeping amid thousands of writers, from journalists to dictators, would have been easier than among all those strangers in Zakiya's house. Men of ink can be closed at will.

One thing I do have trouble with in Dutch libraries is the quiet. The distance between a person and a book is small, but the distance between people is huge. In Iraq, the mosques are full and the libraries are abandoned, while in the Netherlands, the churches are empty and the libraries full. Nowadays, when I travel I visit a country's libraries and places of worship, to see which its people have chosen. The way of many books, or the way of just one.

When the library was closed, I would go to the Surinamese takeout restaurant Rola. It was run by a couple, and sometimes their children. Their food stayed warm for half an hour, and their hearts for an eternity. Sometimes they invited me to eat my takeout meal in their house behind the shop, and sometimes they refused to take my money—then their takeout was their hospitality.

It was there I met a young guy named Paresh. Our stomachs were the reason we met. They brought us at around the same time, at least once a week, to Roti Shop Rola. After about our tenth roti chicken, Paresh and I exchanged telephone numbers. But we did not need them for some time, because the roti continued to bring us together. One day, though, Paresh phoned me to ask if I could fill in for him at the moving company where he worked, because his mother was in the hospital.

So for a day, I worked as a mover for Erwin van Houten. I asked Erwin to pay my hours directly to Paresh. He thought that was okay and Paresh thought it was more than okay.

Paresh could laugh about anything. He had the knack for listening to the most dire problems, and then laughing like mad. And it didn't matter to him whether the other person laughed along. He had the deepest respect for everyone, which he showed by making small jokes, and later, bigger ones. Paresh's laugh was civilized, never offensive. It was great to have a friend who was neither Iraqi nor Dutch, and therefore had nothing to do with the world of asylum seekers, a world in which I felt trapped.

Asker Shaheen and his family had become like a benign spider, who builds her nest around you with the intention of protecting you—but with every strand, you lose a bit of yourself and have to pretend to feel safer. I wanted to free myself from Asker Shaheen, because the more he trusted me, the more he owned me.

You see, if you work for a Dutchman, you give him work and he gives you money. If you work for an Iraqi, then you become sucked into his life. As I said, Asker had got it into his head that I should marry his daughter. When Ferdous got wind of this, she contacted me behind her parents' backs. She phoned me once and said she wanted us to meet.

So we made a date the way Iraqis do: we would happen to be taking the same train somewhere, and happen to sit in the same compartment, and happen not to know each other.

51

Ferdous was wearing tight jeans, a tight blouse, and a tight jacket. Tight on tight over tight. On her head was a modest black satin headscarf.

"You're also going to Amsterdam?" she said with a smile.

"Let's not play games with each other," I said. "I'm sitting here because you wanted to see me."

"Fair enough. So listen, my father wants us to get married. He thinks he can choose someone for me." She looked at me and said, "But you don't want to, right? I should warn you that I'm totally crazy. And I don't want to get married." She lowered the tray table in front of her and pulled a makeup bag from her purse. She started polishing her nails. After every finger, she blew on it.

"Why do you polish your nails on the train, and not at home?"

"At home? Are you kidding?! My mother would be like, who are you doing that for?" she said, imitating her mother.

The conductor came by to check our tickets.

"What if you come home later with painted nails?"

She took another bottle out of the bag. "Nail polish remover."

Twenty minutes later, Ferdous removed her headscarf and shook her hair loose. At once she had another face. The conductor came back up the aisle and stopped.

"Tickets, please."

She showed him the ticket, he looked at it and smiled.

Then she got out a small mirror and began applying eye shadow.

"So, what have you decided?" she asked.

"I have no desire to marry you."

"Why not? Just out of curiosity."

"Because if you're two people in this train and can confuse even the Dutch conductor, how many women are you in your marriage? Twenty?"

Ferdous burst out laughing. "Oh, good! I don't want to be the one who refuses to get married. You're the one who has to refuse. That way I won't have any trouble with my parents."

"And what am I supposed to tell your father when he asks me to marry you?

"Tell him you have a girlfriend."

"But I don't have a girlfriend."

"That doesn't matter," she said, irritated. "It's just a white lie. At least you won't have any trouble from me for the next forty-five years."

"Good point. But I can't do without the work your father provides me. I need money and a roof over my head. So I'm not going to be the one to refuse."

End of conversation.

Ferdous knew what she did not want, but not what she did want. Whenever her parents were around, she looked lethargic. When they weren't, she was energetic. She spoke the Iraqi dialect in a way that made you think she did it wrong on purpose, and used as many Dutch words as possible.

Once we arrived in Amsterdam, she confided in me that she had a date with her boyfriend at three o'clock. She went off to her date, and I took the next train home.

After our "date," I became the problem between Ferdous and her father. He dropped hints that she fancied me and that she would be glad to marry me, and I dropped hints that I also really liked her, but was not ready to settle down. He started inviting me to have tea and meals at their home.

"Marry an Iraqi, it's better," he said. "If you marry a Dutch woman, your life will become a business and your wife will be not only your colleague but your boss and the job itself."

"If marrying a Dutch woman makes life a business, then

marrying an Iraqi woman makes life a war," I replied. "Maybe not with her, but certainly with her family."

He looked at me and smiled. "You're right about that."

Then he invited me to go to his grandson Seef's birthday party. Because, he said, there would be Iraqi food. And he wanted me to meet Ferdous. He did not know I had already met her, both with and without a headscarf.

52

It was three o'clock when Asker Shaheen, Zakiya, Ferdous, and I arrived at Rebecca and Ehaab's place for Seef's birthday dinner, which was only due to start at six. It was going to be a long afternoon. No one was home: Ehaab and Rebecca had promised to take the children to McDonald's. We sat at the picnic table under the walnut tree in the yard. Zakiya went into the house and came back out complaining. She said it stank inside, and couldn't understand how anyone could live in such a pigsty. She opened the windows and got Ferdous to help her tidy up and clean the house.

"They're doing this to make a point of how much cleaner Iraqis are," Asker Shaheen said. "If Ehaab's wife had been Iraqi, none of this would be going on. Boy oh boy."

I got a kick out of hearing Asker Shaheen say "boy oh boy." He even used it in Arabic. It was one of his favorite little expressions.

The family got home at five o'clock. I could tell that Rebecca was annoyed by the open windows and doors, but she pretended not to notice.

"Why does that Hollander take her children to McDonald's when she knows we always cook for birthdays?" Zakiya grumbled in Iraqi.

"Sew your lips shut," Asker reprimanded. "The children will be hungry again soon enough."

She stopped her muttering when she saw Asker was annoyed. What am I doing here, I thought, but it was too late to think up an excuse to leave.

At six o'clock the three children ran to a great big Volvo that had pulled up in front of the shed. Grandma and Grandpa Noordhoek got out with Diane, Rebecca's twenty-eight-year-old sister. Grandpa was wearing a suit without a necktie, and glossy, pointed-toed dress shoes, and Grandma and Diane were both in skirt suits, Dianne with stiletto heels. They each carried a gift.

"Have you ever seen Hollanders dress like that?" Zakiya hissed. "They're doing it to make us feel like asylum seekers. And look how the children rush over to them! They don't run up like that to greet us. It's the fault of that Dutch son of yours. He hasn't raised them to be Iraqis."

"That's how they greet us, too, *yuma*," Ferdous said to her mother. "So stop complaining."

Zakiya only bellyached even more.

"They run, they don't run, they do this, they do that ..." Asker said. "Do we have to time how fast they run to greet you? Just shut up already." His words were angry in the quiet Iraqi manner. If a Dutch person were to see him talking, they would think he was saying, "What fine weather we're having! No chance of rain today." Zakiya stopped when she determined her husband was now pumped up with her anger, which appeared to satisfy her.

The Noordhoeks greeted us, introduced themselves to me, and sat down at one end of the long table across from the Shaheens. I sat on the Noordhoek side, because for me, not being part of the family, it would be improper to sit with the Shaheen women. The Shaheen family started eating and talking all at once, to break the silence. It was clear that the Shaheens were more fun, and the Noordhoeks more proper. The Shaheens talked a lot and said nothing; the Noordhoeks talked little and said a lot.

Diane, like lots of Dutch people, understood bad English better than good Dutch. There's nothing more irritating for a foreigner than to have Dutch people constantly saying "What?" after every sentence. It feels like they don't *want* to understand. Diane talked only with Ehaab and Ferdous, and no matter how hard I tried to strike up a conversation with her or her parents, their faces refused me a visa.

Diane took tiny little bites of the food Zakiya had prepared.

"Is it greasy?" I asked her.

"Sorry, what?"

"The food. Is it greasy?"

"What?"

"He asked if the food is greasy," Rebecca said.

"No, it's delicious," she said.

"She pretends not to understand your Dutch," Zakiya said to me in Iraqi. "Not because she doesn't understand, but because she doesn't want to answer you."

I saw Diane shoot us an inquisitive glance, because it was clear we were talking about her.

"Grandma says you understand what Samir says, but that you pretend not to on purpose, because you don't want to answer him," blurted little Seef, who to everyone's amazement had picked up more Arabic than they had realized.

Asker burst out laughing. Grains of rice spurted from his mouth. Grandma and Grandpa Noordhoek observed the scene in silence. Diane's face went from arrogant to timid, until the point that she didn't look my way at all.

The three children seemed to do their best to fit in with Rebecca's family. If Zakiya called them, they ignored her; if she wanted to shower them with kisses to prove she loved them more than the other grandparents, they shied away from her. They were standoffish to the one set of grandparents, and extra well behaved for the other set.

As I observed them, it became evident that Grandma Shaheen stood for what was possible, and Grandma Noordhoek for what was forbidden. Grandma Noordhoek's stern look made them think twice before digging in to dessert before it was time, or moving to eat with their hands like their Iraqi grandparents. While Grandma Shaheen pumped sweets into the children to make them leap around like monkeys, Grandma Noordhoek's quietly powerful glance was stronger than a kilo of sugar.

After dinner it was time for the presents. Every Noordhoek had a gift for Seef, and together they had brought a book for the younger siblings. Grandpa Noordhoek's present was a LEGO set, Diane's a wristwatch, and Grandma Noordhoek gave him a football jersey. Here, too, Grandma Noordhoek was strict with the children, but so imperceptibly that the youngsters did not even notice.

"Look at all that paper," she said. On the surface it sounded lighthearted, but her look said it all: each child promptly tidied up their wrapping paper.

Then it was the Shaheen family's turn to give their presents.

Asker's present to the birthday boy was a half-meter-long laser sword. "So as not to fall into danger, you have to be a danger yourself," he said in Dutch. "With this sword you'll stab all your enemies one by one. There's no escaping your vengeance!"

Grandpa Noordhoek swallowed, Grandma Noordhoek dabbed her forehead with a hankie, and Diane's face went as pale as old turmeric.

Asker then gave Ayid a realistic-looking toy gun. Little Senna got nothing. She looked expectantly at her grandfather, but he seemed to have forgotten her. He took his wallet out of his back pocket and handed her fifty euros.

"Sorry, Senna, sweetie, I didn't know what to get you. You choose something yourself."

Senna took the money, but didn't look all that happy with it.

Grandma Shaheen's gift for Seef was a radio-controlled army tank. "With this tank you'll run over your enemies' corpses, after you've killed them with Grandpa's sword. You'll make mincemeat of them, and crush their bones into flour!" she said in her asylum-seeker Dutch.

Ayid also got a kind of pistol from her, "to help your brother wipe out your enemies." She gave Senna a dress.

Ferdous gave Seef a computer game. "Don't listen to Grandma and Grandpa Shaheen," she said. "They're crazy. You don't have enemies. And if you do have them, you just call the police."

Shortly after that birthday party, I knew my days with Asker were numbered, because I got the bad news that Zakiya liked me. Staying would mean getting sucked into the family, and having to marry Ferdous.

Also, there was no privacy in the mini-ASC. Arabs—and I am one, too—have no concept of privacy, because they equate it with loneliness. The Dutch, on the other hand, have a great respect for privacy. I really needed my own space. Was I becoming a Hollander?

Landlords want reliable tenants. So they are generally not that keen to rent to an asylum seeker. But luck was on my side, thanks to my friend Paresh. He knew of a studio apartment in a complex that I could sublet for cheap from Malti, a young woman who was going to Suriname for an internship. I told Asker of my decision, and as soon as I could, I moved into Malti's flat.

53

I now had a third-floor studio to myself. A window where I could have the curtains open and look out at the canal with a cup of tea. A key of my own. A shower of my own. A toilet of my own.

And aside from a forty-five-year-old man, adopted from Bangladesh as a child, the entire building was Dutch. Living among Dutch people was wonderful. I paid for the studio, but I had the entire building, including cats, dogs, and hamsters (but not mice, rats, or cockroaches, because there were none).

Everything in this building was perfect. *Too* perfect. This building filled with Dutch people seemed to clean itself, because I never saw anyone doing the work. And yet it was always clean and quiet. I did not find dirty diapers in the stairwell, not a single letter scrawled on the walls with pencil or marker or spray paint, not even a wayward housefly. Moreover, doors never suddenly flew open, and you never heard a war between brothers or between a cat and a dog or between enemies from the other side of a wall. No smell of spices from open windows, no stench of a backed-up drain or a forgotten frying pan or balcony barbecue. This struck me as strange, because in the student house, practically everything and everyone was incredibly filthy.

When I mentioned this to Paresh, he told me that there had been a nasty smell in the building once. When they went looking for its source, they saw worms crawling out from under the door. There was no answer, the police came, and they discovered it was the resident himself who had become that smell and the worms. He had been dead for days, without anyone having missed him. That building was permeated with something no cat could chase and gobble up, something not even the strongest Wi-Fi in the world could suppress. It was more powerful than war: Tedium. And that dead, dreary tedium hung in the air, day and night.

At least three dogs and five cats lived in that apartment building, but I never heard them—except for Bikkie, who belonged to the young guy in the ground-floor apartment. Bikkie barked whenever he saw me, or even smelled me. I only saw the cats behind windows, sleeping or yawning. I hardly ever saw the rest of the residents either, and whenever we did happen to meet, I would occasionally get a quick nod or a friendly hello, but just as often, people pretended not to have seen me.

Willem Jan Bouwman, a man of around sixty, was an exception, but a strange one. I knew his name from his mailbox. On my very first day, when I went out for groceries, he stopped me in front of the building.

"You're the new guy upstairs, aren't you?" he said with a smile.

"Yes, my name's Samir. And you?"

"Where are you from? You don't sound like someone who was born here."

"Iraq."

"Oh, Iraq, dangerous place. I understand," he said.

What exactly he understood, I did not know.

"So, do you have a job? Or are you studying Dutch?"

"I'm looking for work," I said. "And you, what do you do?"

"Good stuff, good stuff."

I didn't know what was "good." He was wearing a cap that covered half his forehead. His dog did not bark.

"You've lucked out, an asylum seeker getting a flat in our building this fast," he said.

"I'm subletting the studio temporarily."

"From your welfare?"

"I don't get welfare."

"You don't get welfare? So how do you pay the rent, with no welfare and no job?"

"I manage. And you, are you a renter or an owner?"

"I get it," he said. "Holland is expensive."

Again, I did not know what there was to "get."

"Nice to meet you. Max, come!" And off he went.

That evening I saw Willem Jan at the foot of the stairwell, talking to one of the neighbors. I wanted to greet him, because now we were on greeting terms, but he seemed to have disappeared under his cap. I approached, and he disappeared even further. His movement was barely perceptible, but he turned, like a sunflower that turns to face the sun, until his back was to me. Max, recognizing me, wagged his tail, at which Willem Jan Bouwman gave the leash a hard tug. This extinguished the dog's enthusiasm.

I walked on. He was probably having a serious conversation and didn't want to be interrupted, but the same thing happened when I passed him on my way back. I came to the conclusion that he was prepared to chat with me outside the building, but indoors, he pretended not to know me. If I kept trying to make contact, poor Max would pay for it with a sore neck.

Outside, he often suddenly appeared with his dog.

"Hey—what's your name, again?"

"Samir. And yours?"

"Found work yet?"

"No, I'm still looking. What kind of work do you do?"

"Good thing they give you welfare here in the Netherlands. And a roof above your head. I'll bet there's no welfare in Iraq, is there?"

"No, not in Iraq."

"See? Lucky for you you're in Holland. There's no war here, at least. But the Netherlands is an expensive place. More expensive than Iraq, right?"

"Yes, absolutely."

For me, being ignored as an adult foreigner in the Netherlands was really the worst. In my culture you only ignore someone if you've done him wrong and he's still your friend and you don't want a conflict. At first, I didn't understand that ignoring people is part of daily life in the Netherlands. But by the time I figured out how it worked, it had already broken a good thirty-five percent of my soul. Someone you chat with, with whom you're on a first-name basis, who lives next door or whom you sat next to in the bus, that same person can, a few hours or days or weeks later, suddenly pretend not to know you, and look the other way even though you know for sure they've seen you. For me, this is the gravest of insults, and I could spend years wondering what I did to deserve it. Now I know it's not about me.

The building would start quietly coming alive at 6:30 a.m. A door, a shower, a flushing toilet. Aside from that, all you heard was silence. Except for in the weekend between eight in the morning and six thirty in the evening, those first weeks felt like the building was mine alone. Sometimes I dared go down to the mailboxes in my pajamas to pick up Malti's post. I gave it to Kimatra, Malti's mother and my landlady, when she came by to pick up the rent.

One day, when I went down for Malti's mail, I stood reading all the nameplates on the mailboxes, as a sort of introduction to the neighbors I did not get the chance to meet in person.

When I turned around I saw a man eyeing me suspiciously. A dog next to him. The man put the collar around the dog's neck, and the dog began to bark and pull at the leash. The man kept looking at me. Was it impolite to read the names on the mailboxes?

I went over to him and stuck out my hand. First he looked at my hand as if I had just picked up a turd. He cautiously returned the gesture, as though he had to first convince his hand to introduce himself.

"Day ... Fah ...," he said. His voice was like gargling, and it was mixed with the shrill yapping of his dog.

"Pardon?" I said.

"Day ... Fah ..."

"Dayfah?"

"Dave Faber."

I turned to the mailboxes and saw his name.

"Oh, Dave Faber," I said, smiling, enthusiastic at having discovered his name, but he just looked at me, irritated, and the dog kept barking.

Dave Faber had a crewcut and stubbly (but nearly invisible, because of the blond color) beard. His skin had the color of a plastic heron. Had he ever eaten any healthy food? There was aggression in his eyes that surely had to escape now and then, otherwise it would devour him from the inside.

When I later described him to a friend, she asked if he was a druggie, or a neo-Nazi. I had no idea. It's often hard to size people in a new country.

54

Dave's dog Bikkie always seemed to want to bite me, and for no reason. The only thing I ever heard Dave Faber say when he saw me was, "Bikkie, inside." That became Dave's greeting. Bikkie barked at me from behind their front door even when I entered the building. I did my best to avoid Dave and Bikkie, but did not always succeed.

So, even if the entrance and the stairs were not mine but Bikkie's, the studio apartment I sublet from Malti was my kingdom—until the war, the ASC, and Leda moved in with me. The war and the ASC with their interminable history, and Leda in brief flashes. She tended to wait patiently on the fringes of my thoughts, and when I was alone and unawares she would burst in. I hung her picture near the window and gazed at it. The leash wrapped around her left hand. Diesel alongside her, his tongue hanging out of his mouth. Leda, smiling at the camera. The ground covered in autumn leaves. Leda could fill the entire studio apartment.

Paresh would drop by occasionally, but never stuck around for more than half an hour. He often took me to eat at his mother's. Maybe he was bored eating alone. I had no idea where Paresh lived, so I couldn't drop in on him.

He came by whenever it suited him. If I called him up, he did not answer and did not call back. For a while I thought he didn't want any more contact, but that wasn't so, because in his own time he showed up again, or called to say to meet him at his mother's house. I often went around in the hope of finding him there, usually without success. But I did get warm Surinamese food out of it. There was not a millimeter between Pallavi's heart and her pans. She gave love not with words, but by the spoonful. I asked Paresh why he ate at Rola when his mother cooked even better. He said his need for food was greater than his need to see his mother. She always went on about wanting to live in Suriname, but said she couldn't convince Paresh to go. Paresh, on the other hand, told me he would be happy to go to Suriname, but his mother wouldn't budge. They each used the other as an excuse to stay in the Netherlands.

One gray winter day, terrorists in Iraq blew themselves up, killing 476 people. My mood was heavy, and I was sick of the chronic boredom surrounding me. So I went to pay a visit to Pallavi. I knocked and, to my amazement, it wasn't Paresh's mother who opened the door, but a young woman. Before I could say anything, she introduced herself.

"Cindy Nijman."

When the door opens on a chilly, gray, dreary day and you see one of the most beautiful creatures you've ever laid eyes on, and she smiles and says her name is Cindy, then that name becomes magic. In just one second, the terror vanished, not just from my own body but from the entire world.

Cindy not only knew she was pretty, but she also knew what beauty meant.

She wore contact lenses. I didn't know this at first, but when I started visiting her at home, I noticed she sometimes wore glasses. In fact, this made her even more attractive, as though her face wore lingerie of glass. She had green eyes, like grass after rain. Her long, straight hair was bathed in a red glow.

Cindy invited me in, and I learned how her friendship with Pallavi had been born. Cindy and Paresh had known each other since high school. Whenever Cindy went through difficult times, she went to Pallavi and not her own mother, because Pallavi always had time for her, while her own mother worked and had to "make time." And making time sometimes took too long, and by then the problem was already resolved.

I got the impression that she and Pallavi had been discussing something personal when I showed up, and I said so.

"Sit down," Pallavi commanded. "It was unimportant. Cindy was telling me about Bruno."

"Bruno is my former ex," Cindy explained.

"And what's your current one's name?" Pallavi asked.

"He's also an ex."

"Okay, but what's his name?"

"Walter."

"She was telling me about Walter," Pallavi said. "She's mad, you know. She has a fit at the sight of a mouse, but she smiles at a wolf." Then she looked at me and said, "You look hungry. Have you eaten?"

"I've eaten."

"When?"

"A few days ago."

She hoisted herself out of the chair, pushing up on her knees, to make me something to eat. Alone with Cindy in the living room, I was so overcome by her beauty that I dared not look at her. She took out her cell phone and started tapping and reading. Only then did I dare look at her.

"Paresh told me about you," I said.

She looked up, smiled, and returned to her phone. I got the impression that she wasn't interested in what Paresh might have said. She's not only afraid of a mouse and glad to see a wolf, I thought, but she dives into her cell phone when she sees an asylum seeker.

Pallavi came out with food, and when I had finished and brought the plate back to the kitchen to wash, I said goodbye and left. That evening, Pallavi's warm food and Cindy's cool beauty had rescued me from the jihad.

55

Integrating into a new culture is easy, if it doesn't bark at you. Whenever I went out or came home, all I could think of was: How on earth am I going to integrate with Bikkie? When will he be satisfied? What did I need to do to keep him quiet? He smelled me even before I opened the front door, and then the barking started. If I happened to bump into Dave Faber on his way in or out, he would look at me apologetically. Then he would take the yapping dog's head in his hands, caress it, and say things like, "Aw, Bikkie, are you scared?" or "Oh, Bikkie, why are you barking at this nice man?" I almost started to believe he meant it, and figured the way to appease Bikkie was to become friends with Dave.

"Good afternoon," I shouted.

"Afternoon," Dave said, keeping it short. He clipped on Bikkie's leash.

"Would you like to come up for tea sometime?" I asked.

Dave pretended not to hear, and kept petting and reassuring the dog.

"You're always welcome to stop by for tea," I said. "Number 31."

"Thanks," he said.

I went off hoping he and the dog would drop in sometime. I even bought dog biscuits at the supermarket and a bone at the pet store, just in case.

A few days later, the doorbell rang. Could it be Bikkie? I said, "Who's there?" through the intercom.

"Talib." The jokester from the ASC.

"That's a pity," I said.

"Why a pity? Man, man, have you forgotten your old comrades?"

"I haven't forgotten them, but I was expecting a dog. Instead, it's an asylum seeker."

I went downstairs and we embraced. Talib looked at his watch.

"I have to be getting to work. No time to tell you everything right now. Later, maybe."

A man was standing next to Talib.

"This is Youssef," he said. "A good guy. His brother was badly injured in an attack in Baghdad, and is in the hospital. Youssef wants to go to him to say goodbye. He needs to get his hands on an IND card, so that he can ask for travel documents."

His phone rang, and he went off.

I wondered how Talib knew I had bought an IND card, but I didn't press the subject and called Asker. But before I could fix them up, Youssef called to say his brother had died, and the IND card was no longer necessary. From that moment on, however, Youssef started visiting me.

He became my friend in the Arabic manner: first he visited me to thank me for the trouble I had gone to for him. The second time he visited me it was because he had already been there once before. And the third time he visited because we were acquaintances, since we had already seen each other twice before. Starting a friendship with Youssef was easy; it was ending it that was hard.

I did want to have contact with people, but Youssef ... He had this horrible way of ringing the bell. He did not ring to see if I was home or not. I *had* to be home, and *had* to open the door. At first I just ignored it. The intercom button in my apartment to buzz open the downstairs door didn't work, which in this case was handy, but he would just keep ringing and ringing and knocking, until one of the neighbors went out to see what the commotion was. Then he would ask that person if I was home, and let himself in. I could not get rid of him.

I once mentioned to Paresh that I was lonely sometimes.

"Call Cindy," he said. "She's a really sociable person."

I hesitated, because I had only seen her once, very briefly, but she surprised me by phoning me herself and asking if I had time for a drink. What a question. As if I would say no, even if I had something else to do!

"I have time," I said.

"Okay, when?"

"Now."

"Tomorrow too?"

"Yes, tomorrow too."

"You sure are flexible," she said. "I'll come around tomorrow at three to drink tea with you."

I had the studio all to myself and a date at three o'clock with the prettiest girl I knew. I bought enough tea for an entire rugby team.

Cindy arrived at 3 p.m. sharp. She looked as if she had walked out of a fashion magazine. Everything about her was just so: the colors of her clothes, her shoes, her socks, her necklace, her makeup, her hairdo.

"Paresh said you drink white wine," I said. "I have wine, would you like some?"

"It's a little too early for wine, but thanks anyway. Tea is fine." When I went to make tea for her, at exactly that second, the air resonated with the drawn-out sound of the doorbell.

56

I ignored the doorbell, but soon enough there was a pounding at the door, as though a polar bear from the Arctic had rolled and slammed against it.

"What's that?" Cindy asked.

Now it was like an elephant from the savannah was rolling against the polar bear, while an excited chimpanzee had also discovered the door and rattled it with all his might. A safari at my doorstep.

"What's that?" Cindy asked again.

"A rhinoceros with a mustache," I said.

I had no choice but to open the door, and there stood Youssef, at the worst possible moment.

"Why didn't you open, man? I've probably broken my hand knocking. Where have you been?" He walked in and when he saw Cindy sitting on the sofa, he said in Arabic, without taking his eyes off her for one second, "Why didn't you tell me you got a Dutch passport?"

"I don't have one."

"It's sitting right there. Not the usual dark red kind, but a blonde one. Ah, Samir, this passport will even get you into heaven."

Youssef went over to Cindy and she introduced herself.

"Cindy Nijman."

Youssef took her hand in his big hands and just stared at her. I was afraid Cindy would think I had mistakenly double-booked, and didn't know how to make it clear this was not the case. Cindy did not seem at all disconcerted. She sat back down, crossed her legs, and took a sip of tea.

"How do you guys know each other?" she asked.

"Are you asking me, or him?" said Youssef.

"Both of you."

"Should I answer her, or you?" Youssef asked me in Arabic.

"You go ahead."

"But she's your visitor. Can't you?"

I explained, without going into details, that a mutual friend had introduced us.

"Do you have a husband?" Youssef asked.

"No."

"Me neither," Youssef said.

"You don't have a husband either?" Cindy laughed.

Youssef gave her an angry look. She had offended him. She realized this, and her face softened. "I meant, you aren't in a relationship either."

"No, no relationship," he snapped. I was stuck in the middle and sensed that this date was going in another direction than I had planned.

There was no way Cindy could not regret having visited me. Her face had changed from "cozy-with-hot-tea" to "nervous-with-two-Arabs-one-with-mustache." Cindy was clearly feeling less and less at ease, and Youssef retreated into himself and grumbled things like, "Those Dutch people. You do your best to speak their language and they still pretend not to understand."

Eventually, Cindy said she had to get going, and since Youssef also got up at the same time, I walked them down to the main entrance.

When we got outside, Cindy's beauty only increased (because I was sure I'd never see her again) and Youssef's ugliness got worse (because I knew I *would* be seeing more of him, and because he had managed to scare Cindy off). Bikkie barked.

"Samir," Youssef said in asylumseekerese, "that dog barking always! Why not people in building complain for so?"

"I've never heard him bark before," Cindy said.

"He only barks when he knows I'm nearby," I said.

"He barking when I too here," Youssef piped in, and he added, hissing, in Arabic: "Dirty racist dog. He barks at foreigners because it's actually his owner that wants to bite us."

I said goodbye and watched them both cycle off in opposite directions, the dog barking as I walked back to my apartment.

The next time Youssef appeared at my door, he told me that "the dog under" would no longer bark at any foreigner.

"Did you kill it?" I asked.

"Of course not. But now he's had his civics lesson."

He laughed loudly. His mustache looked like a raven spreading his wings against a gray sky. Youssef would not elaborate on Bikkie's civics lesson. But when I bumped into Dave and the dog later that day, he shrunk back from me a bit, pulled the leash tight, and after one yap I never heard a peep out of Bikkie again.

57

To my amazement, Cindy called me up a week later and said it was high time we drank tea together again. Before she came to my place, I listened to the news from Iraq in order to distract myself from the date. I hardly dared look at her for the entire two hours she spent in my apartment.

"Who is that?" she asked, pointing to the photo of Leda and Diesel. She bent over to get a closer look. "Do you think she's pretty?"

"I don't know, but I would like to spend the rest of my life with her."

"Why?"

"I ask myself the same thing."

Cindy started asking me all kinds of things about Leda and me. In this way, Leda brought me closer to Cindy. It was like this every time she came to visit. Cindy got closer, and Leda kept her distance.

Paresh showed up during the good times and stayed away during the difficult times. So I only ever saw him cheerful. With Cindy, it was just the opposite. So I mostly saw her when she was down.

Sometimes she would just sit down and stare out into space. She seemed far removed from everything around her. I could say something, and she didn't hear. Her beauty became a mystery and a burden. As though it were concealing something, something infinite. Whenever that happened, I would keep to myself so as not to disturb her. I was dying to know what it was that made her sink into thoughtfulness, but didn't dare ask.

I was too ordinary for Cindy. And she was too special for me. For her body, I was the departure and arrivals terminus, and for me, she was a marvelous station stop. Our occasional contact offered us both a welcome diversion from painful matters of the heart.

One day she told me her mother would be going away for a week with her boyfriend. If I wanted to, we could spend a weekend at her mother's house. It was a detached house at the edge of the woods, a big house with a sauna, three vintage cars in the garage (none of which was in working condition), a sunroom, a veranda, and a large fishpond. There was a wood-burning stove in the living room, and on the veranda was a pile of firewood and an ax. On the bookshelves were family photo albums.

She did not want to have any physical contact in the house. But that was compensated for by the fact that I could touch her past. We were sitting in the sunroom, the wood stove was crackling, and Cindy sat staring outside the way I had seen her before, in a sort of trance, removed from time and space. As if she were posing for a sculptor, who would transform her into time eternal.

I startled her out of her reverie by asking, "Can I have a look in those photo albums?"

"What was that?"

"Those photo albums. Do you mind if I have a look?"

"Go ahead, just remember to put them back just as you found them. My mother is a perfectionist."

I took out the albums one at a time, and after going through each one, I put it back in exactly the right spot. It had started to rain. Cindy was more engrossed in her thoughts than in the sunroom, her eyes focused on the woods beyond the back fence. I tried to feel the pain she felt, or maybe it wasn't pain at all, but somberness or sorrow.

I was curious where that feeling came from. Was it her own, or something she had inherited from her ancestors? I looked for it in the albums. There was no trace of her beauty in all the generations that had preceded her. But I did encounter a Cindy in a black-and-white photo from 1899.

The person wasn't exactly Cindy, and was certainly not as beautiful, but she had her presence. I could also see that heavy, fiery light in the woman's eyes. And on her mouth, Cindy's mysterious smile. I couldn't take my eyes off that photo, and did not dare page any further. My eyes wandered over the photo of the woman who came to life because of Cindy, and when I looked over at the real Cindy, it looked like she in turn had retreated into the past.

"You done looking?" she asked with a smile. "Or do you have the hots for one of my great-grandmothers?"

A couple of weeks later, Cindy told me she was in love like never before, so deeply moved and happy for the first time. Not long thereafter, I heard from Paresh that Cindy's new lover lived in The Hague and that she waited impatiently for the weekends.

Soon enough they decided to move in together in The Hague.

So one Wednesday, a day that alternated between gray and sunny, Paresh and I went to her apartment to help her move. A car with a trailer in tow pulled up. Cindy got out, gave me three kisses, exaggeratedly on alternating cheeks. Then she hugged Paresh and also gave him three cheek kisses. Then her new lover got out of the car.

"This is Barbara," Cindy said.

Barbara was a butch woman of about forty. If she had been a wolf raiding a petting zoo, she would have devoured all the roosters, rams, and bucks.

Cindy offered us something to drink.

"We haven't even parked yet," said Barbara, giving Cindy a stern, threatening look, and casting a quick glance at us.

"Okay, let's start, then."

It was as though Cindy left all the decisions to Barbara. I was amazed at how quickly Barbara had taken control of Cindy, even though she had never been the subservient type. It looked like Cindy was more impressed by Barbara's strength and character than in love with her.

"Do you think we'll ever see her again?" Paresh asked.

"Who knows," I replied.

Cindy did phone me occasionally. She talked constantly about her love for Barbara, or about Barbara herself. Once she called in tears. She said she wasn't sure if she was still happy there in The Hague.

Paresh visited her once, on her birthday, and came back furious. He decided never to go again. I too never heard from her after that.

58

Living in Malti's studio in that tedious apartment complex gave me plenty of time to think about the huge change that had taken place within me since my long stay in the ASC. It was, I realized, not only my loss of faith in the world, in myself, and in life. It was that I could not feel grounded anywhere. Somehow or other, my head had turned into an asylum seekers' center. And of course it filled itself with asylum seekers, immigration agents, and receptionists. I had to get out. But after a few days of roaming, or a few hours if it was bad weather, I again felt the need for a roof above my head, and the whole thing started all over.

When I think of all the people I met because I kept moving from one place to the next—Leda, Nellie, Paresh, Cindy, to name just a few—the change did not feel so bad. More like something spiritual. Now, I am like water: if it stays still, it starts to stink; if it moves, it purifies itself.

I was getting myself and the apartment ready for Malti's return when her mother told me I could stay another month, because Malti had fallen for some guy in Suriname.

Head over heels in love, Kimatra said. She didn't know his age, but he did not have children. So I stayed in the studio and kept my eye out for a new place to live, but when that didn't pan out I just crossed my fingers that Malti would stay madly in love. She did. For another month, and another, and yet one more. But now, the longer I stayed in her studio, the more I wished her love would shrink rather than grow, so I would be forced to find someplace else. The whole ASC, including personnel and five hundred fellow residents, was squashed in my dreams in Malti's studio apartment.

When Kimatra came around the next month to collect

the rent, I could read the disappointment on her face. The boy Malti had fallen in love with was not a boy, but a man. Twice married and the father of five children. Malti had booked her return flight and would arrive on the ninth of next month. I could stay for free until the sixth, and Kimatra would use the last three days to get the apartment ready for Malti.

"Where will you go?" she asked.

"I don't know," I said. "It's hard to find a house, and expensive if you do find one. And I'd like to keep living among Dutch people."

"Why is that?"

"To improve my Dutch. And to find peace. Among Dutch people, I am the only problem and the only solution."

This made her laugh. "I'll ask around—maybe we can find you someplace in among the cheeseheads."

And what do you know, three days later she came back with the news that she had found me a place to rent. A friend of hers, Karen Mars, was putting her house on the market and meanwhile would live with her boyfriend.

The house was on the Kievietstraat, the most fertile street in all Holland. Everywhere, there were stuffed half-storks stuck to the windows announcing a new baby. Pregnant women waddled up and down the street like fat ducks, and because it was the first nice day in weeks, there were lots of children out. Sitting, crawling, running, crying. Dogs with loose-hanging tongues looked out of windows. Kimatra sighed as she parallel parked with the skill of an Amsterdam cab driver.

"Do you see those Hollanders you're so keen to live with? They're nuts! They raise their dogs indoors and their children on the sidewalk!"

59

Kimatra rang Karen's bell. The door opened. I think Karen Mars was expecting someone else, perhaps people of another color. She looked at us in silence for at least six seconds.

"This is Samir and he wants to rent your house," Kimatra said.

Karen's face tightened. She shook hands with us both and invited us in.

Kimatra started talking and talking. Whenever Karen looked at Kimatra, her expression was what you'd call a tentative okay. When she looked at me, her face went tight again. In fifteen minutes, Kimatra described every house she had rented in the Netherlands over the past fifty years. Then she said that a good tenant is harder to find than a good partner. After that she talked about her husband, who had not been good to her, and about one of her kidneys, which was also not good.

"I didn't know him," Kimatra continued, referring to me. "He sublet my daughter Malti's studio apartment. At first I was nervous and thought he would be a slob, that the house would turn into a garbage dump and that he'd steal things, but he's on time with the rent and has kept my daughter's place just as he found it. He's an asylum seeker, but a good one."

She uttered the word *asylum seeker* with the most intense pathos she had in her. Then she launched into a monologue about Malti in Suriname. Karen listened and listened, and I could tell Kimatra's endless stories were driving her crazy. She got a glass of water.

"The house is ready to be sold," she said, after taking a big gulp. "And it has to stay that way. That's why the rent's not so high."

"He'll leave whenever you say," Kimatra interjected before Karen could get a word in.

"Fine," Karen said. This meant a roof over my head. "I'll show you around."

After a detailed tour of the house, Karen handed me the key, the Wi-Fi code, and her phone number. We all went outside, and I walked Kimatra to her car. As she drove off I yelled, "I love you!" She honked three times. I know for sure that this meant, "Ha ha ha."

The first thing I thought when I moved into Karen's house was to take a break from everything. I hoped no one would phone me. But even before the first day in my new apartment had passed, my cell phone vibrated. Yelena. She was calling from Brazil. When I asked about her life there, she said it was just like life in Mexico. When I asked about her life in Mexico, she said it was better there than life in Argentina, which in turn was better than in Germany, which itself was an improvement on Belgium. Okay, I thought, I know Belgium a little, so I'll quit asking. Then she chatted about her sister, about a certain Vlad, and some fuss with papers. Then she hung up. Who Vlad was, and how Yelena herself was doing—no idea. But her voice sounded just like in the ASC. Effervescent. Full of life.

What a wonderful person that Yelena is, I thought. Passing through places is her way of staying there. She passes through and passes through, without giving any place enough time to change her. Che Guevara once said that the revolution is like bicycling: if you stop, you'll fall over. That's how it is with Yelena. When she hung up, I suddenly looked around me, unnerved, and thought: where *am* I, and what in heaven's name am I doing here?

60

In an Iraqi village it's always clear who lives where. Just like a dog marks its territory with urine, Iraqis do the same with gossip and shouting.

A street in Iraq is a river of chitchat, a neighborhood a lake of gossip, and a city an ocean of chin-wag. In Iraq, people stop every meter or so to chat with a face through a window, a door, or a hole in a fence or wall. Houses in Iraq are like newspapers: you skim the headlines as you pass.

A street in the Netherlands is a river of time, a neighborhood a lake of silence, and a city an ocean of hurry. Dutch houses are like the cover of *Playboy*: you glance at it inquisitively in passing and do your best to make sure no one saw.

As I inserted my key into the keyhole, I was startled by a voice right next to my ear.

"Hello, new neighbor."

I turned and saw Eva. Eva Dijkhuis. Her front door was next to mine. With only the occasional exception, the doors were exactly the same size and exactly the same dark green as all the rest of the doors in the Kievitstraat.

She immediately started telling me about herself and her personal life. She had two daughters who lived alternating weeks with her and their father. She had met her new flame Marco online, because since becoming a mother she had no time to meet people any other way. "Handy, isn't it, the internet?" He, Marco, was adorable and sweet, and he had an adorable, sweet cat. After two months, he and his cat had moved in with her.

In return, Eva Dijkhuis wanted to know everything about me. I told her three times that I was renting the house until it was sold. I told her twice that I was an asylum seeker, and four times that I was not on welfare. I answered all her questions. At a certain point, Eva Dijkhuis looked at her watch.

"Sorry, neighbor, but I don't have much time. Nice to chat with you and all, but we here in the Netherlands have things to do."

She said the words "we here in the Netherlands" in such a way that it did not sound personal.

This marked the end of my making Eva Dijkhuis's acquaintance, the longest such meeting both until then and since.

I went inside and the only thing I wanted was to find two aspirins as quickly as possible. I drank half a liter of water and lay on the sofa until my headache receded.

A few days later, Eva rang the bell. She said in a tired voice that there was a lot of noise coming from the kitchen, and that Marco was very sensitive to noise. When I told her that the noise came not from my kitchen, but from the one behind us, her expression changed from tired to as if she'd just told a joke. She chuckled.

"Here in the Netherlands, neighbor, we're so preoccupied with things that I don't even know where a noise comes from. How stupid is that!" Then she proceeded to tell me that the neighbors at number 43 were always making noise. Never after ten in the evening, but it was irritating all the same. She told me that "we here in the Netherlands" do not make noise after ten, unless we've warned the neighbors first. She looked at her watch. "Sorry, but I really have to go."

This is how my second conversation with Eva ended: as though she hadn't knocked on the wrong door to complain, but as if I had made noise last night after ten and was now chatting more than necessary. My contact with Eva Dijkhuis was like the contact between a car and an accident: with her "we here in the Netherlands" she could always claim to be the car. Which is why I gave her a wide berth in that street, where I was the only foreigner and where everything ran according to plan.

But after a few days she sank back into her busy life. I had no more trouble from Eva at our shared front step.

61

In all my time on the Kievitstraat, I couldn't put my finger on who actually lived there and who was just passing through. I would make tea and sit on the living-room sofa. When I looked outside, I could see not only five and a half meters of street, but the entire house of the neighbors across the way, from their living room through the kitchen and into the backyard. The windows were so big and so clean that I could almost tell what kind of plants they had out back. All I wanted was to look out onto the street, but my curiosity was drawn to the neighbors' home. Their house was the fitness club of my curiosity.

I therefore decided to sit in my small backyard, fenced in on all sides. Except for when it rained, Eva Dijkhuis and Marco spent all their time in their backyard. Eva wanted him to feel like he was incredibly witty and oh so interesting. Even if he said he'd forgotten to charge his laptop so he couldn't watch a movie in the train, she would act astonished or laugh. "Really? That's *awful*." If Marco said he had bought bottled water at the station snack kiosk and only realized in the train that it was carbonated and made him burp, she would roar with laughter to let Marco know how hilarious he was.

To the right was a young couple without children. They were standoffish but friendly. If they greeted me, they would do so and then quickly look away, a technique used in the Netherlands if you have to greet someone you'd actually rather not know. At first, I did not understand that this was how Dutch people showed they were keeping their distance. So I mistook their aversion for grumpiness.

The couple to the right was very quiet. Even their enormous dog was quiet. Except on weekends, particularly

Saturdays. Then they would invite friends around to sit in the backyard. One of the regular guests was a woman named Margreet. I only heard her when Ton said anything. Then Margreet would correct whatever it was he said. If Ton was a book, then Margreet was his lifelong editor.

"It was such nice weather last Saturday," I heard Ton say.

"Friday was nice, but not Saturday," said Margreet.

"Quite right. It rained all day Saturday."

"No, not all day. Only in the afternoon and evening."

I noticed that when the neighbors to the right talked, the neighbors to the left were quiet. And when the neighbors to the left talked, then the ones on the right were quiet, or talked in low voices. Not only do Dutch people respect one another on the ground, I mused, but also in the air. There, too, they wait their turn.

Occasionally I would take out my photo albums and carefully remove the photographs. On the back I would write where they belonged and then shuffle them like playing cards. I made a game of trying to match the families by looking at the faces. This face belonged here, that one belonged there. This one is a child of that one. These two must be the same person. This one vanishes and then reappears two generations later. After spending hours in the past and its various faces, I separated the newly formed families and tried to replace them in the albums. This always went wrong. Because the hearts that had brought the faces together in the first place weren't there anymore, and sometimes it was difficult to pair up faces that had so little to do with each other without the hearts as reference points. It was painful to see a friendly face suffer alongside a harsh one, or to see an extroverted face buried alive next to an introverted one. Or to see a radiant face become paralyzed alongside a gloomy one. There is no glue as stupid as the heart that forces disparate faces to stick together.

Oh, how much easier it was to live among Dutch people from the past. Each time, my journey through the faces ended with me finally getting them all back in the proper place and albums, after having spent hours in another time and place, with those faces as my ships.

After a while, I noticed that the neighbors were also secretly watching me, the way I was secretly watching them. And then I caught on that basically all the neighbors were peeking at one another from across the street. Every pair of facing houses were two theaters that took turns performing daily pantomimes. These performances were repeated day after day, with the same staging, the same decor, the same scenario. Two plays going on at once, with two audiences who could watch their daily lives in the performance across the road being played out by different actors.

I learned that I could simply look outside to see what time it was. This Dutch street was a clock that needed no batteries or cord, and did not break when cars drove over it or when left out in the rain.

If Bimba the dog barked twice and Stijn shouted at him to keep quiet, then it was precisely 7:15 a.m. If the engine of Peter's Citroën purred, it was just before 7:30. If Arjan walked past, then it was either 12:20 or 1:10, depending on which way he was going, but if Dirk walked by, it was exactly 4:15. It could be that Dirk chose that specific time so that he wouldn't bump into Aryan or Peter. From ten o'clock until a quarter to three, no one at all passed. Not an insect. Not a dog. Not even Eva Dijkhuis.

I started to adapt my day-to-day routine to the Dutch people's habits. If I saw Bo jog past my window, then I was happy because that meant it was Friday and I could go to the market to buy a *lekkerbekje*. Eric was a walking weather report: if I saw him walking his two dogs, I could tell by his clothes whether I should bring sunglasses or an umbrella.

This boring and tranquil street, free of mortars falling out of the sky, free of mujahideen and soldiers, was heaven for me. A paradise of peace and quiet.

62

At a certain point I needed money, so I went out to find work. I took the ID card Asker Shaheen had bought for me and headed downtown. I was nervous. Would the employment agency be able to tell I'd bought that card? And if they did, what would they do?

I walked past various employment agencies and studied the faces of the people working there. One unpleasant-looking face and I would discount that particular office outright. With serious faces, I decided to make a mental note of the address, but not go in quite yet. Finally, at an employment agency called Cityworks, I saw two women, each at a computer. One of them had red hair and a smile on her lips. The other one was blonde, and yawned. The combination of a yawn and a smile gave me a good feeling, and I decided to go in. I sat down on one of the colorful chairs against the wall. Pretty soon the red-haired woman called me over. She introduced herself as Jessica. I told for my name and said I was looking for work.

"May I see your ID?" she asked. This was the moment of truth. I nervously handed her the card. She set it down next to the keyboard, typed the information on the card into the computer, and handed it back to me. Now I knew for sure how valuable that card was. It worked!

"What was the last job you had?" she asked.

"Full-time asylum seeker," I said.

Jessica burst out laughing and said, "I have work for you."

From then on, Jessica and her colleague sent me to various temporary jobs. Whenever I was in town, I would drop in at the agency. My way of talking made Jessica laugh. If she heard someone say "it's shitty weather," she did not laugh, but if I said "the weather shits," then she did.

What I liked about Jessica was that she wasn't official or formal at work. Sometimes I bumped into her at the Saturday vegetable market, and she did not ignore me, but stopped and chatted, as though we were acquaintances, friends, or colleagues. She even did this if there was someone else with her, without first going to great pains to explain to the other person who I was and how she knew me. Nor did she ever say anything that would give away that we knew each other through her job. I do not personally know any royalty, except from Shakespeare's plays, but I believe Jessica had the character of a monarch. She was the most genuine person I ever met in the Netherlands. Someone else's opinion had absolutely no influence over her. When she sent me out to a new job, she always wanted to know afterwards how I thought it was, while everyone else wanted to know what the boss thought of *me*. If there was one person who did not treat me as an asylum seeker, but simply as Samir, it was Jessica. Oh, how I would love to have been able to look through her family albums. Not to see where her red hair comes from, but her white smile, which was in no way like ice, and her warmth, which not even a roaring fireplace could match.

The longer Jessica knew me, the less she sent me to do boring or repetitive jobs. It was thus via a temp job from that employment agency that I discovered the magic key to Dutch society. I became a dog walker.

Vincent the dog knew where he was going, how fast, down which street, and who he should stop at and who not. Take ten thousand asylum seekers who have been in the Netherlands for three and a half years and let them loose in the wet, multicultural Dutch streets where thousands of Big Brothers are watching you, and they won't be able to find their way like that dog did. He knew exactly which window he had to look through, which tree or wall to raise his hind leg at. He knew where he was welcome and where he wasn't. Where they thought he was a cute doggy and where he was seen as the devil. The Dutch people who knew Vincent started to greet us. With Vincent at my side, I got only smiling faces and friendly waves. I felt more like a pop star than an asylum seeker taking a dog to the park to poop.

Vincent seemed to be well acquainted with one particular tree in the park. He squatted there and pooped. That's that, I thought, and assumed he would move on. But he didn't. An invisible leash tethered him to his turd. I called him, but he just stood there looking at it and then at me, and then back at his turd and again at me.

"Yeah, Vincent, I know you pooped!" I called. "Good boy! Now, come!"

But Vincent just stood there looking from me to his excrement. For the first and maybe the last time, he barked.

"Don't you have a baggie with you?" said a gentle female voice next to me. A woman of about twenty.

"A baggie?" I asked.

"Yes, a baggie. Here, take this one."

She handed me a small plastic bag, and only then did I remember that Vincent had wanted me to take something out of the drawer before we left. Aha! So that was it. I felt so dumb—for years I had been impressed with how clean the Dutch streets were but never noticed, even after seeing all those thousands of dog butts on leashes, how they got that way.

I took the plastic bag from the woman and found myself in one of the most awkward situations ever. How in heaven's name was I supposed to get that turd into that little bag? It would be easier to get the dog himself into it. Vincent looked from me to his turd. The woman also looked at me, smiling. I went in search of two sticks, far away from the poop, to get away from the smell.

"Looking for something?" she asked.

"Two sticks to get that poop into the bag," I said.

She laughed, took the bag back from me, stuck her hand

in the bag, and in less than a second the turd was no longer on the ground, but in the bag. And her hand on the outside. It was perhaps the most unromantic moment of my life.

"Monique Oudshoorn."

"Samir van Vincent."

"Huh?"

"Samir. *S* as in Saddam, *A* as in Al-Qaeda, *M* as in mujahideen, *I* as in ISIS, *R* as in—"

"Stop! What an awful name. Is that your dog?"

"He's not my dog. I'm his human."

She was pretty, and got prettier the more she talked. Vincent was the leash connecting me and Monique. Otherwise she wouldn't have given me a second glance, and I would not have dared to come even a centimeter closer. She had a buzzcut, as though she did not need hair to be pretty. Her right ear was pierced all the way up, a large safety pin hung from her left earlobe, and there was another ring in her nose. As soon as I started telling her about my love of dogs (before she could discover that in truth I don't like them at all), Vincent gave me one last look and walked off.

I called to him. "Vincent! Vincent! Darling Vincent! Come back!" But he did not listen. "Wonderful Vincent, my best friend! Come!" But Vincent was already out of sight. "Ciao, Monique," I said and ran after the dog.

"Damn dog," I hissed as I chased him. "Your shit is better than you are, you stubborn animal. Your shit helped me meet Monique, and now, thanks to you, I have to leave her behind."

But Vincent had taught me something about Dutch society that no language lessons or civics course could. For those ninety minutes, that dog was my face, allowing me to greet more Dutch strangers than in the previous ten years altogether. This was the magic key to the Netherlands: a dog. And a baggie.

63

The most unusual temp job Jessica sent me to lasted for two weeks: as a cleaner at an old-age home.

In Iraq you have old people, but no old-age homes. If they do exist, they are not government-run, but set up by a charity. And I can tell you that these are filthier than the prisons. The residents are society's castoffs who have no family and no money to hire someone to care for them. Being old in Iraq means finding someone who will care for you; otherwise, death is a more merciful option.

An elderly person in a house in Iraq is more important than poles are for a tent. Just as every house in the Netherlands has central heating, every house in Iraq has an elderly person. Many generations live under one roof, so it doesn't feel like having an old person in the home.

On my first day, I passed the empty reception desk leading on to a large room where tables and chairs were scattered about at random. There were only a few people there. Each had a bowl of soup, an identical bowl, and a piece of bread. They each had a bib tied around their neck, so that the soup would not splash from their quivering spoons onto their quivering outfits. A woman in a white nurse's uniform spoke to a woman in a wheelchair, and her gestures were explanatory and threatening at the same time, as though she were talking to a three-year-old child.

Eventually she noticed me and told me where I should start. She repeated a few times that I had to make sure to dry the floor after mopping it, so that the residents did not slip. "A fall could be disastrous for our residents." I didn't tell her I already knew this, because I grew up in a house where there were always four elderly people, and if one of them died, another one would get old soon enough and take over the empty room.

Not just from day one, but from the very first hour, I felt that I was not in an old-age home, but in an alternative Holland. A Holland without haste and without civil discrimination. Where a person is not an iPhone that gets an update every six months. There was patience and respect. Outside that old-age home, I saw bodies that needed a soul in order to live, and inside I saw souls in need of a body.

I became acquainted with the living history of the Netherlands. There, I believed that the country did have tolerance, but that its tolerance had grown old and had ended up in an old-age home. There, I learned the wisdom of the Netherlands, which no one takes the time to listen to anymore.

Most of the residents' minds were still intact, but their bodies had more or less atrophied. The chairs and the beds moved more than the residents did. They inhabited small rooms with large windows, which opened and shut easily, but beyond which life was no longer reality. Every room had real flowers on a table and a wall full of the past: photos of the old days, of children and grandchildren. I saw that the old people got more visits from words than from bodies. Cards and letters were pinned up everywhere. I have visited many museums in my life, but I never saw one like that place, with living statues, ones that tremble and struggle to breathe. A museum where you don't need an audio tour. The artwork speaks for itself.

Not every room had photo albums, but every room *was* a photo album. Therefore I peeked inside an open door whenever I could. If one of the residents called me, I went in and tried to stick around for a bit, even though I was supposed to be working. It was fascinating to watch an elderly lady shuffle across a room whose walls told me how beautiful she was when she was a queen who reigned over her own life.

One old person died in the first week I worked there. So I thought this was normal, that someone died every week, but I was told that this was a coincidence and that sometimes months passed without anyone dying.

The person who left the building for good that week was Colette van Woerkom. Her memory and her hearing were as strong as ever. She was eighty or ninety and as thin as a rail. When I approached the building before my shift, she would be sitting at her window, and sometimes she waved. Other times she would sit on a bench in the hallway. It looked like she was waiting for someone. She once asked me where I came from, and when I said Iraq, she beckoned me to her room. She had been there once before, in 1957, the year before Iraq became a republic. There were no photos or cards on her wall. On her table was a vase of yellow flowers.

She pointed to a thick photo album, which I set on the table in front of her. Her nearly transparent hands opened it and paged to a photo of herself, taken in Baghdad and dated April 8, 1957. A pencil-thin finger pointed to something in the picture. Her quivering hand, a dried-up river of hours, touched her then-hand, a wellspring of years, and I got the sensation that those two times embraced one another.

When she died, no one came to take anything from her room. I asked the man from the thrift shop if I could take the photo album. He nodded. That album was the only thing in her cupboard. When I leafed through it at home later, I noticed there wasn't a single photo of anyone else. No grandfather or grandmother, no father or mother or brother or sister or boyfriend or girlfriend, no dog, no cat. Only photos of her. Every few years, another picture was added, but she had apparently stopped adding pictures before her hair went gray, as though she had decided that a certain period of her life was over. I closed the album and realized why no one came to clean out her room: she hadn't taken anything from another person, no memories, no moments. And all she left behind was tenderness.

64

Karen Mars called to say that someone would be coming to view the house tomorrow at ten fifteen. She asked if I would put back the weaker light bulbs before they came. How did she know I had changed all the living-room lamps from 60 to 100 W? Okay, so I changed the light bulbs, washed the windows, moved my things out of the shower, and made the place look like no one lived there. I put my belongings in the back shed. When Karen arrived at a quarter to ten the next morning, the house was ready to be shown. She was satisfied, and I cleared out for the morning. When she called me after lunch to say I could come back, she told me the house had probably been sold and that the new owners wanted to move in on the first of the month. This meant I had seventeen days to find a new place to live.

By now I was getting used to life among the Hollanders: I was able to remain an outsider, which is what I wanted. But even though I had an ID card I knew I could trust, and had money for rent and a deposit, I simply couldn't find an apartment. I searched high and low, and only after I returned to Karen Mars's place did I think of Talib, the old friend from the ASC who had foisted Youssef on me. I call to ask if I could stay with him for a few nights. He lived a few kilometers away.

"Come on, man, what's with this 'a few nights' stuff? I have a place for you, you can stay for free as long as you like, or until they discover the secret."

"Where?"

"In Elvis Presley!"

I figured he was making another one of his crazy jokes, but he swore it was true. We agreed to meet at the Aldi, the second meeting place of asylum seekers after the train station. We cycled off, leaving the city center behind us, and crossed through a large park.

"Look, Samir, on the one side of the park live regular Dutch people, and on the other side, the antisocials," he said. "You can spot the difference right away."

On the far side of the park were identical apartments or houses. We cycled through that neighborhood, and in the distance I could see enormous apartment blocks like the kind you see in old Soviet movies.

"That's Elvis Presley," Talib said, pointing to one of them. The closer we got to it, the more it looked like a giant gray cement box. There were four other buildings just like it next to Elvis Presley. If you asked someone where Elvis Presley was, they would say, "Behind Ruud Gullit." And if you asked where Ruud Gullit was, they would say, "Next to Rutger Hauer."

In front of Elvis Presley was a dilapidated, litter-strewn playground. Behind it was a row of shops: Turkish, Moroccan, Chinese, Somali, Russian, Syrian, and Ethiopian. Every ethnicity in the neighborhood had its own supermarket with products from home. There was also a day care, a primary school, teahouses full of men, and takeout restaurants with delivery motor scooters parked outside. The women were either pregnant, carrying small children, or elderly. The men, almost without exception, all had a beard.

Elvis Presley had ten stories. Along one side were the outdoor walkways, and on the other side you saw countless balconies with satellite dishes and clotheslines, as though that's what the balconies were made for. As I parked my bicycle, I heard an unexpected sound, desperate and melancholy, from a nearby balcony. "Meeeehh." I looked up and among the clothes hanging out to dry I saw the head of a sheep sticking out between the rails. I glanced questioningly at Talib.

"Yeah, some of the folks in Elvis Presley use their balcony to keep sheep or chickens. Don't be alarmed if you see blood streaming off them, that's where they slaughter them, too," Talib laughed.

Elvis Presley had a large glass front door. Next to it lay shards of shattered glass. We entered the bare, creepy entrance hall, which smelled like the ASC did during the weekend when social services weren't on duty: food, rotten vegetables, diapers, and dirty toilets. There were crying and whining children on the public walkways and in the stairwell, and the voices of screaming mothers drifting from the apartments. The walls were full of children's drawings and yellowish grease stains from the kitchens. If I closed my eyes and meditated a bit, this brought me back to our house in Iraq.

We stood for a while waiting for the elevator, but it didn't come. Talib told me that children liked to play in it between the third and sixth floors. They would just keep pushing the buttons, and therefore it sometimes it got stuck between floors. So we walked up five filthy flights of stairs. We passed a fat old woman wearing a headscarf, who panted that the elevator was broken again.

"Those stupid Hollanders, why don't they fix the elevator?" said an old man with a cane in Arabic. "As though we're animals, not humans!"

"You're right, Hajj Hassan, but don't you worry: I heard that the council is going to add two more elevators, then we'll have three," Talib said.

"Why three? One is enough, if it works."

"They're going to make one marked with a beard, only for men. And one with a headscarf, only for women. And one for the kids to play in between the third and sixth floors," Talib said, and the man laughed as he shuffled down the stairs.

We stopped in front of a door with the name *Abud Alami* on the nameplate. We knocked, but no one answered. We knocked again, and still no one came.

"Maybe there's nobody home," I said.

"Of course there is. They assume I'll use my key, but I left it inside."

"So call them."

"I forgot my phone, too."

He started shouting that it was him and they should open the door. So his voice, too, was a key.

"Who is Abud Alami?" I asked.

"An old Iraqi guy. Dead and buried in Iraq, but here he's very much alive," Talib said. "That is the secret."

65

Abud Alami was already an old man when he fled Iraq during the Gulf War. He made his way to the Netherlands, and after six and a half years was given humanitarian asylum and an apartment in Elvis Presley. Because Abud Alami was too old to care for himself and had no family, the other asylum seekers in the ASC had taken care of him. There was someone who did his shopping, another who cooked for him, and yet another who washed his clothes. When he left the ASC, he repaid their kindness by opening his home to whoever had been rejected by the IND or faced deportation. In 2003, when Saddam Hussein fled Baghdad, Abud Alami decided to return to Iraq.

He did not want to have to kick the illegals and deportees out of his apartment. So he stayed registered there. One of those asylum seekers was a lawyer from Tunisia. He understood the rules in the Netherlands, because he had spent years in the system. He pored through Abud Alami's papers, figured out exactly what had to be done to keep the old man registered with the city council and the landlord without him actually living there. He did not have to practice forging Abud Alami's signature, because it was just a straight line.

The Tunisian lawyer figured it would be a matter of a few months before they caught on. But by now it had been much longer than that. Once in a while the lawyer would have Abud Alami call the city council from Iraq, so this ruse went on for years without the authorities getting wind of it. Even when he died and was buried in Najaf, he stayed alive in the Netherlands and continued to reside in Elvis Presley. Everyone in the building knew this, and they collectively kept Abud Alami alive so that there would be a safe haven for rejected asylum seekers and undocumented immigrants.

He had left his IND card, his bank pass, his passport, and everything he had needed to live in the Netherlands with the Tunisian lawyer. Those few numbers and pieces of paper were enough to keep Abud Alami immortal in the Netherlands. Every time I hear the Dutch cabaret song "There is Life After Death," I have to think of Abud Alami in Elvis Presley.

The atmosphere in the apartment was just the opposite of that in Asker Shaheen's wife's house. The pseudo-presence of that woman made us perpetually uneasy, while Abud Alami's omnipresence created—as it did when he actually lived there—a welcome feeling.

On the kitchen counter was a contribution tin. The money got deposited in Abud Alami's bank account, and paid for the rent, utilities, and even the insurance. I'll bet Abud Alami is the only person on earth with insurance but without a body.

Every room in the apartment was filled with men of all ages and from different countries, but each with the same problem: they were not welcome in the Netherlands.

"This is Samir," Talib announced.

The men went quiet, got up, and shook my hand.

"Is he a newcomer?" one of them asked.

"No," Talib answered. "After four governments, he's still an unwanted alien."

"Welcome!" they all shouted at once.

"Don't worry, brother, you don't need the Hollanders here," one of them said. "There's food, tea, and a bed. And everything's free until you're able to pay your own way."

"The only thing you have to know," said another, "is that our life here relies on a little secret. Maybe Talib already told you. If those bumbling Hollanders find out, we'll all be thrown out on our ear."

"Enough of your chitchat, you all are as bad as the Dutch," said a young man who came in with a tray of tea cups, which he passed around.

After the tea, Talib gave me a tour around Elvis Presley. Or, at least I have to say it was a tour, as I wouldn't know what else to call it.

"Forget your Dutch here, my friend," he began as we walked up to the top floor. "In Elvis Presley you'll get by fine with Arabic, but you could also easily pick up some Turkish, or Berber, or Polish. And if you need new shoes, you should learn some Romanian. It's important that everyone in Elvis Presley knows you live here, then they'll leave you alone. I can't promise that this also goes for the police. In that respect they are a lot like the police in Iraq, except here you can't bribe them. Anyway, you'll see plenty of them. You'll also have to watch out for the antisocial Hollanders who live in that antisocial neighborhood further up, the Bloemenwijk, on our side of the park. They're cowards when they're alone, but dangerous in a group. They are convinced that every foreigner is a tick that's come here to suck their blood. They think they're antisocial because of us, not because of the Dutch city folk."

When we reached the top floor, he pointed to a door that led up to the roof.

"It's been locked ever since some Hollander just waltzed in here, went up to the roof, and jumped."

We took the stairs back down, and he told me something about each floor as we passed it. How funny it is, I thought, that Elvis Presley is filled with Muslims, immigrants, sheep, chickens, clotheslines, women with headscarves and burkas, crying children, and broken glass, but nothing that sounds even remotely like rock and roll.

"In this apartment," Talib whispered on the sixth floor, "you'll occasionally hear screams of pain and anger. The pain belongs to Farhaan and the anger is from his wife, Anber. They both have a rough, masculine voice, because they both smoke all day long, so you won't know who's who. Don't pay any attention, just keep walking. Just so you know, Anber, the wife, is the one doing the hitting, and that Farhaan screams in pain, and not the other way around. She does that because after twelve years in the camp, Farhaan is addicted to hash and turns their life with their four children into a daily argument."

"What about the children?"

"The eldest, a son, ran away at sixteen. The Hollanders gave him a room with some other boys. He is addicted to beer. But their three daughters still live at home. The mother doesn't want them to leave. She's afraid they'll take off their headscarves and drink alcohol, like their brother, and then their uncle will have to come from Germany to kill them."

I listened to his various stories until we reached the second floor.

"If you lose your bike, then you can buy it back here for ten euros. But you have to be quick about it, before they cut through the lock. Then you're out another ten euros for a new lock. If you hear a metal grinder, then you know it's too late. Don't get into a discussion with him about it being your bike. Just pay him and know that your ten euros are not so much to buy your bike back, but are more like anti-theft insurance. Because he never steals a bike he's already sold. And if you steal one yourself, then you can borrow his metal grinder for one euro per lock."

We arrived at the first floor.

"You can buy back stolen scooters here, and stolen Tom-Toms there," he said, pointing to two apartments. "And if you happen to see a poor Dutch woman outside with a walker who wants her purse back, then you have to go in there."

By now we were on the ground floor, where a young man greeted us and asked if we had fifty cents for him. We gave him a euro.

"That guy needs five euros a day for hash, otherwise he gets aggressive and Elvis Presley turns ugly," Talib said.

We walked out through the glass door, past two men from the city council who were repairing the window panes. A man with a beard greeted us. Talib told me he was the imam from the Moroccan mosque. There were three mosques: a Moroccan, a Turkish, and a Saudi. The Moroccan and the Turkish ones were similar and not so strict, but the Saudi one was another story. Officially it was called the Al Sahabe mosque, but everybody called it the Saudi mosque. The Turkish and Moroccan mosques were built with money collected from the local community, but the Saudi one was built with money from the Saudi embassy, and was the biggest in the neighborhood.

A boy walked past us and Talib told me he was a dog thief. If I ever saw Dutch people searching frantically for their dog, then he had stolen it. He resold them in Germany or France and was good at guessing their ages, because he never stole any dogs older than three. They younger, the better. Sometimes he even stole the dog's name along with the dog. He would first follow the owner and wait until they called the dog, and only then would he steal it.

Just as Talib had predicted, every few minutes a police car passed and the officers glowered at us from the car. The Kievitstraat and Elvis Presley were at most five kilometers apart, but I felt as though I had left the Netherlands far behind me, without even crossing the border. Even now, if I hear a song by Elvis Presley or see a picture of him, I think about that golden opportunity I had to live inside him.

When the light went out that first night, Talib called out in the dark amid the snoring of the sleeping men and over the whispering of the smoking men, "Samir, I know I told you once already, but I'll say it again: don't go to that antisocial Bloemenwijk. Even if the most irresistible tattooed legs try to lure you there!" I wanted to ask him why, but I yawned and before I fell asleep I realized he had piqued my interest in the Bloemenwijk. What I didn't know was that my curiosity would later fill our balcony with song.

66

Except for the toilet, Abud Alami's apartment was chocka-block. The two bedrooms were filled with mattresses, clothes, blankets, sheets, and pillows. The living room with chairs and rolled-up mattresses during the day, which at night would offer room for a few more sardines. The clothesline on the balcony was filled with attire in various sizes; on the floor were shoes and bags of stuff left behind by previous residents and never retrieved. The current housemates rifled through these bags whenever they needed something, to see if there was anything that fit, and sometimes they would put in something they no longer needed. Aside from the balcony, the house stank, but after a few days you didn't smell it anymore.

Most of the men in Abud Alami's apartments were mosque-goers. A few went to the Turkish one, a couple of others to the Moroccan one, and one man, Abdullah, went to the Saudi mosque. Everyone agreed that it made no difference which mosque you went to, in all three you prayed to God, but as soon as the conversation turned to politics or jihad, suddenly there were three Gods again. This happened especially when Abdullah was around.

The Turkish God was more European; he looked like a meeting place for the soul. The Moroccan God was more religious: go to prayers five times per weekend and you would be sent to heaven. But the Saudi God was political. For him, you had to fight, and only then was he satisfied. The men who came together via their stomachs with halal food were separated via their hearts by the God with three mosques.

The chatting in the apartment never really developed into a discussion. It was repetitive and boring, just like the incessant talk of doping during every Tour de France. It always started with the IND and illegal work, and then proceeded to politics and smugglers. A glass of tea or hot food put the talk on pause, so you only heard chewing, and then someone pushed play again and the chitchat resumed.

I soon tired of all that. You couldn't retreat to the balcony, because it was so full of junk, to go to a bar you needed money, and I could not fall back on the Dutch friends I had made. In the Netherlands, friends are friends if they want to see you, acquaintances if you want to see them, and if they don't need to see you, they forget you.

Abdullah was the only one in the apartment who tried to turn the small talk into a serious discussion. He was always afraid that God would be angry at him, or at us, or at Elvis Presley. We were all wary of him, because although we could take his anger, the anger of his God was too much.

I heard that Abdullah had lived in Italy for five years. After some problems with drugs there, he moved to the Netherlands. The police had picked him up because he had no residence permit, so he asked for asylum. He was put in an ASC, where he spent his days picking fights with the staff, bickering with the other residents, and getting into arguments with the locals. So rather than trying to fit in, he opted for a life on the street. He was regularly arrested for causing trouble, sent to prison, and then back to the ASC, where he picked more fights and ended up on the street again. This was Abdullah's life circle.

Elvis Presley had broken that circle. One time during Ramadan, a Saudi sheikh came to the Saudi mosque. Apparently he took Abdullah by the hand and said, "Turn this hand toward heaven and say, 'God, I give you this hand, give me happiness.'" Since then, he was a new man. He went to the mosque five times a day, where he prayed and he listened, and was transformed from a criminal and troublemaker to a Salafist Muslim. Not only had Abdullah himself changed, his aggression had too. Whereas it once came out as fighting, alcohol, theft, and drugs, it was now expressed as love for Islam, for God, and for the jihad. He had shaved his mustache and left his beard. He wore a djellaba. I heard the police now let him be. Abdullah claimed that this was because God protected him, but the housemates knew it was because he no longer smoked joints and drank. After a few weeks in the Saudi mosque, Abdullah appeared to have a personal friendship with God. If only he, and not his aggression, had become a Muslim, this would have been a perfect solution for Abdullah, for Elvis Presley, and for the universe. But when his aggression also became Muslim in the Saudi way, he seemed to need more and more jihad to get rid of all the anger that the drugs and alcohol had put into him.

You know, being alone is hard enough, but the inability to be alone is even harder. Sometimes I could shut out the other men in the apartment, but Abdullah and his jihad only became more and more present. I took daily bike rides around the city, looking for somewhere to rent, but the only thing I found was the library. Once again, just like my first month in the Netherlands, the sacred library was the only place where you could sit for free. Where no policeman ever checked what a person was reading, where no civil servant ever said you couldn't come in, where no bouncer said you had to wear different trousers or shoes to be allowed inside. You could even go in without reading glasses. If it rained, I stayed in Elvis Presley, and because it rained a lot, I didn't get to the library as often as I wanted to. I bought a Koran in a Turkish shop and read it a few times, but unfortunately there were no other books to be had in the neighborhood.

In Elvis Presley I automatically ended up doing under-the-table work. Sometimes Jessica called me for a job, but when she left the employment agency to move in with her boyfriend in Dordrecht, work from her agency dried up.

Finding work in Elvis Presley was easier than finding it in the Netherlands. In fact, the work found me. I made the acquaintance of Ibo, a Turkish guy with a shop selling electronic equipment, mostly satellite dishes. I helped him install the dishes he sold. Sometimes I worked in the shop, after a while even on my own, and sometimes I went with him on a job. Ibo was a slippery one. He could wriggle out of a situation at just the right moment, so that he was neither part of the problem nor part of the solution. This was mostly because he could always keep his curiosity under control, and would sneak off from a conversation as soon as he could.

Whenever you saw Ibo, you assumed he was busy with work, always on his cell phone, focused on his call. But the only thing he was really occupied with was women. For him, work was a short break in between women, or the big excuse between them. He had three combs: one in the shop, one in the van, and one in his pocket. When he was on his way to one of his women, he would comb his mustache, which made him look like a man from the previous century, even though some of Ibo's women were very modern.

Among the hundreds of people living in Elvis Presley and the surrounding buildings were a few well-known criminals. The police were on patrol day and night. They constantly checked these hundreds of people, whereas they would have been better off nabbing those few criminals. It was awful to leave Elvis Presley and see the police glaring at you as though you'd just done something against the law, or were about to blow yourself up. My fear grew along with my belly, because I was worried they might think it was a belt bomb. So I did my best to lose weight. The friendlier you looked at a policeman, the more hostilely he looked back at you. Elvis Presley was like an ulcer on the healthy complexion of the Kingdom of the Netherlands. We foreigners were the bacteria and the police were the antibiotics.

There were more police cars driving around Elvis Presley than flash bulbs at the Oscars. I couldn't get used to it. Police cars, with or without shrieking sirens, would drive so fast that little children took fright. Or else they would creep past, so that you didn't see the car, but rather the police officers' angry faces. But sometimes, when it rained, the police cars would stay away, so I started to look forward to the rainy Dutch weather.

Once I got stopped by a police car. I had been cycling without a lamp, he said. This was clearly not said for my own safety, but rather because I had broken a rule. They checked my ID card and I was given a fine. The next day I bought two bicycle lamps—a white one for the front and a red one for the back—and a week later they stopped me again. This time in a small police van. The burly agents came over to me with their bulging muscles and said I was cycling without lamps. I pointed to the two lamps I had just attached to my bike, but realized then I had put them on the wrong way round. Red on the front, white at the rear. Instead of having a good laugh about my mix-up and just asking me to switch the lights before I rode off, they wrote out another fine. So because of those two fines I always double-checked myself before leaving the apartment. I made sure I had my ID card, and even if it wasn't dark I checked that the bike lamps were in the right position.

So it happened that while in Elvis Presley, the police took up residence in my head, and worked overtime.

67

Every time Abdullah came back from Friday prayers in the Saudi mosque, he was more charged up with anger and jihad. His anger only increased during discussions in the apartment. I also had the feeling that every Friday his beard grew longer. There's an Arabic saying that goes, "Drink sour, eat sour, but do not live sour." For me, living in that apartment became more sour because of all the arguing about the jihad. I grew tired of the debates and the others' attempts to get me to go with them to their mosque.

One evening after dinner, the men got talking about the IND and as soon as Abdullah joined in, the conversation turned to Islam and the jihad. The debate was about whether you could make a political cartoon of the prophets, and if Muslims themselves weren't allowed to, could Europeans do so?

"God is very serious, and he prefers to be taken seriously. Jokes anger him," Abdullah said.

"If God is so serious," Talib countered, "why did He create Charlie Chaplin?"

"Who's Charlie Chaplin?" asked Abdullah.

"You've lived in Europe for years and you don't even know what Charlie Chaplin is? And you sit there like you know God personally, even though you've never been to heaven?"

You could count on Talib for a laugh. But Abdullah did not think it was funny.

"God is everywhere. I don't have to go to heaven to get to know Him."

"Aha, so God is also in laughter. And if He is in laughter, then He likes jokes."

"And I like eating," said one of the others as he came in with a tray of steaming food.

Everyone stopped arguing and ate, but as soon as we

were finished eating, the discussion continued. I couldn't take it any longer. I opened my bag and took out the leash and rubber ball I'd been given by Leda. The men stopped talking and looked at me.

"What's with the leash, Samir? Are you going to buy a dog, like a real Hollander?"

The others laughed.

"This is no leash, it's a magic rope," I said. "I'm sick of the stench of your socks and the jihad. You all talk about God as though he's Wi-Fi and you're the only ones with the password. You go to the Turkish mosque and come back talking like Erdogan, you go to the Moroccan mosque and come back talking like Hassan II, and you go to the Saudi mosque and come back mimicking Osama bin Laden. Enough! Stop!"

Only Abdullah did not laugh.

"So what are you going to do?" someone asked.

"With this magic rope," I said, holding up the leash, "I'm going to bring Holland into this fucking apartment and get it to drag me back out." And I launched straight into the Dutch national anthem. *"Wilhelmus van Nassouwe, ben ik van ..."*

They laughed even louder now. They did not know I was dead serious.

I decided I had a dog. The dog's name was Rocky. I had googled dog breeds and looked for ones that suited me, until I found two breeds that resembled my own character, so that I could talk about myself as though I were talking about my dog. My dog Rocky was part dachshund and part Frisian Stabyhoun.

After studying these two breeds online, I started going for walks carrying the ball and the leash. Sometimes I would whistle or shout "Come!" If anyone asked my dog's name, I would say proudly, "Rocky. He'll be three on August 9."

If you want to know how wrapped up Dutch people are in their own heads, go out for a walk carrying a leash and pretend there's a dog attached to it. Aside from my housemates, no one realized that Rocky did not exist.

I would sit on a bench in front of Elvis Presley, wrap the leash around my left hand, and hold the ball in my right hand. I put on the expression of someone keeping an eye on his dog, and at certain intervals I would whistle, or shout, "Rocky, no!" or "Here, Rocky!" My housemates thought I had gone crazy, and gave up trying to get me to go to their mosque with them. This was the first liberation Rocky brought me, and the first miracle.

After a few days of walking around holding the leash and the ball, the second miracle happened. I was sitting on the bench in front of Elvis Presley when two policemen approached. I whistled and called out, "Rocky! Where are you?"

For the first time in all my years in the Netherlands, the policemen gave me a friendly look and said hello. That was the moment I also believed that Rocky was not imaginary, but rather very real indeed.

"You know what it is," I explained later, up in the apartment. "As soon as they think you have a dog, you might be a Muslim, but you're a good one, not hardcore or scary. Once they see that a dog can live with a Muslim, then they realize that they can, too."

A few days after that, the third miracle happened. I was walking with the leash and the ball to the Moroccan shop to buy some meat. About ten meters ahead of me was a dog, playing. Again, two policemen walked in my direction. One of them greeted me, and the other said, "Nice dog."

"Thanks," I said, as I looked at the leash.

68

After all those miracles, I decided to make the fourth miracle happen. By now I had more faith in the leash and the ball than in Dutch society. I decided to take the leash and the ball with me to Bloemenwijk, which I had been curious about for a while now. Why did they call it an antisocial neighborhood? And why did they keep warning me about it?

The houses in Bloemenwijk all looked exactly the same. The fences bordering the small front yards too. I noticed that there were older people living in some of the houses. Not alone with their loneliness or with a dog or cat, but with a family. I also noticed that with the police, it was just the opposite of how it was at Elvis Presley: in Bloemenwijk, the police were friendly to the people and the people gave police the dirty looks.

This antisocial neighborhood didn't seem too antisocial at all to me, but thanks to Talib's warnings I didn't dare walk through it without Rocky.

One day, someone greeted me.

"Lost your dog?" he asked.

"No, but he's stubborn."

"Is he castrated?"

"No."

"Aha, then he must smell the other dogs. If you want him to be more obedient, you'd better have him castrated."

"No can do," I said, not because I'm against castration, but where would I find an imaginary veterinarian to remove Rocky's imaginary testicles?

"Obedience school?"

"Done it. But of all nine puppies, mine was the worst."

"Call him louder then," said the man, whose name was Jeffrey.

"I've been doing that for more than three years."

Jeffrey was just shy of thirty years old, and had the look of someone born with *Heineken* tattooed on one side of his stomach, and *Grolsch* on the other. It was never a problem to strike up a chat with him, or to end it. Within a few minutes you were one of his acquaintances, but there weren't enough years to become his friend. He was not only filled with beer, but with joviality. Jeffrey was a wheeler-dealer of anything that could be dealt. But he didn't let on. It felt like he was just shooting the breeze, but in fact this was his clever way of working you. Half an hour later, he led me down a narrow alley to a fence behind his house.

The backyard was filled with small aviaries and birdcages. Even the shed was in service as such. He showed me loads of canaries and informed me at great length as to the different varieties, how much they cost, what they sang. Malinois, Mosaic, Gloster, Lizard, Raza Española. He had several in every variety. The price varied from seven to eighty euros per bird. While he was talking, his entire family crowded around us. His father, also named Jeffrey, his mother Chérie, and four of his children. One of them twelve years old (a teenage slipup), one of them nine (a post-teenage slipup), and two more, six and three, with his wife, from whom he was divorced. Then there was Jeffrey's sister Patricia, and another sister named Mylena. You could tell the character of each family member from their tattoo. Jeffrey Jr.'s tattoos were songbirds, his sister Patricia's were growling or pouncing tigers. Mylena also had tigers, but they were lying down or looking about, so they appeared a little more chill. Chérie had all of the above—chill tigers, angry tigers, and birds—as though each of her children inherited one of her animals. The children did not inherit anything from Jeffrey Sr. He was covered in snakes, scorpions, and skulls.

This antisocial family in that antisocial neighborhood was the friendliest and most sociable family I'd ever met in the Netherlands. Patricia brought out a case of beer, as though I was an old friend they hadn't seen in ages. Not only a friend of Jeffrey's, but of all of them. Then another girl showed up, her name was Patricia too, and she was Jeffrey's niece. She joined us at the table. Whenever Chérie said "Patricia," the two Patricias seemed to know from the tone of her voice which one she was talking to.

"Aren't you going to drink your beer?" Chérie asked me.

"I don't drink alcohol."

"Patrice, make him some coffee," she said, and her daughter went to the kitchen and brought back a cup of coffee for me. I listened to their stories about canaries and children. Finally something other than the IND, war, and kebabs. For the first time in my life in the Netherlands I was sitting among people without having to change who I was, and without having to first carefully suss out the way you were supposed to tell them something—not too loud, not too soft, not too long, not too short, and not too repetitive.

When I got back to Elvis Presley, I had the leash and ball in one hand and a caged canary in the other. Jeffrey had convinced me that it sang better than André Hazes. I nodded, without realizing that for Jeffrey, nodding meant that I had bought the bird.

The canary really did sing better than André Hazes. And it cost me, including the cage and a week's worth of food, €35. A bargain, according to Jeffrey. A week later he called me and asked if I had bought more food. When I said that I hadn't, he said, "Come around for a drink, and I'll give you some birdseed to take home."

So there I was again, at Jeffrey's family's place. And they brought me coffee again. Two hours later I went back home with a new canary, and a week's worth of food for two canaries. I hung the second canary's cage alongside the first one's on our small balcony.

At my third visit, Chérie said to Jeffrey, "Don't go selling him a canary every time he comes for coffee." At the door, when I left, Jeffrey asked if I didn't want to exchange my two canaries for another one, which was more expensive and sang exquisitely. I nodded. The next time, I brought him the two canaries. I'm still waiting for the one who sings so beautifully.

Two canaries later, I was friends not only with Jeffrey's family, but with their neighbors, too. If I dropped by unannounced for a cup of coffee and no one was home, then the neighbors would call me over. I also became friendly with the neighbors' neighbors. Now I started going around without the leash and ball, and there was always one or other "antisocial" Dutch person who would invite me in for a drink and a chat. This is how I got to know about Dutch popular music and Dutch food: croquettes, *frikandellen*, "everything" fries, endive *stamppot*, and *snert*. I learned nothing about Dutch silence, but rather about Dutch life and Dutch hospitality. I learned how the system deals with various social problems. I met people who unequivocally either love you or hate you. If they are your friend, then they are a true-blue friend. If they hate you, then you're their worst enemy. You don't have to wonder where you stand. You're not just two ears that listen and a head that nods. For the price of just two canaries, I became one of them.

69

The Bloemenwijkers considered themselves "normal" Hollanders, and the *others* to be the "antisocials." Think of the Netherlands as a ship. The residents of Bloemenwijk were the rugged sailors, the simple crewmen, and the others were clever captains, the officers. The residents of Elvis Presley were not the mice and rats who should be thrown overboard once the cheese is finished and they start gnawing on the wood, but the passengers who were required to sit quietly in the hold or on deck. The ship was filled with captains who all wanted to be in charge, and mariners who all felt the need to be brawny and tough. The voyagers had simply to keep to themselves until the ship arrived at port, and then quietly slip ashore—not because they were no longer welcome, but so as not to be onboard if the ship happened to sink, taking them with it.

I often went to the park with the leash and the ball. One day Malik, a boy of about eight who lived with his parents and two sisters on the ninth floor of Elvis Presley, came up to me. I intrigued him, and we often chatted. Now he saw me holding the leash and the ball. "You've got a leash. And you shout 'Rocky! Rocky!' but I've never seen your dog."

"That's a secret. If you promise not to tell anyone, I'll share it with you."

"I promise," he said.

"My dog," I whispered conspiratorially, "is invisible."

"That's impossible! I don't believe you."

"Ah, but it's true. Come with me to the park and see for yourself."

He called up to his mother that he was going with me to the park, and she waved back that it was okay.

When we got to the park I said, "All right, here's the secret: I don't have a dog."

"See? I told you. But you walk around with a leash and a ball. You think you have a dog. You're crazy."

"You know what it is, Malik? With a leash in your hand, the Hollanders think you have a dog. Then they think, maybe he's a Muslim, but a good one, not so hardcore and scary."

"How weird," Malik said.

We sat down on a bench. Soon enough, a Dutch man and his dog walked past. He said hello and went on his way. Malik started throwing the ball, and I brought it back. When in the distance we saw a young woman let her dog loose, we took our places on the bench. Malik sat in nervous anticipation.

She greeted us. Her little dog came over and sniffed the leash and ball in my hand. The woman called, "Chica!" and the dog trotted back over to her. She clicked on Chica's leash. "I have to hold on to her, she's afraid of other dogs."

"Rocky is very sociable," I said. "And he's really good with other dogs." I pointed to some bushes behind the bench where we were sitting. "He's looking for moles."

"Is he a Frisian staby?"

"Part. And part dachshund. Actually, his front legs are too short to get to the moles."

Chica started barking, and she and her owner walked off. Malik's jaw dropped open. "You really made her believe you have a dog!"

"Not only her," I said, "but her dog, too. The Netherlands is a wonderful country. All you need is a leash, and you have a dog." We laughed and walked back to Elvis Presley.

I began to notice what time of day Chica's owner brought her to the park. So you could find me in the park at 10:30, 2:30, and 7:30 p.m. carrying the leash and the ball. But instead of Chica's owner, I saw three different men walking Chica. I fantasized that I might become Chica's fourth walker. And once, after many 10:30s, 2:30s, and 7:30s, I finally saw Chica with her owner. She smiled at me, stopped to ask how Rocky and I were doing, and walked further. The next time we bumped into each other, she shook hands and introduced herself as Irene. She told me all about Chica. And I talked about myself, except instead of the words *I* and *me*, I said *he* and *Rocky*.

"He's from an asylum. A sensitive creature, really. He values his privacy, but has none in the place where he lives. He's really sweet, but has been through a lot in life. And he's allergic to policemen."

"I hear ya," she said. "The asylum does that to you."

"Yes, his soul has been damaged, but he still has faith in beauty, especially in the park."

Each time I talked about myself and substituted *Rocky* for *I*, it was like getting a step closer to Irene.

One time, Chica came up to me, wagging her tail. Irene never seemed to think it was strange to see me without a dog. The leash was enough.

"Rocky does his own thing," I said. "I try to let him know he's free, after all that time in the asylum. So he tends to go off on his own."

"So I've noticed."

I can't remember at what point I started talking about myself and saying *I* instead of *Rocky*. And Irene also started talking more about herself and less about Chica. We became friendly enough that we exchanged telephone numbers, and she called me up once to ask if I could take Chica for a walk. So I *did* become the fourth man! Irene was a sorceress. She turned men into dog walkers.

Once, when I was walking back to Elvis Presley carrying the ball and the leash, I bumped into her again. She was wearing a miniskirt and a jacket. The jacket made her look like she was chilly, but if you looked at her legs, you'd think it was summer.

"Where are you headed?" she asked.

"Home."

"Where's Rocky?"

"I've lost him. I think he's already gone home. He's probably sitting at the front door waiting for me." She walked with me and we talked until we reached the front door of Elvis Presley. The windows that had just been repaired were broken again. I asked her if she would like to come up for a drink, and she nodded. But when the words left my mouth, I thought: What have I done? I remembered Youssef with his mustache in Malti's studio apartment, and realized here I had an apartment with ten or more Youssefs. Not only with a mustache, but a beard to boot. This would be a disaster. But once words leave your mouth, it's impossible to put them back in.

70

Irene walking into Abud Alami's apartment was like an ice-cream cone entering hell. When Chica saw nine beards and five mustaches she leapt anxiously against Irene. I realized I had to come up with a quick excuse, and I told her today was my birthday, and that all these men were my karate club teammates.

"Karate?" she asked, surprised.

"Yes, the Islamic karate school where we train," I said. She congratulated me with the traditional three Dutch cheek kisses.

"I birthday also," said one of the other man, and she gave him three kisses as well. Suddenly it was the birthday of all my teammates from the Islamic karate school. Chica was still scared, and the men were dumbstruck: a girl in a dress like that, with legs like that, in Abud Alami's apartment, where no woman had set foot over the threshold in years ...

A man came over and whispered to me, "One question. May I borrow that leash and ball of yours sometime?"

"After Abdulrazaq," I said. "He's just reserved them."

"What is your job?" asked one of the men. "Dog groomer," answered Irene.

"What?"

"Dog groomer."

"What?"

"Dog. Groomer."

I translated it into Arabic. One of the men began to whine and yammer. "Oh, dear woman. What a pity you are a dog barber, not a Muslim barber. We all suffer from hair trouble. There are no barbers for us."

"What did he say?" Irene asked.

"He says," I translated back, "that he wished he was two

dogs, then you could groom him twice."

"What did you tell her?" asked the man.

"I told her you would like to be one of her clients."

"Oh, yes, yes, tell her that." After Irene had had her fourth or fifth cup of tea, from the fourth or fifth housemate, she left because her shift started in forty-five minutes, and, because it was Thursday, they would be open until nine. I walked her down to the front entrance.

"Next time, come over to my place," she said. "And bring Rocky with you."

Nellie from the student house, remember her? She phoned to say a registered letter had arrived for me. I cycled over straight away, because I had been using the student house as my official address and I didn't want the city to find out I didn't live there any longer. I got a chilly reception along with the letter.

It had to do with my integration process. So I called the telephone number. The woman said I had not yet signed up for Dutch lessons and a civics course, and it was high time I did so.

"Sorry, ma'am, I've never had anything to do with civics courses or the city council. And as you can hear, my Dutch is already good."

"Maybe so," she said. "But if you don't sign up soon, you lose your welfare and your apartment."

I wanted to tell her that I didn't get welfare or have an apartment from the government, but I couldn't get a word in edgewise. She made an appointment for me with the integration people. "Next Tuesday, a quarter to two."

So that Tuesday afternoon at just past one thirty, I was sitting in the waiting room at the "integration" section. "My" integration consultant, Caroline Ommen, did not come to get me at quarter to two, but at eleven before. Four minutes late.

"Mr. Karim, you have one month, and no longer than that, to begin your civics course." She gave me a strict look. "It's really important to learn Dutch and become acquainted with Dutch culture."

She wore glasses, but when she spoke she looked over the top of the frames. So it felt like she was looking at me with two pairs of eyes.

The funny part was that Caroline Ommen from integration insisted I take a course in the language we were effortlessly conversing in. On top of it, she had been four minutes late, according to her own clock on her own waiting-room wall. Hardly the kind of Dutch punctuality they expect new immigrants to master, if you ask me.

"You haven't had Dutch lessons either, I see. How have you managed to get welfare all this time without a language and civics course?"

I thought to myself: what a twit. Was I supposed to tell her that I do not get welfare, and never did? That would be saying she wasn't doing her job properly, and that is the last thing you should do with a Dutch person. Then she'd only go out of her way to prove she *was* doing her job properly, and get even stricter. She kept going over my dossier in the computer, until she got up and asked me to come with her. Outside on the sidewalk, she took out a pack of cigarettes, lit one, and took a long drag. She looked at me as though we were old friends standing outside a bar, having bumped into each other after many years.

"Listen, Samir," she said. "You speak good Dutch and have done great all these years. But you're lucky the IND hasn't found out you haven't done your civics course yet. Just make sure you do the test before they catch on." She no longer called me *Mr. Karim* or used the formal *you*. "Good luck, okay?" she added with a smile.

I thanked her and walked off. I thought: if the integration section can turn this woman from a twit into an angel just like that, then surely it's possible for integration to turn an asylum seeker into a citizen.

The fast-track exemption test was the quickest and cheapest option. I was sure to pass it, after all my experience in the ASC and the time I had spent among Dutch people since then, so I went to Groningen to take the test.

The test was administered in a room with separate tables and computers. A woman named Jannie Draaisma gave us the instructions. She announced, loud and clear, that we had forty-five minutes, "and not one minute more," that the test would automatically shut off at that time, that we were not allowed to leave the room, "also not to visit the toilet," that we were not allowed to take pictures, copy down questions, or tell anyone else about the contents of the test afterwards. Then she said the computers would be turned on and the test timer would begin. "Now."

After the first few minutes I asked myself why I had been given nine years, nine months, one week, and three days to prove I was an asylum seeker, and just forty-five minutes to prove I was a citizen.

The fast-track exemption test consisted of thirty questions, all of which began with a short video and a bit of text, after which came the question. All this took quite some time, and the videos kept freezing. Jannie Draaisma said you had to "just wipe the mouse dry and then it would work." When one of the other test-takers asked if he couldn't just use his own laptop because it was much faster, she took it as an insult. And when another asked if she could use her own ear buds because the headset they provided hissed (mine did too, by the way), that wasn't allowed either. With more time, it would have been a matter of just being patient, but with the seconds ticking away, that three-quarter-hour was shrinking fast. You can't ride the Giro d'Italia on a granny bike either, can you?

But what amazed me most of all were the questions themselves. This was the Netherlands, not Morocco, where I had never been. Yet more than half the questions were about Mo and Amal, two Moroccans who had come to live in the Netherlands, and their housing aid and welfare and child support. Things I had absolutely nothing to do with.

Jannie Draaisma marched through the room with her hands clasped behind her back. Here and there, she answered a question (with "No") and checked to see that we weren't cheating with our cell phones or crib notes. She was, however, so kind as to inform me that the time was running out. Every second took a bite out of me as a citizen. After twenty-five minutes I was still at question 7. So I raced through the rest in the last twenty minutes, and failed.

To retake the test was more expensive. I had to buy books and study them. This exam consisted of five different tests. So I bought the books and studied them, not to understand the Netherlands, but to understand the integration test. After many months and many euros—I will spare you the details—I passed my integration exam.

Integrating was certainly a learning experience. Just like vaccines infect you with a weak form of a disease, so you don't get sick from the strong version, I integrated so as never to become a full-blown citizen. I stopped trying to make friends with the Hollanders, but rather focused on how to keep my distance.

I started to appreciate Elvis Presley. There, I was a person. There, the canary did not have to be a parrot, and the parrot did not have to lay eggs like a chicken.

The integration test made me positive. I saw the police who were constantly patrolling around Elvis Presley differently. Not like they were protecting the Netherlands from Elvis Presley, but Elvis Presley from the Netherlands. I stopped going to the park to see Irene, and quit hoping to find a place to live among Dutch people.

Unfortunately, the situation of a cow in McDonald's is clearer than mine in integration. The cow goes into McDonald's as a cow and comes out as a hamburger, but I went into the integration process as an asylum seeker and came back out as an asylum seeker.

Shortly after my civics tests, I opened a post on Facebook from a man whom, at first, I did not recognize. When I read the post, I felt that one thin strand that kept me connected to the Netherlands snap. It happened after Malik disappeared from Elvis Presley.

71

The jihad in the Middle East started to exchange residents of Elvis Presley. Some families disappeared without notice, others showed up, uprooted, in their place. If Elvis Presley had not been the building, but the singer, he would have been happy with the change. He'd become less radical on the inside.

One evening, Abdullah came in and stood in the middle of the living room.

"My dear brothers, if I have ever wronged you, please forgive me. I come to say goodbye. Tomorrow, after morning prayers, I am leaving. My dream has finally come true. I am glad I see the day that the Caliphate has been announced."

Everyone embraced Abdullah.

"Brothers, pray for me that I reach my destination and do not get caught at the border and sent back."

Malik's family was one of the first to leave for the Middle East. His parents had asked me to teach him classical Arabic. So while I was sitting around idly in Ibo's shop, Malik would often drop by for an Arabic lesson. I would give him a half-hour lesson, then would read to him for another half hour from the legendary Dutch children's book writer Annie M. G. Schmidt, because I thought it was a pity that the jihadist Abu Bakr al-Baghdadi had come to Elvis Presley, but not Annie M. G. Schmidt.

Malik's father gave me a watch as thanks for the lessons, when he came to tell me Malik would no longer be coming. And after not seeing them for a couple of weeks, I heard from Talib that their apartment on the ninth floor was empty. Talib had the key, and we could stay there as long as no one found out.

Talib looked both ways down the hall and opened the

door. We hurried inside and closed the door behind us. The apartment was tidy and looked lived in, as though the residents had only just stepped out. Talib said they left everything as it was on purpose, so that if they were nabbed on their way to the Caliphate they could say they were just going to Turkey on vacation. Malik's father had given the key to Talib so he could sell their things and send the money once they had safely arrived in the Caliphate. There was still hot and cold running water, electricity, and gas, and even working internet and telephone. On the walls were photos of Malik and his two sisters, including their swimming diplomas.

"The Netherlands taught the Muslim children to swim in water so they don't sink and drown," Talib said. "And there, the mujahideen will teach them to swim in blood, so that others can drown in it."

We looked at those swimming diplomas in silence. Even Talib's little joke could not lighten our mood.

"There's one thing I don't understand, Samir, and I'll never understand it. Parents who flee a war zone to take their children to a safe place, this I understand. But to flee a safe place like this to go to a war zone? With three small children? I don't get it."

What would Malik's life be like in the Caliphate? How would he look at all the horrible things that happened there? Would he think back on Annie M. G. Schmidt's Patterson Pepps or Jip and Janneke?

"You can sleep here for a while," Talib said at last, "but no one's allowed to know."

"I would rather sleep in Abud Alami's apartment. He's still alive in death, but these people are dead in life," I said, and went outside.

I was supposed to work in the shop that day. I still had another hour before my shift started, and it was raining. I decided to make some tea and surf the web. On Facebook I saw a message from someone called Lazar Azikiwe. I did not recognize that name.

Hello Samir, it's your old friend Calvin here. I just heard that Leda threw herself under a train. Sorry for the delay. Be strong.

I looked at the photo of Lazar Azikiwe. It was indeed Calvin. I reread the message and was paralyzed. It was as though a speeding car only just missed hitting me.

I shut the laptop, got dressed, and cycled off, without feeling the rain. Only at the train doors did I realize that the cold rain had seeped all the way to my bones. I realized I hadn't bought a ticket yet, and on the stairs thought I should buy some flowers. Outside the station florist, I saw a white bouquet. I took it out of the bucket and headed for platform 5.

"Sorry, sir," came a young woman's voice from behind me. I turned. "You haven't paid for the flowers." I gave her twenty euros. "Another two ninety-five, please." I looked in my wallet, handed her a ten-euro note and walked off to wait for my train. The rain pounded on the station roof. On the platform, my bouquet dripped.

In all my life I had never felt such peace or experienced such clarity. I saw everything around me so clearly, as though I had just taken off dark glasses. I saw the people with their drenched faces, the cigarette butts on the cement floor tiles, some of them stubbed out, some still smoldering, others extinguished by the wet platform. I saw a small plant among the glistening stones between the rails. Even the woman's voice announcing train delays—I had heard it for years—came across as new. The train stopped, and when I boarded, I thought of the ticket I hadn't bought. I sat down and when the conductor asked for my ticket, I handed him fifty euros. He asked where I was going.

"Then you owe me another three euros and seventy cents, because there's a thirty-five-euro fine for not having a ticket. I felt in my pants pocket, gave him four wet euro coins. He took a notebook out of his breast pocket, wrote out the ticket and fine, and gave me thirty cents change. "Have a good day," he said before walking off.

When I arrived, I took the same bus Leda always did on those Friday evenings, and I got out at the bus stop where Diesel and I would wait for her. I walked to the Van der Weerdes' house along the road where I first cycled with Calvin. Nothing had changed. The faces, the gray hair, the windows, the curious old dogs and cats.

I knocked. Danielle opened the door. She had aged about twenty years. When she saw the white bouquet, she said in a choked-up voice, "You've come for ..."

"Where is she ..." I wanted to say *buried* but the word came out as tears.

"Wait, I'll take you to her."

She went inside. Diesel lay sleeping in the hallway, as though the energy that made him dance around Leda was gone. Danielle came back out with the car key and we drove in silence to a church just outside the village. We got out. Even if I had all the words in every language from the beginning of time, I still could not describe the sorrow I felt as I walked to the gravestone where Leda had changed into her name.

72

It was late by the time I got back to the apartment. Someone was lying on my mattress. I found an empty one and flopped down on it. I closed my eyes and thought of all the people I had lost. They all had Leda's face. At eight thirty the next morning, Ibo called to ask why I wasn't at work. When I told him I was tired and might be sick, he said, "Get some rest and call me when you can." He did not ask any further. I slipped back into a deep sleep.

At five to twelve, I woke up and without bothering to wash my face or drink tea, I put my belongings in my bag and fifty euros in the household can. I took the garbage bag full of photo albums and called a man on the seventh floor of Elvis Presley who ran an informal taxi service. As I was waiting outside, I heard Talib shout from above, "Where are you going with that garbage bag?"

"To a monastery."

"What? Everybody leaves Elvis Presley to go to the jihad and you're going to a monastery?"

I nodded.

The monastery had been the right place to go when I lost Leda, and now it was the right place to go when she lost herself.

"How long will you stay this time?" asked Lea, the woman at the reception desk, whom I remembered from the previous visit.

"I don't know. Last time I was here for three weeks, but now ..."

"I remember you."

"I've got ..." I said, checking my wallet to see how much money I had.

"We're not so full at the moment, take the time to find the

peace you're looking for," Lea said. "Money is not so important. If you want to do something while you're here, you can
do some gardening if you have the energy for it. But only if
it brings you peace. Would you like the same room as last
time?"

"Yes, please."

Lea led me through that huge, silent building to my
room. Oh, checking in to heaven is so serene.

Exhausted, I dropped my things, took off my shoes and
jacket, and crawled under the blanket.

That night I dreamt the same dream as during the first
night in the Van der Weerdes' shed. I was an animal and was
walking in the dark. The tip of my tail was illuminated and
I kept turning around, following that little light. I heard my
eldest brother shout, "Wake up! Quit chasing your tail!"
And like back then, no matter how hard I tried to wake up,
I fell into an ever deeper sleep. I heard the cawing of crows
and thought, are they cawing in my dream, or for real?
"Samir! Samir!" I heard Calvin shout.

When I woke up, it was a quarter past four in the morning, and I had a splitting headache. I recalled there being a
first aid kit next to the refrigerator in the kitchen. I took two
aspirin and made myself a cup of tea. I sat under the kitchen
window drinking tea and looking out into the darkness. By
the time the trees in the monastery's garden started to
become visible, my headache had gone. I went back to my
room, hung Leda's photo on the wall, and looked at it. The
leash in her right hand, the ball in her left. Diesel looking
up at her with his tongue hanging out of his mouth, Leda
smiling at the camera. Autumn leaves covering the ground
around her.

I remembered that Lea used to sing classical music during
her lunch break, and that her voice filled the reception area
and the corridors. Her voice turned the roof into windows,
through which you could see heaven. Every day at noon, I

would go sit on the stone bench near Reception and listen to her sing. After a few days I felt relaxed enough to do some work in the garden. I raked leaves, trimmed branches that hung too close to the windows, and tidied up dead branches in the orchard.

And at noon I would listen to Lea. I sat on the stone bench until she finished the song "Amarilli Mia Bella" and went back to the garden. I tried to dig up a dead tree, but the roots were too deep. I dug and dug, but the tree would not budge. I suddenly stopped wrestling with the dead tree. Something had snapped inside me. I went back to my room and carefully removed all the photos, one by one, out of the albums. Leda had to be reborn from the best memories from all the generations and the most cheerful faces I could find.

I searched the photographs for living faces. I separated families, letting one face move to another family. I matched smiles, and let them reinvent one another. I let the twinkling eye from one generation be transplanted to another. Sometimes I saw a smile in a faraway moment be transported to the present, or I would take a laugh and send it back in time, so it could meet that other smile. I could not let a single smile slip into somberness.

I stopped working in the garden. I spent hours, days, and nights staring at the photos, trying to fathom the souls behind them, so that Leda might have the chance to reenter this world through a soft doorway. I shuffled the photos like tarot cards, went through them at random and changed the order. This face must go here, and that one there. If I wasn't sure where a certain face belonged, I strolled under the trees in the orchard, thinking of Leda in that far-off winter, until I knew what to do. Sometimes a face appeared in my thoughts. Then I searched until I found it, and placed it in the right spot in Leda's new life. Sometimes I woke up, having just dreamt that a different man should be Leda's grandfather, and I dug around in the photos until I found him. Or I dreamt that Leda told me who she should be when she was ten, and which photos suited her when she was fourteen. After a while it felt as though Leda, that beautiful, good-natured girl who had made my heart beat faster, and still did, had come to live with me in the monastery and started thinking about her new life with me.

To that girl I could not give my life to, I gave other people's lives. There, in that time, in the eternal seconds of others who had become smiles, Leda lives and will live always.

73

The Netherlands changed me. That change is greater than when a bamboo stalk becomes a flute. The bamboo stalk is uprooted. And it gets a few holes. It can no longer grow and dance in the wind, but in return it can, with the help of someone else's breath, make music. I have lost my roots, my ground, my water, and my air. I have holes everywhere, in my soul, in my heart, in my hand, in my back. That is the price someone pays for fleeing, for leaving his country behind, when it needs him to stay.

On the thirty-seventh day in the monastery, my cell phone rang.

"Hey, Samir, where are you?" Yelena asked.

"In a monastery."

"What number?" she asked.

"I live in a monastery, not on a street," I said. "Where are you now?"

"Amsterdam. I want to see you. We're staying with Vlad's sister. Send me your address."

An hour later, my phone rang again.

"We're here. At a church. But the address isn't right."

"Wait there, I'm coming."

Outside the wooden gate to the monastery I saw a car with a German license plate. At the wheel sat a blond man who looked like he had just got his driver's license at Madame Tussaud's and was out on his first spin.

She had not changed. Perhaps that had to do with her eyes. Mostly I realized how much I had changed.

"You've gotten old and ugly," she said. "Come on, let's go have a drink."

Instead of getting back in the car, she first walked

through the monastery gate and stuck her head inside.

"Dutch people are really strange, you know," she said to me. "They've got a reception desk in there." She opened her eyes wide, the way she did when we lived in the ASC. "Not only does the camp have a reception desk, but in Holland, Jesus does, too!"

She gestured at the car. I opened the door.

"No, not that one."

I opened another door.

"No, wait, don't sit on those things. Put this over there. Careful. It's designer stuff. Give it here, I'll lay it in the back."

The man in the driver's seat was about thirty-five. He shook my hand, gave me an impassive look, and turned back.

"His name is Vlad Dovoryanchikov."

The man nodded when he heard his name, like a telephone that vibrates when you tap in the right PIN code. I said my name and he repeated it twice, with precisely the same accent as Yelena. He smiled and said nothing more.

"Do you know anywhere we can get something to drink where there are no Dutch people?"

"Alaska."

"You and your jokes," she said. "You're exactly the same as in the ASC in 1998." When she uttered that year, the tears streamed down her cheeks. She turned away. I directed Vlad to a teahouse in a wooded area along the riverbank.

"It's tricky to remember, Dovoryanchikov. His first name is a lot easier," Yelena said, patting him on the shoulder. "His last name is no longer Dimitriev, difficult, complicated. He's not Dimitriev anymore, but Dovoryanchikov. My last name isn't Novakova anymore, but Reyntiens."

She chattered as though she was afraid of silence, and that her emotions might take over. She nattered away and Vlad and I listened. She looked at her watch. "One more hour," she said, and continued chattering.

"You called me when I was working as a chicken catcher,

and said you had news," I said. "I'm curious what that was."

She looked at me sadly, and then again at her watch. "Another hour."

Was she just not listening, or did she not want to talk about it? She jumped from one subject to the other. She was like a USB stick with lots of information on it, but no screen to show it on. Every time she reached a sensitive moment in her monologue, she said, "I'll tell you about that next time."

Suddenly she turned and looked straight at me. "Get out of this country," she said, softly but decisively. "You're still wearing the same jacket and the same shoes as in the camp. At least not the same socks."

"That's not true," I said. "They're the same socks, too."

She laughed, but her laughter soon dissolved into tears. When we parked the car and went into the teahouse, she went straight to the ladies' room. She came back fifteen minutes later. I could see that she'd retouched her makeup.

"Sorry about that, Samir, I only wanted to cry when we left, but I couldn't hold it in any longer."

"Why did you cry, then?"

She started to tell me, but then the tears came again. She asked if we could go for a walk, said something in Russian to Vlad, who nodded and stayed behind as we walked out to the river.

"Why don't you talk? Why don't you say anything?" she asked. "Did you learn that from the Hollanders?"

"I don't say anything because you sit there looking at your watch the whole time, saying, 'One more hour.' It feels like you're in a hurry."

She looked at her watch again.

"I'm not in a hurry. We still have an hour." She started to cry again. "What's this river called?"

"The Vecht."

"You used to read a lot in the camp. Do you know a poem about a river?"

"Yes, by a Dutch poet."

"No, I hate the Dutch and their poems."

"By a Polish poet, then."

"I hate the Polish, too."

"I know a poem by a Yugoslavian, and don't say you hate the Yugoslavians, because Yugoslavia doesn't exist anymore."

"Go on, then."

"*Every man should be a river, come without wanting to stay, go without longings.*"

"How pretty. Who's the poet?"

"Rutger Koplanowich."

She started tapping something into her phone. I looked at her, that girl, an old dream, and then thought of another old dream of mine: Tarifa. She looked at her watch and spoke to Vlad in Russian.

"He'll pay and come pick us up. So what are you going to do?"

"There's a city way at the southern tip of Spain. Tarifa. It's windy there all the time. I wanted to go there to live after I left that ASC, but never got round to it."

"Go," she said.

As I waved when they drove off, she rolled down the window, stuck her head out, and shouted, "Samir, *go!*"

I needed that Russian breeze.

74

"So you're leaving," Lea said when she saw me walk into the reception area with my bag.

"Yes, I've found the peace I needed."

"Where are your photo albums?" she asked, smiling.

"They've become just one album. Now it fits in my bag."

I don't think she understood. I gave her all the money I had, but she pressed it gently back into my hand.

"You'll need it on the outside. And besides, you did a lot of gardening. We're really grateful for that."

How rich that monastery is, I thought. Rich poverty is richer than poor prosperity.

I took the train to Schiphol without thinking of papers or money. The time I spent in the monastery taught me to believe in small, everyday miracles. In the past, I had always looked for someone to sit next to in the train. Now, I looked for a place to be alone. But the train was full. I sat down next to a Dutch man.

"There's more room in the quiet car, but it's more sociable here, isn't it," I heard him say.

He could have been talking to anyone. I kept quiet and looked straight forward.

"Do you understand Dutch?" he asked. Now it was clear that he meant me.

"Yes, mister," I said. "The language, but not the culture."

At Schiphol I saw a young guy with Rasta hair, a takeout coffee, and a laptop. Next to him was a large backpack with black smears and a sleeping mat fastened on top. It was clear he had a long wait before his journey continued: he didn't look around, or at his watch.

"Can you do me a favor?" I asked him in English.

"Sure."

"I'm looking for a ticket to Malaga, as cheap as possible."

"Wait a sec." He typed away at his laptop, and a few minutes later he said, "You're in luck. Forty-nine ninety-five for a one-way to Malaga. Only thing is, it's tomorrow morning."

"Do they check passports to go to Malaga?"

"If you check in online and only have hand luggage, you can go straight to the gate, and if it's busy at security they only check your passport photo and sometimes just the boarding pass. Depends on the moment. Don't you have a passport?"

"No, but I do have an IND card. It's the first time I'll travel with it."

"Do you have a credit card to pay for the ticket?"

"No, but if you could do it, I'll give you the cash straight away."

"Sure thing."

He took the IND card to get my information. I handed him fifty euros in cash and within a few minutes I had a ticket to Malaga.

"One more small thing …"

"You want me to do your online check-in?"

"If you please."

Just five minutes later, the boarding pass appeared on my telephone. I chatted with him for a while, and when he wanted to get some sleep, I walked off. The next morning, as soon as I saw that things had started to get busy, I headed to security. I got through with no problem and walked across the transit hall.

I looked out through the huge windows of the airport, thinking back on when I landed here with China Airlines, all those years ago. The grayness outside was the same, but I was not. I thought about that change. I had started as a man and ended up as an asylum seeker. It cost me my life, like how for other people it cost them time, money, and sometimes their humanity. I heard my flight being announced and walked to the gate. I was the last one to board. The woman scanned my boarding pass, wished me a good journey, and asked me to hurry on board to seat 27A.

I arrived in Malaga airport at 11:30. I took the bus into town, walked around a bit, and found myself at 1:20 that night in a park abutting the sea. I rested my head on my bag with its new life and Leda inside, and slept. After waking up to the chatter of parakeets, I asked a passerby which bus went to Tarifa. I got choked up as I stood at the bus stop. I was just one bus, no more, away from achieving my old dream. In the bus I paged through the Teach Yourself Spanish book Leda had given me. Spanish was no longer a language, but a memory. I thought of her voice that time she read the César Fernández Moreno poem back in the shed.

When I got to Tarifa, I missed feeling the wind I went there for.

But I did see the white houses they showed on the internet, and which I often dreamed of. And the little balconies full of colorful flowers, and the bougainvilleas climbing the walls. I ambled past those white walls and spotted an empty café terrace on a small square. I sat down and ordered tea. I looked up and for the first time saw the sky the way I wanted to see it: as a tourist. That surprised me, it was like I had never seen the sky before. How deep it was, and how far it stretched. And so different from the gray Dutch sky, which sometimes hung so low you could reach up and touch it.

"Are you from India?" the waiter asked in bad English.

"Yes, I'm from India."

"Tourist?"

"Tourist."

"Is it nice weather there?"

"Beautiful."

Two other people came and sat down on the terrace. I looked at the walls around me and took a deep breath.

Tarifa, the most beautiful city in the world. Once, it gave me a dream, and just now it gave me India. I drank my tea and placed three euros on the table. One and a half euros for the tea and one and a half for India. I walked over the white-sand beach, stood straight up, and took a deep breath of the sea air. Across the water, there where the Mediterranean and the Atlantic meet, I could see Africa.

When the sun went down, I walked down a road familiar to me, although I had never walked on it before. A small stone stairway led down to the beach. I slowly walked into the water, my shoes and clothes still on. I felt the red of the sun touch me with a hand of water. Standing among those endless waves that lapped against both the sun and my life, I took the photos from the album and placed them, one by one, onto the water. There in the waves, I watched the smiles from which Leda had been reborn disappear, after the red of the sun had brought them to life. At last, a breeze picked up. When I got to the photo of Leda, I looked at it until it got dark, bent forward, and laid it gently on the water's surface.

Dreams don't know you got there too late.

... Samir, who was an adolescent, who was me. Who had walked life's path with the many wounds of ignorance. Who was robbed of his life by books and tongues. How I would love to sit with him for an hour. A minute. And I would tell him this:

"Samir, friend, listen. The world is bearable if it's under your shoes, and not in your head."

JONATHAN REEDER, a native of New York and longtime resident of Amsterdam, enjoys a dual career as a literary translator and performing musician. Alongside his work as a professional bassoonist he translates opera libretti and essays on classical music, as well as contemporary Dutch fiction by authors including Christine Otten, Marjolijn van Heemstra, and A. F. T. van der Heijden. Other notable translations include *Rivers* and *The Pelican* by Martin Michael Driessen, *The Lonely Funeral* by Maarten Inghels and F. Starik, and Rodaan Al Galidi's previous work, *Two Blankets, Three Sheets*. Other World Editions titles translated by Reeder are *The Last Poets* by Christine Otten and *Sleepless Summer* by Bram Dehouck.

Book Club Discussion Guides are available on our website

On the Design

As book design is an integral part of the reading experience, we would like to acknowledge the work of those who shaped the form in which the story is housed.

Tessa van der Waals (Netherlands) is responsible for the cover design, cover typography, and art direction of all World Editions books. She works in the internationally renowned tradition of Dutch Design. Her bright and powerful visual aesthetic maintains a harmony between image and typography and captures the unique atmosphere of each book. She works closely with internationally celebrated photo graphers, artists, and letter designers. Her work has frequently been awarded prizes for Best Dutch Book Design.

Mississippi, used on the cover, is a gradient font, which means that it dynamically increases and decreases letter height to control the rhythm of the words. It is inspired by the aesthetics of mid-twentieth-century America, with its blues music, endless highways, and bold advertising. It is designed by Nikola Djurek and published by the Dutch type foundry Typotheque. The drawing of the teetering man is loosely based on the physiognomy of the author Rodaan Al Galidi and was created by Annemarie van Haeringen, an internationally renowned Dutch illustrator. Unlike the silhouette on Al Galidi's other book published by World Editions, *Two Blankets, Three Sheets*, this one is walking downstairs, towards the edge of the cover—towards freedom.

The cover has been edited by lithographer Bert van der Horst of BFC Graphics (Netherlands).

Suzan Beijer (Netherlands) is responsible for the typography and careful interior book design of all World Editions titles.

The text on the inside covers and the press quotes are set in Circular, designed by Laurenz Brunner (Switzerland) and published by Swiss type foundry Lineto.

All World Editions books are set in the typeface Dolly, specifically designed for book typography. Dolly creates a warm page image perfect for an enjoyable reading experience. This typeface is designed by Underware, a European collective formed by Bas Jacobs (Netherlands), Akiem Helmling (Germany), and Sami Kortemäki (Finland). Underware are also the creators of the World Editions logo, which meets the design requirement that 'a strong shape can always be drawn with a toe in the sand.'